DARK CORNERS

Alex Walters

Also by Alex Walters:

Trust No One
Nowhere to Hide
Late Checkout
Murrain's Truth (short stories)
Candles and Roses

Writing as Michael Walters:

The Shadow Walker
The Adversary
The Outcast

DARK CORNERS

Copyright © Michael Walters 2016
Michael Walters has asserted his right to be identified as the author of this Work in accordance with the Copyright, Designs and Patents Act 1988.

This is a work of fiction. Names, characters, places and incidents are a product of the author's imagination. Locales and public names are sometimes used for atmospheric purposes.
Any resemblance to actual people, living or dead, or to businesses, companies, events, institutions or locales is completely coincidental.

For Helen

PART ONE

CHAPTER ONE

Now

What did he remember? He remembered a song.
Between the salt water and the sea strand.
That was where the child's body was found. The thin twisted limbs half-buried in the moist sand. The soft pulse of the incoming tide against the pale skin. The foaming waters stained pink with drifting blood.

They had described it to him, over and over, until the imagined image of the child's body was burned into his mind. And the image was forever linked with the words his mother had sung to him, as a lullaby, every night before he slept. He remembered that, vividly. Remembered her soft soprano voice breathing the words as if weaving a spell to ward away all harm.

He remembered that, though he'd been little more than a baby. It was almost all he did remember of his mother. The voice and the spell that failed.

He recalled that, but he didn't remember the body. He had told them that. He had kept telling them that. But they hadn't believed him. They had kept describing the body. Kept describing it until he was no longer sure what was memory and what was dream.

So what did he remember? He remembered the child's scream.

He'd been in the woods, on the damp ground, his back against one of the wind-blown oaks, listening to one of his dad's old tapes on the Walkman he'd got for his last birthday. He'd been sitting there for ages, as bored as he'd been every day on that endless holiday. Playing the same three or four tapes over and over until he'd stopped hearing the music or words. Waiting for the clouds to break, for the sun finally to appear. Waiting, really, just to go home.

At least, that was what he told them. That was what he thought he remembered.

But they told him that couldn't be true. They told him what had really happened. What he'd done.

All he could do was nod, and say yes, and wonder how his life could have changed so suddenly, so unexpectedly. Wonder how he couldn't have known, couldn't remember. Wonder how his mother's whispered spell could have failed so completely.

Even now, everything that came before remained lost, but the child's scream was burned in his memory. Some nights he woke to the soft sound of his mother's voice crooning in his head. But more often he woke with that scream still echoing through his skull. In those first moments before he was fully conscious, he was always certain the echoes had faded only just as he opened his eyes. He lay in the darkness, haunted by the past, half-expecting the anguished voice to resume, before slowly dying into silence, just as it had in that distant, damp summer.

It was as if the scream had woken him, then as now. Now, he would lie in the unexpected silence, trying to piece together whatever dreams might have preceded the sudden awakening. But the memories were stubbornly out of reach, wisps of thought that slipped from his consciousness as he tried to grasp them.

It had been the same then, all those years before. When they'd questioned him about what had happened, what had preceded that awful discovery, he could offer nothing. Only fragments of imagery — the green canopy of trees, the wash of the sea, the cool softness of the sand. That, and a slowly-growing sense of dread. The knowledge that, whatever he might remember, something had happened, something bad, and he must be the one responsible.

Between the salt water and the sea strand.

CHAPTER TWO

Now

DCI Kenny Murrain stood on the hilltop, at the edge of the road, staring down into the valley. It was late afternoon on a fine spring day, and the low sun sent his elongated shadow down the grassy slope into the shadow of the woodland. Behind him, the western edge of the Pennines ringed the skyline.

He was hoping for something up here, some feeling or sensation he could use, that would give him some direction. But so far there had been nothing, no trace of the familiar electricity. Just a mental silence as empty as the blue sky above.

The young boy's body had been found just outside their jurisdiction—they were just over the border into Derbyshire here—but the Derbyshire Police had been fully co-operative and sent over all the requisite paperwork so he'd been able to confirm the details. As far as he could judge, they'd handled the scene and the follow-up with the same thoroughness Murrain would have expected of his own colleagues.

The remains had been discovered by the farmer who owned the fields on this side of the road. Murrain could see the roof of the farmhouse on the far side of the trees, a thin plume of white smoke rising from its chimney. He'd make his way over there later and introduce himself. The farmer had already given a statement detailing how he'd stumbled across the body while out checking the fences that bordered his land.

One question was why here. It was a remote enough spot, admittedly, the first stretch of open moorland after leaving the densely-packed stone cottages of the village below. This might be the spot you'd pick if you were in a hurry, panicking about what you'd done or what you were going to do next. But it was, in every sense, close to home. Close enough that they perhaps couldn't yet even be absolutely sure this was even the crime they suspected. It was unlikely, given the circumstances, but it was still conceivable that the whole thing was just a dreadful accident.

For Murrain, it was also an odd coincidence.

Three years earlier, he'd been standing—well, not quite on this exact spot, but a half-mile or so further up the same road, gazing into this same valley. Then, as now, he'd been speculating as to how a dead body had ended up among that stretch of woodland. In that case, there'd been less doubt about the accidental nature of the death, though some uncertainty as to the cause. Ryan McCarthy had been an experienced motor-cyclist, the bike itself in good condition, and it had been a fine, dry night. Even though he'd been with colleagues in the pub earlier in the evening, there'd been no trace of alcohol in his body. In the end, there'd been insufficient grounds to justify further investigation, and the inquest had recorded McCarthy's death as accidental. The case was still theoretically open on the off-chance that some further information might emerge. Fat chance of that now, Murrain thought.

He had stood then as he was standing now, hoping to feel something. It had been a little earlier in the year, the air a little warmer, but otherwise a similar clear, sunlit afternoon, a soft wind rippling the moorland grass. He'd stayed here for an hour or so, eventually trudging down the hillside to the spot where the bike had come to rest. But—nothing. Another of the many occasions when his supposed gifts had let him down. Or perhaps not, he told himself. Perhaps the absence of any intuition, any sensation, had simply confirmed the truth—that McCarthy's death had indeed been another unfortunate accident.

Was that the same conclusion he should draw now? It was possible. Young Ethan Dunn had gone missing five days earlier. He'd disappeared at some point in the short walk from the main road where the school bus had dropped him off up to his parents' house in the small new-build estate at the bottom end of the village. The walk was no more than fifty yards up a straight road visible all the way from the Dunns' front windows. Ethan's distraught mother had told Murrain that, up to this year, she'd always walked down there to meet the bus. But Ethan, having reached the grand old age of eight, had demanded more independence and insisted on walking up by himself. Most days, his mother said, she continued to watch him through the window as he approached, ready at the door to meet him. But that day she'd lost track of the time and had been a few minutes late approaching the window.

At first, she'd assumed the bus was late. Then she began to worry it had broken down or not turned up. She'd phoned the school but the reception had been closed, her calls transferring to voicemail. After another few minutes, she'd walked to the end of the avenue to peer down the main road into the village. The traffic seemed no heavier than usual, but there'd been no sign of the bus.

Eventually, anxiety beginning to gnaw at her, she'd phoned another mother who lived further out into the hills. And received the confirmation that escalated the anxiety into a clutch of cold fear. Yes, the bus had been and gone, and, yes, the mother's own daughter had arrived home safely at the usual time.

For another five minutes, Mrs Dunn had stalked up and down the avenue calling Ethan's name as if the boy might have hidden himself away somewhere among the rows of box-like houses. She'd returned home and begun frantically phoning around the parents she knew, hoping against hope that Ethan might for some reason have decided to go to play with one of his friends after school. She'd known even then there was no point to this. Ethan would never have gone to a friend's without telling her. Fifteen minutes later, having exhausted all the names she could think of, she called her husband at work. Without hesitation, he'd called the police.

Murrain had become involved later that evening when it was becoming increasingly undeniable that something bad had happened to Ethan. At first, the police had largely focused on calming Mrs Dunn while working pragmatically through the possible explanations for Ethan's disappearance. They'd contacted the school and the head-teacher and obtained a contact-list for Ethan's class, systematically calling each parent to check whether, against the odds, Ethan had made some unexpected after-school detour. They confirmed that Ethan had caught the school-bus as usual and that, as far as any of his friends could remember, he'd alighted at the usual spot. When the police made contact with the bus-driver he recalled Ethan getting off. The driver remembered he'd had to stop the bus ten or fifteen yards further down the road because a van had been illegally parked in the usual pull-in. As the evening wore on, and it was increasingly clear that there was no straightforward explanation for Ethan's absence, CID became involved and serious questioning of witnesses began.

Murrain had been duty officer that evening and had pulled the case even though, as a missing person enquiry, it didn't strictly fall within his remit. Child disappearances were different—more urgent, more sensitive—and Murrain's team was already investigating recent reports of attempted child abductions across the south Manchester area.

They made frustratingly little progress in the first twenty-four hours even after the reports went out on the local TV news. It was a night of following up supposed sightings, gathering witness statements from Ethan's friends and neighbours, conducting door-to-door enquiries through the village, tracking down and checking local CCTV coverage including footage from the school-bus which confirmed definitively that Ethan had travelled and alighted at his usual stop. The next morning, at first light, they began a search of the countryside adjacent to Ethan's home —the hillside and woodland behind, the river Goyt and its banks on the opposite side of the main road. In those early hours, the river had been a key focus. Although no-one put the assumption into words, an abduction was seen as less likely than the possibility that Ethan had come to grief in the steep drop down to the river.

They found nothing. It had been later that afternoon that Murrain had received a call from the Derbyshire force, with whom they'd been liaising on checking CCTV and vehicle reports in the neighbouring villages. A child's body had been found by a local farmer out carrying out fencing repairs on his land just a few miles up the road. Murrain had immediately felt the physical shock, the pulse of energy through his veins, that told him that he at least needed no more formal confirmation of the body's identity.

Now, three days later, he was standing on this windy moor-side, gazing down into the green shade of the woodland, hoping to recapture that feeling. He'd been up here on the day, of course, liaising with the officers from the Derbyshire force who were overseeing the management of the scene. He'd hoped to feel something then, but any sensations were lost in the bustle of police vehicles and white-suited SOCO officers.

Ethan had drowned in the stream that ran through the woodland to the Goyt below. There was bruising to his face and head, but no other evidence of physical or sexual assault. The drowning might conceivably have been accidental—it was possible to construct scenarios that could have resulted in the boy tumbling headfirst into the steam—but the pathologist's view was that the boy had been forcibly held under the running water. Even if the drowning had been accidental, there was still the question of how the eight-year old came to be here, several miles from home in the midst of this bleak moorland. There was no doubt that this was now a murder investigation.

Murrain stood for a moment longer, drinking in the view, seeking that re-connection. Then he made his way back up along the dry-stone walling that marked the boundary of the farmland to where he'd left his car at the roadside. Somewhere below, he heard shouts and the sound of dogs barking. A moment later, a new-looking 4x4 came tearing up the rough driveway from the farm buildings, scattering gravel. Murrain watched as it pulled on to the main road without pausing for any oncoming traffic and then sped out, well above the speed limit, down towards the village.

Curious, he climbed back into his car, pulled back on

to the road and turned into the farm entrance, slowing as his tyres hit the uneven hardcore. His battered Toyota was less well designed for this terrain than the 4x4.

As he approached the farm buildings, a stocky figure emerged, his hand firmly wrapped around the lead of the German Shepherd dog barking angrily beside him. Murrain pulled to a halt and opened his window.

'You can bugger off an' all,' the man said, angrily. 'Before I let go of Buster here.'

Murrain held out his warrant card. 'Police.'

The man stared back at him, not obviously mollified by this revelation. 'Right,' he said, finally. 'Thought you were another of those buggers.'

Murrain climbed out of the car. 'Who were they?'

'Journalists,' the man said. 'Well, journalist and a photographer. Some national rag. Not the first we've had down here.'

'It's a big story. If you have any more trouble, give us a call.'

The man snorted. 'Like you'll be here in a flash. Took you two days when we had a break-in.'

'This your place?'

'Yeah.' As if he'd decided he'd goaded Murrain enough, the man suddenly smiled and held out his hand. 'Pete Tanner. Impoverished sheep and dairy farmer.'

Murrain smiled back and shook the proffered hand. 'DCI Murrain. I'm the officer in charge of the enquiry.'

'Poor little bugger,' Tanner said, presumably referring to Ethan Dunn rather than Murrain himself. 'I was already interviewed by two of your blokes. Gave me quite a grilling.'

'I know,' Murrain said. 'I've read the notes. They were from the Derbyshire force. I'm GMP.' He waved a hand in the direction of the valley below. 'Kid was from down in the village, as you've no doubt heard. Greater Manchester jurisdiction.'

'Ah.' Tanner looked concerned. 'Does that mean I've got to go through the whole rigmarole again?'

'Not at the moment. I just came down to introduce myself.'

Tanner squinted at him. 'You were here the other day, though? After they found the body. I remember you now.'

Murrain knew he cut a memorable figure—tall, heavily-built, slightly ungainly, with a mop of tightly curled greying hair—but was surprised Tanner had noticed him among the melee. 'That's right. But I left my Derbyshire colleagues to run the show. Didn't want to tread on their toes.'

'Assumed you'd come back because I'm a suspect.' It wasn't a question.

Murrain hesitated. Tanner was right, of course, at least about his being a suspect. As the individual who'd discovered the body, he was bound to be on their list. But he'd been able to account for his time since Ethan Dunn's disappearance, either with his wife or members of the farm staff, and he'd been out working with a young labourer when they'd stumbled across the child's remains. So unless something emerged to call his alibis into question, he wasn't high on their list. 'We have to eliminate all possibilities, obviously,' he said, after a moment. 'But I don't think you're seriously in the frame, Mr Tanner. I just came down to say hello and maybe have a little look around the site before it gets dark.'

'Thought the crime scene people had already been all over that.'

'They have,' Murrain agreed. 'Very thoroughly. I just

wanted to get a sense of the lay of the land. It's not easy to do that when the place is crawling with police officers.'

It was true enough, as far as it went. He couldn't tell Tanner that his real reasons for being here were slightly more esoteric. He wanted, as always, to see if he could tap into those — whatever they were, those feelings, intuitions, sensations that so often intruded unsummoned into his mind and body. It was something that couldn't be forced. It would come or it wouldn't. But in the right place and in the right frame of mind, it could provide him with insights he could never achieve by more conventional methods. He'd wanted to meet Tanner for the same reason. He couldn't be sure — maddeningly, he could never be sure — but the absence of that sensation as he stood here helped confirm his assumption that Tanner had no part in this beyond his accidental finding of the body.

'Be my guest,' Tanner said. 'Do you want me to show you where I found the poor little bugger?' In other circumstances, Murrain might have found Tanner's phlegmatic attitude surprising, but he guessed a livestock farmer was accustomed to dealing with death. The sight of a body, even a young human body, probably hadn't fazed him too much.

'If it's not too much trouble,' Murrain said. 'Don't want to go trampling in the wrong places.'

'Not much damage you could do to this place.' He led Murrain along the side of the farm-buildings and down a muddy slope into the heart of the woodland. As they walked, he pointed ahead. 'My land ends over there. You can see the line of fence-posts through the trees?'

'Who owns the land the other side?'

'There's a private care-home further down the hill.

They own the remaining woodland. There are a couple of fields the other side they let for horse-grazing, and then there are the gardens for the home itself. One of those retirement places.'

Murrain felt a momentary tremor, some passing sense of significance. His team would already be checking these facts out, and for the moment he was simply making conversation. But he knew that, at this early stage, anything might help.

The two men trudged down the muddy slope towards the stream, which snaked through the bottom of the valley on its way to the River Goyt below. They'd had a wet couple of months and the waters looked relatively full, maybe a metre wide and a similar depth. A little way ahead of them, where the hillside dropped more steeply, there was a small waterfall with a shallower pool of water beyond. That was where the child's body had been found. 'Does it always run this fast?' Murrain asked as they stood watching the currents.

'Comes and goes,' Tanner said. 'Never dries up entirely, or at least I can't remember when it has. But this is what it's usually like when we've had a bit of rain. And we get plenty of rain up here.'

Murrain had studied the photographs taking by the Scene of Crime Officers. The body had been found lying face-down below the waterfall, still dressed in the school uniform and brightly-coloured anorak he'd been wearing when last seen alive. 'Where were you when you spotted the body?'

Tanner pointed at the line of wire fencing silhouetted against the pale blue sky. 'Just up there. To the right of that tree. Working on the fence. It was Conor who spotted it.'

'Conor?'

'Young lad helps out on the farm. Good worker. We were taking a bit of a break and he pointed out this red object in the water. We thought it was just a plastic bag or something at first but—well, it didn't look quite right, so we went down to check it out.' He shook his head as if the reality had only just struck him. 'Nasty business.'

'Very nasty,' Murrain agreed. 'You think that's where he got in? Whoever did this. Through the broken fence?' That was what Tanner's statement had suggested, and the Derbyshire police had accepted it as a plausible assumption. The Crime Scene people had checked it for forensic evidence, but Murrain wasn't hopeful they'd find much.

'Looks likely. Not often we get a fence broken down. Mostly it's just wear and tear. Replacing the odd rotten post and the like. This looked like it had actually been forced down.'

'Would that require some effort?' Murrain said, peering up at the fencing. For the first time, he was beginning to feel something. Something of the sensation that suggested this was worth pursuing. Some elusive image.

'A bit, and some care. It's a barbed wire fence, after all. But nothing you couldn't achieve with a stout pair of size tens. The fence is designed to deter animals and mark the boundary rather than as security.'

'You could see someone doing that to gain entry down here?'

'Well, the only alternative would be to come past the house and that would have set the dogs off. They're our real intruder alarm. We've occasionally had tramps break in through the fences at the back to sleep in the barns, so it's not unheard of. And we've had teenagers from the village damage stuff for the hell of it after a few bevvies. When we first saw the damage we assumed it was something like that.'

Murrain stomped a few more steps down the bank to where the pool lay beneath the bubbling waterfall. The water here was probably two metres wide, and no more than half a metre deep in the centre. It glittered in the shady sunshine, clear and inviting. He could feel the sensation here strongly enough, the familiar tingling through his skin, but that was no surprise and told him nothing, except perhaps to confirm they were indeed dealing with a murder. When he'd first reached the site, two days before, the body had already been removed. It was hard now to envisage that it had ever been there, a grotesque intrusion into this peaceful scene.

'He was just there,' Tanner said, as if reading Murrain's thoughts. 'A couple of feet out. Right under the waterfall. Face down. You got kids, Mr Murrain?'

'That's a long story,' Murrain said, his face expressionless. 'But I know what you mean.'

'Yeah. It's a bugger. Saw his parents on the news. You wouldn't want to be in their shoes.'

'No,' Murrain agreed. 'You wouldn't.' His eyes were still fixed on the sparkling surface of the water.

'You reckon it was definitely murder, then?'

The appropriate answer was that they were still pursuing their enquiries and waiting for the pathologist's report. Murrain said: 'Unlawful killing, anyway. We don't yet know exactly how he died. Could have been murder. Could have been manslaughter. Could even have been an accident. If he was abandoned up here, he might have just stumbled into the water while he was trying to find his way back up to the road.'

'But he didn't come here by accident? Or by himself?'

'Quite. And he didn't kick down that fence of yours.'

Both men stood in silence watching the motion of the ever-changing water, the dappled sunlight on the underside of the shaking leaves.

'You'll get the bastard, won't you?' Tanner said, finally.

Murrain didn't respond at first. Then, after a second, he said: 'If it's in my power, yes, we will. We'll get him.'

CHAPTER THREE

Two Years Earlier

'You think he's ready for release?' Greg Perry's voice was muffled as he fumbled for something in the bottom draw of his desk. She watched, fascinated, as he emerged clutching a box of dog biscuits and, without pause, tossed one nonchalantly over her head. From behind, she heard a yelp as Bonnie dashed out from under the large meeting table, snatched the biscuit, and promptly vanished again.

Cabaret, she thought. Perry was a man going places in the Service who wanted you to register his ascent up the greasy slope. She couldn't always follow his thinking, but she had little doubt he had it all figured out.

Bonnie was just one of his mild eccentricities. Some of his staff had asked pointedly whether they'd be allowed to bring their pet dog into work too. Perry's response was that when they'd made it to Governor-in-Charge they could do what they bloody well liked. In the meantime, the privilege was his alone.

Kate Forester suspected that Perry wasn't even particularly fond of Bonnie. But the presence of the little Highland Terrier, or whatever the hell breed she was, helped humanise his dour Yorkshire demeanour. And made him seem a more interesting character than he perhaps really was.

He'd say that was typical of a bloody psychologist. A dog couldn't be just a dog. It had to be the key to the workings of his inner psyche. Whereas maybe Greg Perry just wanted to throw dog-biscuits.

He sat up straight and looked at her, making it clear he'd noted her failure to answer his question. 'Well, what do you think?'

'It's not up to me, is it? It's up to the Parole Board. If he was a normal case, he'd have been out years ago.'

'But he's not a normal case. Not in any way.' He opened the file in front of him but made no effort to look at the contents. 'I know in practice he's going out anyway before too long, whether we like it or not. That wasn't the exam question.'

'No,' she acknowledged. Perry hated management-speak, except when he threw it into the conversation to wrong-foot you. 'You asked whether he was ready for release. And the answer's yes, definitely. Unless it's no, not in a million years. One of the two.'

He sighed. 'That's the thing about you psychs. You make life too easy for those of us who have to make operational decisions. Go on, then. Explain.'

'I genuinely don't know, Greg. I'm generally good at reading people—'

'That's what we overpay you for.'

She ignored him. 'But like you say, he's not a normal case. Most of the time, he seems fine. Well adjusted even. But I don't know what's going on in his head.'

'Lucky bugger, then. You've got the rest of us sussed. You think he's hiding something?'

She hesitated, wanting to express her thoughts accurately. 'I don't think so. I mean, you can't be sure in a case like this. It may be he's been stringing everyone along.'

'If so, he could have made life easier for himself. If he'd expressed some remorse, he'd have got parole well before now.'

'It doesn't always work that way. It might be about game-playing. It might be about maintaining control. It might be about preserving his own self-image.'

'It might be about time to go home.' Perry glanced pointedly at his watch. 'But you don't think he's being devious?'

'That's my feeling. I think he's been honest from the start. I don't think he knows what's lurking in his head any more than I do.'

Perry tapped the file with the end of his expensive-looking fountain pen. 'That's feasible, is it? I've read the psychobabble in here but I'd rather hear it from someone who talks English. Or at least from you, since you're the closest I've got.'

She knew he'd have read and digested every word in the file. 'Of course, it's feasible. Shock can do all kinds of things. It's not unusual for people to suppress all memory of a traumatic event. Psychogenic amnesia, to use the babble. Commonly happens to victims of assault or abuse.'

'And to the perpetrators?'

'It depends on the circumstances. We don't know what went on here, what actually led to the death—'

'Because he's the only one who could tell us.'

'My point is that, whatever did happen, it might have been as traumatic for Carl as it was for the victim.'

'Except that Carl's still here to tell the tale. Or, rather, not tell the tale. But I take your point. And it could remain buried even twenty years after the event?'

'It could remain buried forever, in theory. Or the memories might come back, either with help or just through the passage of time.'

Perry was doodling small concentric circles on the

pad in front of him. 'You think he's a danger if he's let out?'

She considered. 'My instinct says not. But it's not much more than instinct.'

'Helpful as ever,' Perry noted. 'But you must have your reasons?'

You didn't get to Governor without the ability to ensure your arse was covered, she thought. 'He doesn't display any of the patterns of behaviour that might lead me to think he was still a concern. Apart from a few unsubstantiated anecdotes at his trial, there's no other significant evidence of childhood psychopathic behaviour—'

'That we're aware of.'

'That we're aware of. And there's been no evidence of such behaviour since he's been inside.'

'He's not been a model prisoner, though. Not throughout.'

'Who is? More sinned against than sinning, in my opinion. He was no trouble at all in the Special Unit. When someone had the brilliant idea to move him to a YOI, he was identified—Christ knows how—and attacked before we'd got our act together. He had the bottle and the nous to fight back, that's all, as far as I can see. There were two or three similar incidents—at least one apparently with the collusion of an officer, according to the report at the time. Then we finally got our backsides in gear and started looking after him properly. Since when he's been, in your words, a model prisoner.'

'So I see. Applied himself with enthusiasm and alacrity. GCSEs, A-levels. An almost completed OU degree. In—what was the subject again?'

She'd known this was coming. 'You know full well,'

she said. 'You know that file even better than I do.'

'Oh, yes.' He was smiling. 'A degree in Psychology. Like every other nutter.' He paused, the smile unwavering. 'Sorry. Politically incorrect.'

'Just incorrect,' she said. 'Only a few of us are real nutters. And your question is, if I'm mind-reading you correctly, has he learned enough gobbledegook to pull the wool over the eyes of a poor innocent professional like me?'

'It's a reasonable question.'

'Anything's possible, Greg. He's a smart cookie and he'd probably be able to work out which buttons to press to win me over. But he's almost got a first degree. I'm a Chartered Psychologist with relevant postgrad qualifications and ten years dealing with the worst kind of what you refer to as nutters. I think I'm likely to see through him.'

Perry nodded, apparently satisfied. 'OK, so you think he's not likely to be a danger to society. Then why don't you think he's ready to be let out?'

'I don't know how he'll handle it for one thing. It's a big hard world out there. The last time he was part of it he was just a child. Life would have been small and safe and secure. We're throwing him back out there, twenty years on, with no friends, no family. Even the most stable personality might struggle.'

'It's not our choice, Kate. All we can do is help him make the best of it.'

'No, well, that's obviously my job. But a few months chatting to me isn't going to make all that go away. All I can do is help him prepare for it.'

'I'd put my money on you to help him more than anyone else,' Perry said. 'But there's nothing we can do once he walks through the gate. That's probation's job.'

'And they'll do the best they can, I'm sure. But this isn't just any prisoner walking back out into freedom. Carl doesn't have a community to go back into. He'll have a new identity. He'll be banned from the places he might once have known. Even if he had friends, he wouldn't be allowed to make contact with them. He's no family left. There's nothing.' She paused, conscious of her rising emotions. 'I know there's nothing we or anyone can do about that. The only people likely to have an interest in Carl are the bloody tabloids. It's probably only a matter of time before some smart-arse news editor works out he's due for release. Then they'll loose the hounds.'

Perry was watching her with interest. 'Not like you to get so personally involved, Kate.'

'Not my usual detached self? You know it's never as simple as that, Greg. You have to remain objective, but you also have to engage, find a way of empathising with what they're feeling. How else can you help them?' She went on, before Perry could interrupt. 'Like you say, he's a unique case. I normally know how best I can help. With Carl, I'm still a long way from figuring it out.'

'There's only so much you can do. In an ideal world he'd have got a lot more support but as it is we've got him for a few months. You can't expect to unscamble his brains in that time. Maybe just concentrate on the practical stuff. Help him think about how he's actually going to survive out there.'

'I'll do that, obviously. But the two things aren't unconnected. He can't prepare for the future if he's still mired in the past.'

Perry tossed another dog biscuit casually over her head. Behind her, there was the familiar yelp and scuffle of feet as Bonnie snapped up the unconsidered trifle. 'If it were anyone else, Kate, I might worry you were letting your idealism get the better of you. But you've never struck me as a bleeding heart.'

'You say the nicest things, Greg. I just want to be a professional. I know we've limited resources and we have to have limited ambitions. But that doesn't mean we should set out to do a half-arsed job.'

He smiled. 'Fair point. OK, Kate. I know you know what you're doing. Get out there and give it a go.' His smile grew broader, and she knew he wouldn't be able to resist the punchline. 'And give it both cheeks.'

CHAPTER FOUR

Now

It was the kind of environment in which Murrain felt most uncomfortable. Not the immediate circumstances, though Christ knew those were as unpleasant as they could possibly be, but the whole set-up. He could cope with the apparently obsessive tidiness. That was second-nature to him, as Eloise would frequently testify in irritation. It was one of his ways of coping with his own unique demons. But he did wonder about the state of mind that would have led Mrs Dunn to reach for the vacuum-cleaner on that particular morning.

The box-like sitting room felt too small for his shambling frame, as if he were likely to bang his head against the ceiling or his shoulders on the door frame if he moved too quickly. Then there was the clutter. Every highly polished surface in the room was filled with rows of ornaments — trinkets, mirrors, a souvenir of this place and that. It didn't look like a room that would easily accommodate a child.

Of course, for the foreseeable future, it would no longer need to.

Murrain shuffled awkwardly on the over-patterned carpet and glanced at Milton, who was staring blankly at the couple sitting on the sofa opposite. They looked shrunken themselves, as if physically oppressed by Murrain's substantial physique.

'I appreciate how difficult this must be for you—' Murrain began.

'Do you?' Alan Dunn said. 'Do you really?'

Two days before, Dunn had been taken to the mortuary at Stepping Hill hospital to confirm the identity of Ethan's tiny body. Not many people have to experience that kind of ordeal, but Murrain had been closer than most. Now, though, he said only: 'Of course not, Mr Dunn. But we'll do whatever we can to support you through this.'

'Except leave us alone,' Dunn said, belligerently.

'We won't trouble you any more than we can avoid,' Murrain said. 'But you'll understand we need all the information we can get. Anything that might help us track down the person responsible for this.'

'And as far as you're concerned, we're potential suspects too.'

It was a recurrent pattern that Murrain had noted in murder cases, especially those involving children. Those involved often seemed unduly keen to insert themselves into the frame, if only to demonstrate unequivocally why they shouldn't be there. It had been the same with Tanner earlier in the afternoon. 'We have to consider every possibility,' he said. 'Even if just to eliminate it. We have to be systematic.'

Dunn looked as if he were about to argue, but his wife placed a firm hand on his arm and he closed his mouth. Murrain suspected that, for all Dunn's bluster, he wasn't the dominant personality in this marriage.

'How can we help you?' Susan Dunn said. 'We've both already given statements to your colleagues.' She glanced across at Milton who had been responsible for taking the formal statements from the couple at the start of the investigation.

'We appreciate that, Mrs Dunn,' Milton said now. 'We always try to take statements from the key witnesses at the earliest opportunity, while events are still fresh in their minds. But we also sometimes find that people recall more — or at least different things — as time passes. As the investigation proceeds, we may also have different questions to ask.' And, he added silently to himself, we sometimes discover more when Chief Inspector Kenny Murrain is the one listening to the answers.

'Your statement was extremely helpful, Mrs Dunn,' Murrain said. She had described, in detail and with apparent precision, the sequence of events surrounding Ethan's disappearance. Murrain had read hers and Alan Dunn's statements over several times and had been left feeling slightly uneasy. He'd felt something. Some incongruity, something that sat awkwardly. But it had been no more than a passing fancy, and he'd felt no trace of the more intense sensations that might have suggested either had been directly involved in their son's disappearance. That wasn't necessarily definitive, as he well knew, but it suggested that, for the moment, the police might be better concentrating their attentions elsewhere. 'All I want you to do, if it's not too painful, is just to think again about the events of that afternoon. When you first became concerned, you went out to the main road?'

She nodded. She was dressed a little over-formally, Murrain thought, as if to receive visitors, and her face was carefully made-up in a style that, to his inexpert eye, seemed old-fashioned. He imagined that, like the house-cleaning, this was an attempt to maintain some normality in the face of these devastating events. She seemed remarkably calm but Murrain's years of experience had taught him that everyone mourns in their own way. 'I'd been trying to call the school. I thought perhaps the bus had broken down or delayed. It's happened once or twice before. Then I walked down to the road to see if the traffic looked particularly bad. They had roadworks down by the junction last year and everything gridlocked. So I went to have a look...' She trailed off.

Murrain could imagine the state she'd been in that afternoon, desperately hoping for some simple explanation for Ethan's non-appearance. He could remember his and Eloise's anxiety the day their own teenage son had failed to return home from school. Another story with no happy ending. 'Can you try to think back to what you saw? Was there anything unusual?' She would have reached the main road only a short time after Ethan had gone missing.

She closed her eyes as she tried to envisage what she'd seen that afternoon. Her husband looked as if he might be about to interrupt, but Murrain shot him a look and he remained silent. 'I don't think so,' she said, after a moment. 'From the corner you can see right down into the village. The traffic was running normally. Mostly cars on the school run, I suppose.' She stopped, as if to control her emotions. 'There weren't many people about. It was a dull day. Not raining, but threatening to.' She paused. 'I'm sorry. I don't think this is much help to you.'

Murrain shook his head. 'We don't know what might or might not be helpful at this stage. Just tell me anything that occurs to you. What about the vehicles on the main road? Passing by or parked. Any that struck you as unusual or out-of-place?'

She closed her eyes again. 'I don't think so. There were a few cars I recognised. Neighbours' cars that are usually there. But you get all sorts of cars in the village. Walkers, people visiting the cafes. So there are always unfamiliar cars out there.' She hesitated, her eyes still closed. 'There was a van.'

'Where?' Murrain exchanged a glance with Milton, who was silently making notes.

'Where the bus normally pulls in. It's not exactly a bus-stop, but there are double yellow lines on that stretch so it's normally clear. The bus usually pulls in there so it's not blocking the road while the children are getting off.'

The driver had mentioned the pull-in being blocked but had been unable to recall any details of the vehicle in question. 'I was too busy trying to manoeuvre a bloody bus full of screaming kids up that narrow road and swearing at the bugger who'd blocked the stop,' he'd explained colourfully.

'You're sure it was a van?'

She opened her eyes. 'Fairly sure. It wasn't a large van, just one of those small ones. Like it might have belonged to someone doing work at one of the houses or shops on the main road.'

'Can you remember the colour?'

She frowned. 'Dark, I think. Blue, maybe? I'm not sure.'

'Any name or logo on it?'

'Not that I can recall. I was looking down the road at it, so I couldn't really see the sides. But my impression was that it was just plain.'

Murrain had felt the slight electrical jolt when she'd first mentioned the van. The sense that it was somehow significant. But perhaps he'd imagined that, just linked what he'd read in the bus-driver's statement. He'd felt something then, too, but very faint, the echo of an echo.

'Is it unusual for vehicles to be parked there?' Milton asked.

'None of the locals park there at that time of day because we all know the bus uses it. But the parking spaces further down get filled so people sometimes park there if they're calling at one of the shops or something.'

'It may be nothing,' Milton observed. 'But it's worth following up. We can check CCTV footage from the surrounding area, see if we can get a match and the registration.'

They were already doing that, of course, trying to identify all the vehicles parked in the area, along with any that had passed through the village at the relevant times. It wasn't easy. They'd obtained some information from their house-to-house interviews with the street's shop-owners and residents. There was some private CCTV coverage in the village itself and they were persuading the various retailers to give them access to the data. Down on the main road there were more cameras and there was a number-plate recognition camera on the route to the M60. But once past the village, heading into the hills, there was nothing.

But Murrain had felt something, and now he had more reason to focus attention on the van. Who did it belong to, and why was it parked just there? If the driver was involved, there would have been a risk in parking conspicuously. But the registration might be faked and, in any case, people tended to be unobservant. If the driver had stopped with the intention of snatching Ethan or another child, the vehicle would need to have been parked close at hand. And perhaps the driver had deliberately intended to cause the bus to park further up the road, out of sight of Susan Dunn's usually watchful eyes. Which, he added silently to himself, would suggest some premeditation. And also, perhaps, some knowledge of Susan Dunn's routine.

'I don't understand why he'd have gone off with anyone,' Susan Dunn said, her voice low as if speaking to herself. 'We'd warned him often enough about stranger danger.'

Murrain nodded sympathetically, though he'd often wondered whether warnings to children about going off with strangers missed the point. Children were generally much more at risk from those they knew than from a random stranger. 'It's all too easy to distract a child if you're sufficiently manipulative,' he said. 'And there's always the possibility that this wasn't a stranger.'

'So you're back to us again,' Alan Dunn said.

'There may be lots of people around the village who could have seemed familiar to Ethan. Friends, acquaintances, neighbours, people who work in the shops, parents of his school friends, or other people associated with the school. Anyone he might have come across. People who might have been able to persuade him they weren't really a stranger. We're doing door-to-door interviews through the village, and we're talking to the staff and the pupils at the school. If there's anyone else you can think of that we might have missed, maybe you could provide us with details?'

'I can't go accusing people,' Susan Dunn protested. 'Not about this.' She sounded as if her primary concern was a breach of neighbourly etiquette.

'That's not what I'm suggesting,' Murrain said. 'But people know other people. There may be shops you visit regularly, or people you see. Contacts that might not be obvious to us, but which are worth pursuing.'

Her husband had risen to his feet and was pacing up and down the small living room. 'You haven't a clue, have you? That's what this amounts to.'

It wasn't far off the truth, Murrain thought. As Alan

Dunn had implied, the first rule in a case like this was to suspect the parents, but they'd searched the house and garden thoroughly—on the pretext of gathering whatever information they could about Ethan—and had so far uncovered nothing suspicious. The second line of investigation was anyone else close to the family—relatives, close friends, regular visitors. But so far they'd identified no obvious candidates. All they could do was continue to expand their circle of interest, gathering information as systematically as they could. The worst possibility, in terms of their likely success, was that this was genuinely a stranger, just someone passing through, with Ethan no more than a random victim of the fates. Those killers, like the notorious Robert Black who'd evaded the police for decades, were the ones who might never be caught.

'We don't jump to conclusions. We gather and analyse as much information as we can. It's only a matter of time.' Murrain sounded, he hoped, much more confident than he currently felt.

'I hope you're right,' Alan Dunn said. 'I want this bastard caught. Before anyone else suffers.' He suddenly sounded the way he looked—no longer aggressive, but reduced, vulnerable, at a loss. As if he'd been struggling to keep the reality at bay and now it had overwhelmed him.

Murrain remembered how he'd felt when faced with a similar reality. 'That's what we all want, Mr Dunn. I promise you we'll do our best to make it happen.' As he spoke, he momentarily felt that familiar tremor beneath his skin, but he couldn't begin to interpret what it might mean. All he knew was that twice already today he'd made the same promise. A promise he didn't know whether he really could keep.

CHAPTER FIVE

Two Years Earlier

Tell him to buy me an acre of land.
He'd been humming gently to himself when she entered the meeting room, and she recognised the old Simon and Garfunkel song.

'Not long now,' she said. 'How are you feeling?'

He looked up. 'I don't know. Blank, mainly. Emotionless. It doesn't feel real.'

She could understand that. Despite all the attempts to prepare him—the days out on licence, periods in the probation hostel, the endless discussions with probation and other advisors—he probably still couldn't begin to envisage what the future would be like.

'Do you feel scared?'

'Sometimes. Sometimes I wake in the night, and there's a cold hand clutching my insides. I lie there till the panic goes away. But mostly it's not like that. That only happens when the fear takes me by surprise. When I'm half-asleep and not really prepared.'

'You think you're suppressing that fear most of the time? Finding ways of coping with it?'

'Not consciously. But, yes, I must be finding ways of dealing with it. Is that a bad thing?'

In truth, she had no idea. 'It's natural you're feeling scared,' she offered, after a pause.

'Don't psychologists think repression is a bad thing?'

'Christ knows what psychologists think,' she said. 'I just think it's human. It can be good or bad, depending on the circumstances.' As so often in her conversations with Carl, she found herself circling the real issues, looking for a way of engaging in something beyond banter.

'You lot have spent the last ten years trying to get me to unrepress things.'

'But our motives aren't entirely altruistic. Or, more accurately, we aren't concerned only with you or your well-being.'

'You also have a duty to the victim?' he intoned. 'Or the victim's family. For what it's worth, that's always mattered to me too. It's just that there's not been much I could do about it.'

'Is that right, Carl?' she said. 'There was nothing you could do to help the family?'

He appeared genuinely pained by the question. 'I don't expect anyone to feel sympathy for me. But I've had to live with this without even knowing what I was living with.'

'You know what you did, Carl. You know what happened.'

'I know what they told me happened.'

'So what *do* you know?'

He stared back at her as if the question was unexpected, though she had asked variants of it at almost every session. 'Oh, God, Kate,' he said now. 'I know everything except the one thing I really need to know.'

'Tell me about it,' she said. 'The holiday.' They'd discussed this before, but his responses had never been more than superficial.

'Tell you what?'

'Anything. Something you haven't told me before.'

His smile had returned, and she could sense he was taking up the challenge. 'Oh, Christ, I don't know. It was a crap holiday, I've told you that already, haven't I? I didn't want to go. My mother had died. My old man was in a state, had been knocking back the booze like there was no tomorrow. Which in his head there probably wasn't. I just felt like — I don't know, as if the ground had been whipped from under me. As if everything I'd relied on had melted away.'

'And the holiday?' He'd never talked as openly as this before, not about anything this close to what mattered.

'Those months after my mum died were awful. My dad really lost it. At first, he was all right. He knew he had to keep things going. It was just about okay while he still had things to deal with. Organising the funeral. Sorting out the will. While he was caught up in that, he had a purpose. Then he didn't any more.'

'He had you.'

'That was probably what stopped him going off the rails entirely. Things become tough, but he never neglected me. He always made sure I was fed. That I was taken care of.'

'You say he was drinking?'

'Probably more than I realised. And maybe there was something of a nervous breakdown, or depression, or whatever the right word is. He was taking time off work, and in the end they gave him compassionate leave. He couldn't get out of bed half the time.'

'But he didn't neglect you?'

'Not really. It was a shitty time. But it was only a few months. He realised what was happening. He told me later he spoke to the GP, got some help with the depression. He got himself together. Cut back on the drinking. Went back to work. Got his life in order, more or less. Found a way to cope.'

'What sort of way?'

Carl looked up at her, as if he'd only just realised that, in his eagerness to talk, he'd wandered outside his comfort zone. 'Partly religion. He'd always been a devout Catholic.' He spoke the last two words as if they were encircled with ironic quotation marks. 'They both were, my mum and dad. And I suppose I was, by upbringing. But he started to take it a lot more seriously. We'd missed Mass most weeks after the funeral, but he started dragging me along again. He got involved in various church activities.' He stopped and laughed. 'I think he was just trying to meet another good Catholic wife to replace mum.'

'Did he succeed?'

'Not that I was aware of. There were women in and out of his life later but no-one who stayed. I don't remember anyone at this time. I suppose he must have been lonely.'

'He had you.'

'Lonely for adult company. He was never much of a mixer. Not one of the lads. I suppose he must have had friends, but I don't know who they were. Once mum died, he was on his own.'

'And the holiday? Tell me about the holiday.'

'Crappiest holiday ever,' he said. 'At least that's what I thought then.'

'What was wrong with it?'

'Oh, nothing really, looking back. But you know what it's like when you're that age. I was just bored. I was the wrong age. You spend your time just mooching around, fed up with everything.'

'What sort of place was it?' She'd read the accounts in the file but wanted to hear what he thought, what impressions he might have of the place now. Any clues that might be lodging in his memory.

'Oh, God, the worst possible place for a bored adolescent. It was a church thing. My dad's idea, obviously. I don't think he could face the idea of just taking me away on his own. A bit too up close and personal. This was supposed to dilute it. Probably worked for him.'

'And for you?'

'Not so much. It was some sort of youth centre. The kind of place they use for retreats. I'd been there once before with school. It was okay if you were there with a bunch of mates your own age. Less fun for a summer holiday.'

'What sort of people were there?' She was looking for any signs he was about to pull down the mental blinds as he'd done so often before. For the moment, he looked relaxed, or as relaxed as he ever did.

'Families. People looking for a cheap break, I suppose. It was a nice spot. Close to the sea. Sand-dunes. Woodland. Sounds idyllic now after spending my life in these places. But there was hardly anybody my age. It was mostly families with young children. There were a couple of older teenagers who were too cool to hang out with the likes of me. Spent their time smoking and necking illicit booze. There was nobody I could really spend time with.'

'So what did you do?'

'Mooched mainly. I had a Walkman with some tapes and a few books I'd brought with me. If the weather was okay, I went off into the woods and sat reading and listening to music. When it was raining, I tried to find a corner of the Centre to do the same thing.'

'What sort of kid were you? I mean, were you the solitary type?'

He paused, as if the question had never occurred to

him before. She recalled the personality assessments she'd read in his file. In prison, he'd been seen as a loner, but that was unsurprising.

'I don't think I saw myself that way,' he said, at last. 'I was a fairly sociable type at school. Had a few friends, though no-one I was really close to. It's another thing that's difficult to remember. I don't mean it's a blank. But it's hard to put myself back into the head of that child at school. He seems like a different person.'

'Do you remember how you felt on the holiday?'

'Like I say, bored. Unhappy. Isolated. I was pissed off with my dad for insisting we went, and he was pissed off with me for not being happy about it.'

'Why do you think he was keen to go?'

'I don't know. Maybe there was a woman involved. Someone he had his eye on, I mean. I remember him leaving me alone at night while he went out drinking in some local pub.'

'You didn't mind?'

'It wasn't every night. A couple of times he took me along to get something to eat. There was a crowd in there, some locals, some from the site, that he'd obviously got to know.'

She decided it was time to push her luck. He might shut down, but he might do that at any minute in any case. She wasn't likely to get this close again. 'What do you remember about it? The day it happened, I mean.'

She was certain he'd find some excuse to change the subject or end the conversation. But he surprised her. 'Not much,' he said, finally. 'I remember the morning. There was nothing special about it. My dad had been out to the pub the night before. We'd been sharing a twin room, so he'd woken me when he came back in. It probably wasn't all that late. Half eleven or so. But I remember feeling angry and resentful that he'd left me alone for so long. When he came in, I could smell the beer on him. I could tell he was a bit drunk.'

'He wasn't violent?'

'No. He had a bit of a temper sometimes, but he wasn't really the violent type at all, even after a few drinks.'

She gazed back at him, wondering if that was really true, but decided not to press the point. 'But you were angry with him that night?'

'I suppose. It wasn't even that I minded being left. I enjoyed being able to read by myself. It was just that he took it for granted that it was okay.'

'Did you say anything?'

'You don't at that age, do you? I just enjoyed stewing in my own resentment.'

'You said it was just another morning? The next day, I mean.'

'Well, yes. The morning after the night before as far as my dad was concerned. He wasn't great the next morning. A bit surly and taciturn. But we were up in time for breakfast.'

He still sounded resentful, even after all these years. Perhaps more than he'd allowed himself to believe. 'You had breakfast together?'

'Yes, but I skipped off as soon as I could, and he was probably glad to see me go.'

'Where did you go?' She phrased the question carefully. Not 'do you remember?' She wanted him distracted, carried away on the tide of his recollections, not stopping to think about what he might or might not actually recall.

'Into the woods,' he said. 'Grabbed the Walkman and a book and went off to hide. That's what I usually did anyway.'

'You were on your own?' She wasn't sure what made her ask the question.

He paused again, longer this time, and she was certain now that she'd lost him.

'I wasn't.'

She was startled that he'd responded at all, not even beginning to think about what his words might mean. 'Go on.'

'I wasn't alone.' He hesitated again, as if unsure what he was saying. 'I mean—I don't think I was—' Suddenly he sounded less sure of himself.

'Tell me what you remember.'

'There was a kid,' Carl said at last. 'Younger than me. He'd latched on to me. You know how it is. At that age, we all want to be older. I'd have latched on to the two cool teens if they'd let me but they were too interested in getting to know each other. I guess this kid saw me as a cooler older brother. Christ, if only he'd known.'

'This was just that morning? Or before?'

Carl paused, thinking. 'I knew him before. He'd been pestering me. He was just a kid, not that much younger than me, though it didn't feel like that at the time.' He was clearly thinking hard, clutching on to memories in danger of fading away before he could properly grasp them. 'He had a Gameboy. I'd never seen one before. I couldn't quite believe it. That you could play games on something you could hold in your hand.'

She'd been through his file countless times. She could recite some of his statements almost by rote. There was mention of the victim owning a Gameboy, but Carl had never previously acknowledged knowing him before that morning.

'You liked him?'

'I don't know. Not really, probably, if I'm honest. You're ruthless at that age, aren't you? You're happy to take advantage of the access to the Gameboy or whatever it is. But you're still embarrassed by kids younger than you.'

'And you think he went with you that morning?'

'It's like trying to remember a dream. When I've been asked before, I've always felt sure I'd left on my own that morning. I was sure I'd spent that morning on my own in the woods. Reading. Listening to the Walkman. Just by myself.' His face was as blank as ever. 'But I didn't. At some point, there were two of us. I don't know where I ran into him. Maybe over breakfast. Maybe as I was leaving. There were two of us, heading into the woods—' He stopped, as if only just beginning to realise the significance of what he was saying.

'What did you do? In the woods?'

He closed his eyes, trying to will himself back to that day. 'I can't remember. I've just a memory now—an image, really, just something in my head—of the two of us heading into the wood. I don't know if it's even real, or if I'm just imagining it. After that. Nothing. Still nothing.' He sounded almost desolate.

Her mind was still running through what she remembered of Carl's file. She was sure none of the other witnesses had made any mention of Carl associating with other children at the holiday site.

'Who was this boy, Carl? Can you remember?'

'It was him,' he said at last, eyes still fixed on the blank tabletop. 'It was him. It was the boy I killed.'

CHAPTER SIX

Now

'How you doing?' DI Joe Milton slid himself into the chair opposite Marie Donovan's desk.

'Knackered, but otherwise okay.' It had been a tough few days. Endless door-to-door interviews, fingertip searches of the area around where the body had been found, long hours writing up notes and collating intelligence. Exhausting, but exactly what she'd been wanting when she'd joined the team. 'Not much sense of us getting anywhere, though, is there?'

'Not obviously,' he agreed. 'It's looking more and more like we're in for the long haul.'

'With the chances of a result receding by the day?'

'Who knows? It's like always. We just need one breakthrough.'

'Is that a quote from Joe Milton's little book of motivation?'

He laughed. 'More Kenny Murrain than Joe Milton. He'll keep us going. This sort of case, though, you expect there'll be an obvious suspect.'

'The father, you mean?'

'Often enough. Or some close relative. The funny uncle. The creepy cousin. Someone who jumps out at you from day one. You tell yourself not to jump to conclusions. But it usually turns out you were right.'

'You don't reckon the father's in the frame, then?'

'There doesn't seem any reason to think so, except that he's the father. He can account for his time. We've found nothing suspicious in the house. Everything stacks up.'

'What about the mother?'

He hesitated. 'Not sure, to be honest. I mean, no, I can't see it. But there's something a bit odd there.'

'Is this one of Kenny's feelings?' she asked.

'Not really. He said there was something that left him feeling uneasy, but, to be honest, I'd don't think you'd need any special sensitivity to feel that.'

'How'd you mean?'

'It was the house, partly,' Milton said. 'You know what family houses are like. A bit chaotic. Informal. It didn't have that feel. Everything was too neat. Fussy. She'd obviously spent time tidying up even that morning.'

'She could just be house-proud,' Donovan said. 'I've heard rumours of people like that. Or it was displacement activity. Stop herself thinking about what's happened. It's difficult to know what sort of psychological state she might be in under the circumstances. Anyway, who's to say she's the one who tidies the house?'

He smiled. 'Yeah, fair cop. I shouldn't make assumptions. But it felt like her domain. More than the father's. Like I say, I can't really see her being in the frame. There's a period notionally unaccounted for between the time when Ethan got off the bus and when she started phoning round after she got worried, but it's only a matter of minutes. We've checked the records of her outgoing calls and her story stacks up. And we've found nothing untoward in the house. I was just left with an odd sense that there's something she's not saying.'

'Something significant?'

'Who knows? People have all kinds of secrets.'

'So we're back where we started, with someone outside the family?'

'Looks like it. There are no relatives living nearby, and the Dunns don't seem to have any particularly close friends in the neighbourhood. So far we've drawn a blank with all that kind of stuff. Still, you never know what might crawl out of the woodwork.' He shuffled awkwardly on the hard wooden chair. 'Anyway, you're surviving, are you? Not changed your mind about joining us?'

'Too late for that now, isn't it? Think I've burned my bridges.'

'I suppose,' he agreed. Donovan had originally joined Murrain's team in a civilian post on a secondment from the National Crime Agency. Somehow, though, after a few months, Murrain had managed to wangle a permanent appointment for her at her former police rank of Detective Sergeant. Milton still wasn't sure how Murrain had managed this, particularly as the whole force was supposedly facing a recruitment freeze. But that was Kenny Murrain. Unworldly as he might sometimes seem, it never paid to underestimate him.

'But the answer is no,' she added, 'in case you were wondering. Even despite the challenging induction.' It was almost a year since that first case had resulted in an almost fatal outcome for her. But, then, as it had turned out, she'd brought most of that with her. Murrain, endorsed by the force's occupational health advisor, had insisted she take some time off to recover but she'd resisted the offer of extended compassionate leave. She'd been down that route before and it had seemed only to exacerbate the issues. This time she been glad to get back to work and had thrown herself into the routine with enthusiasm.

'That's good,' he said. 'We're delighted to have you. Even Paul, though he might do his best to conceal it sometimes.' He gestured towards DS Wanstead, who was bustling about at the far end of the room, doing his best to hold back the chaos that continually threatened to overwhelm the Major Incident Room. Wanstead had been welcoming enough but she'd sensed he'd been uncomfortable at the prospect of another DS, especially a female one, joining the team. It wasn't so much that he resented her or regarded her as competition, she thought, more just that she'd walked into his territory and he wasn't sure how to deal with it.

'He's been fine,' she said. 'And he's doing his usual bloody good job with this place.' They'd set up the MIR in the old police station up in the larger town that lay above and adjacent to the riverside village where Ethan had lived. It was a 1960s built building, still notionally the base for a police enquiry centre that opened two mornings per week but no longer used as an operational station. The word was that the force had been looking to offload it but had so far failed to find an interested buyer. In the meantime, the building contained a large, mostly unused meeting room which had housed the local control centre in the days before support services had been centralised. Quite how Wanstead had been aware of this was one of those mysteries to which only he knew the answer, but the room was perfect for their purposes. Spacious, close to the crime scene, and — once Wanstead had completed his wheeling and dealing — well-appointed with networking and other facilities. In an organisation where accommodation was in short support, it was a smart find.

The room was already filling up with the detritus that tends to accompany a major investigation. The piles of paperwork that never seemed to reduce however paperless the office was supposed to be. The unwashed coffee cups and discarded takeaway cartons. The coats and jackets left here pending a change in the weather. Most of the team were out conducting interviews, though a couple of officers were pounding away at their laptop keyboards. Murrain's desk, at the far end of the room, was as always pristine.

'Where is Kenny, anyway?' she asked.

'Back at the ranch giving an update to the powers-that-be,' Milton said. 'They've got a press conference with the parents this afternoon. Usual stuff. Anyone with any information. Someone out there must know or have suspicions. After which, we'll no doubt get a call from every nutter and attention-seeker in the region.'

'You never know,' she said. 'We're not exactly drowning in leads at the moment.'

'True enough. We're still trying to track down this van that was supposedly blocking the pull-in for the bus. None of the CCTV on the street catches it. Nobody we've interviewed, other than the bus-driver and Mrs Dunn, has any recollection of it. Doesn't seem to have been visiting any of the local shops.'

'What about the CCTV cameras on the main roads?'

'Those just give us endless possible candidates. We've been checking on the most likely ones in terms of timing, but nothing useful so far.'

'You'd think someone would have seen something,' Donovan said. 'A kid getting snatched. Broad daylight. Mid-afternoon.'

'You'd think,' Milton agreed. 'Though we don't know

it was necessarily like that. Maybe Ethan wandered away by himself first. Anyway, it only takes a moment.' He stared gloomily into space as if contemplating where that moment had led in this instance. Then he blinked and looked back at her. 'Actually, I was wondering if you fancied grabbing a beer once we'd finished tonight?'

It took her a moment to process what he'd said. There'd been a period during the few weeks after she'd returned to work when she'd half-expected him to ask her out. He'd seemed more solicitous about her welfare than she'd expected, and she'd suspected his interest amounted to more than simple comradely support. For her part, she hadn't been entirely averse to the idea. She wasn't sure she was ready for anything serious after everything that had happened, but Joe Milton was pleasant and good company. If he'd asked her, she'd probably have accepted and been content to see where it led.

But either she'd been wrong, or he'd never plucked up the courage to ask. The moment seemed to have passed and their relationship had stayed at the purely professional level. She'd heard from others that there was still a girlfriend somewhere in Milton's life, but he'd never mentioned her and everything he said suggested he was living alone. However pleasant he might be, she'd concluded, she might be better steering clear.

'Tonight?' she said, in a tone that emerged more negatively than she'd intended.

He looked around the MIR. 'No, you're right. Not really the moment, is it? I just felt in need of a break.'

She decided to take pity on him. 'No, go on. Why not? It's been a hellish few days. And it is Friday, even if we're going to be back in tomorrow anyway. Better make it just the one, though. I've got to drive home.'

'Don't imagine we'll be away early, anyway,' Milton said. He looked back at her with the air of a small boy seeking permission to go out to play.

She resisted the urge to laugh at his expression. 'Yeah, why not?' she said. 'What time do you reckon you'll be done?'

Milton peered at the pile of paperwork on his desk. 'Be as quick as I can. You okay to hang on for a bit.'

'I've plenty to be getting on with.'

'Great,' he said, pushing himself to his feet. 'So it's a date—' He stopped. 'Oh, God, sorry. I didn't mean—'

This time, she really did burst out laughing. 'I know what you meant. And I'm looking forward to it.' And as she spoke the words, she realised, with a slight internal start of surprise, that she really was.

***

'You survived the press conference, then?' Eloise's voice said from the car's hands-free speaker.

Murrain saw the lights ahead turning red and slowed to pull up at the junction. 'Just about,' he said. 'Not the most enjoyable hour's work.'

'Always painful in a case like this,' she agreed. 'I watched it on the TV in the Chief's office. Thought you did a good job.'

'Well, I'm glad you thought so.' The lights changed to green and Murrain accelerated through the centre of town towards the station where they'd located the MIR.

'Chief thought so too, if that tickles your ego. He thought you sounded confident and reassuring. And authoritative. Like you know what you're doing.'

'Whereas he and you know better,' Murrain observed. 'He must have said that through gritted teeth.'

'He's got a lot of time for you, Kenny, as you well know.' She allowed a beat. 'More than you deserve.'

'No doubt.' She was right, though, as he knew. Murrain had his run-ins with the senior ranks as most operational officers at his level tended to, but his track-record stood up to scrutiny even if his methods sometimes raised eyebrows. For his part, though he rarely brought himself to say so out loud, he thought the Chief Officers' Group were mostly a capable bunch. They'd been largely successful at shielding the force from political and financial pressures that he couldn't begin to imagine dealing with, and for the most part seemed content to trust him and his colleagues to get on with their work. It hadn't quite felt like that a couple of hours earlier, when he was being grilled by a panel of his Chief Super, the ACC and the Head of Communications prior to kicking off the press conference, but he knew they'd also just been doing their jobs. Everyone wanted to get this one right.

The purpose of the press conference had been to showcase the Dunns' public appeal for information. The parents had coped creditably in the face of the media pack. They'd been emotional but remained coherent, striking the right tone to encourage potential informants to pick up the phone. Murrain had taken questions from the media, most of which, inevitably, had carried the implication that the police really ought to have made more progress by now. Murrain's responses had been positive if non-committal. Presumably that was what the Chief had meant by 'reassuring'.

'I'm assuming you'll be pulling another late one tonight?' Eloise said.

'Imagine so.' He'd reached the turn-off to the police station but, on a whim, continued along the main road, heading out of town towards the neighbouring village. He wasn't sure what had made him continue driving. Not quite one of his usual feelings. But something.

'I've got to attend some after-hours Council thing tonight,' she said. 'So don't reckon I'll be back till eight-thirtyish. Take away?'

'Fine by me. Whatever you fancy.'

Eloise was an operational Chief Superintendent, although somehow her relative seniority seemed to mean she was generally back home long before Murrain in the evenings. But he was fully aware of the pressures involved in her role. 'What I fancy most at the moment is not having to attend this bloody Council meeting. Two hours of sniping and backbiting. But I haven't been able to come up with a decent excuse.'

'It's the price you pay for high office,' he said. 'Better dealing with councillors than corpses.'

'I'm not sure it's always possible to tell the difference.'

Murrain said his goodbyes, and then continued down the hill and over the river into the village where Ethan Dunn had lived his brief life. Once across the river he turned right off the main road into the centre of the village. The road ran alongside the river for a few hundred yards and then rose again, heading up into the Derbyshire hills, towards the area where Ethan's body had been found. The old stone cottages clustered tightly around what once had been no more than a track then the road widened again as the surrounding buildings thinned. Ahead, this route eventually led past Pete Tanner's farm to the open moorland beyond. Before he reached the farm, Murrain slowed and, signalling right, turned into the driveway of an imposing Edwardian villa that loomed over the roadside, incongruous after the clusters of older artisans' cottages that characterised this end of the village.

There was a small car park and Murrain pulled into a space marked 'Visitors'. A couple of other cars were parked at the far end, presumably belonging to staff, and a minibus stood in front of the main entrance. Murrain stood for a moment gazing up at the brooding lines of the building. It was a sizeable place, no doubt built by some rich industrialist with the resources to live a suitable distance from the urban sources of his wealth. The building was surrounded by woodland, and the rear would have an impressive view out across the Goyt valley.

Ethan Dunn's body had been found in the adjoining land, just a couple of miles so up the road. As Murrain stood in the chilly afternoon sunlight, he could feel something, some distant sense of static, but he couldn't for the moment tell whether it was associated with this building or simply stirred by the proximity to Tanner's farm. He waited for a moment and then made his way up the stone steps to the entrance.

Inside, he found a smart-looking reception area, with plush carpeting, comfortable seats and discreet decor. Designed to make a positive impression on those considering depositing their elderly relatives in the place. There was no immediate sign of life but after a few moments a woman in a nursing-style outfit appeared through the double-doors beyond the reception desk, smiling broadly.

'Good afternoon,' she said. 'How can I help you?'

Murrain brandished his warrant card. 'Chief Inspector Murrain,' he said. 'I was wondering whether the owner or manager's available?'

The smile had vanished instantaneously, replaced by an expression which Murrain assumed was intended to convey sympathetic concern. He could imagine her using it when breaking bad news about one of the home's residents. 'Is this about…?' Her voice trailed to silence, but she gestured vaguely in the direction, presumably, of Tanner's farm.

Murrain nodded. 'I imagine you'll already have spoken to one of my officers as part of our enquiries. I just had a few additional questions, so thought I'd call in on my way past.' None of this was strictly true. He hadn't been passing, and, for the moment at least, he had no real idea why he was here or what he was going to ask. He'd simply wanted to get a feel for the place, follow up on the brief instinctive frisson he'd felt when Tanner had first mentioned the care-home.

He'd had Bert Wallace run a check on the place already but she'd found nothing of interest. The home was appropriately registered with the Care Quality Commission, and there were no recorded concerns about its operation. It was an independent business and the most recent filed accounts suggested it was running profitably. A brief check through the local press achieves had uncovered no reports of scandal or wrongdoing. A couple of Murrain's team had been out here as part of the general door-to-door enquiries but no-one had been able to offer anything useful. The staff on duty at the relevant time had seen nothing. The residents were all fully accounted for. The fields adjoining Tanner's land were let to a local riding-school for grazing and the care home staff had no reason to access them. It had just been another property to tick off as the officers worked their way through the village.

'I'll check whether Mr Brody's available,' she said. 'Can I get you a coffee?'

He smiled and declined the offer, then lowered

himself into one of the comfortable-looking seats to wait. He half-expected that Brody might find some excuse not to see him, but a few moments later the double-doors were flung open and a tall, heavily-built man burst into the reception area. 'Good afternoon, Chief Inspector,' he boomed. 'Welcome to our humble institution.'

Murrain took the outstretched hand and found himself subjected to a vigorous and theatrical handshake.

'Finlan Brody at your service. How can we assist you, Chief Inspector?'

It was a good question and Murrain had no immediate answer. Fortunately, before he could respond, Brody ushered him through the double-doors into the corridor beyond into what was presumably Brody's office. It was an elegantly furnished room, with an old-fashioned mahogany desk set squarely on a plush carpet, and a selection of tasteful and expensive-looking artwork adorning the walls. Two large arched windows gave a view over the lawns at the rear to the open space of the river valley beyond. Murrain could imagine some residents and their relatives might be reassured by such visible opulence. Others might wonder what their fees were being spent on.

'I hope we've offered you coffee?'

'Thank you, I'm fine,' Murrain said. 'I won't keep you long.' He'd hoped for something when he walked in here, some confirmation of the sensation he'd felt when talking to Tanner. But for the moment there was nothing he could feel sure of—only a faint background hum, some faint sense of meaning lurking just beyond his comprehension. He was wasting his time, not to mention Brody's. 'Impressive place you've got here,' he said.

'I was lucky. The house was actually an inheritance—

some maiden aunt I'd never met, would you believe? At first, I thought it was too big to live in and was on the point of selling it. But I was looking for a change of career at the time so I decided to move into this business. It was a bit hairy for the first couple of years because I'd had to borrow a lot for the conversion, but after that we've never looked back.' Murrain thought that this sounded like a well-rehearsed routine and was unsurprised when Brody shifted gear into a sales pitch. 'We've invested a lot in the place over the years. Facilities second to none. Really excellent staff. Beautiful location. If you're ever seeking care for elderly relatives, Chief Inspector—' He stopped and smiled. There was something theatrical about his every gesture. His appearance—swept back hair, a neatly trimmed beard, an costly-looking jacket just the right side of casual— were designed to make an impact. He seemed unlikely to suffer from any lack of self-esteem. 'But you've not come to listen to me waxing eloquent about this place. I assume you've come about the dreadful business up the road?'

Murrain had decided his only option was to play to Brody's evident ego. 'I just wanted to introduce myself and perhaps see whether I might pick your brains. I appreciate you've already spoken to one of my colleagues but I thought, given your standing in the local community, that it might be helpful to talk to you directly ' He had no idea what Brody's real standing in the local community might be, but he guessed Brody himself was unlikely to underestimate it.

'Only too happy to help if there's anything I can do. I'm very active in the community. We do our best to ensure it's a place we can all be proud of.'

'I don't suppose you knew the Dunns?' He wasn't

sure what had made him ask the question, but he'd felt the sudden buzz that suggested it was in some way significant.

'The parents?' Brody frowned. 'I don't think so. The name didn't ring a bell when I saw them on the TV. I may have recognised the faces, though. It's a small village. You tend to see people out and about. I suppose they might have had a relative living here but I've no recollection of it. Nothing more than that.' He paused and looked up at Murrain. 'Do you suspect the parents?'

Murrain could imagine Brody as the type to dispense some supposedly insider gossip as he held court in the village pub. 'We've no reason to,' Murrain said, shortly. 'I'm just looking for general background. Anything that might help us identify potential leads. You must know the community well?'

'You mean, can I point you in the direction of any likely child killers?' Brody said, pointedly. 'Can't say I've noticed any hanging around the village.' He shook his head. 'Sorry—that was flippant. But I can't believe it was anyone local who did this.'

Which was always what people thought, Murrain reflected, right up to the point when they discovered what the quiet young man in the flat above or the harmless old chap next door had really been capable of. 'You'll appreciate we have to explore these possibilities, Mr Brody. Despite what the media would have us believe, it's rare that these crimes are committed by random strangers. But I'm not expecting you to inform on your neighbours. I'm really just looking for some insights into the village. Does it tend to be very family orientated, for example? Or are there many people living alone?' The buzz was still there in the back of his head, perhaps even growing stronger. There was something here, he felt, but he had no idea what.

'It's like anywhere, really,' Brody said. 'A bit of a mix. We attract some older people. It's a nice place to retire—picturesque but not remote. We've got young families. There are a couple of decent primary schools up the hill. And a few people on their own—youngsters who've not got hitched yet, the odd widow or widower.' He laughed. 'Even the very odd middle-aged bachelor like me. There's a decent train service to Manchester so we get plenty who commute into the city. We call it a village, but it's a dormitory town really.' He shrugged. 'I hear what you say about the likelihood of it being a random stranger, but we do get all sorts through here. Ramblers who get the train out so they can head into the hills. People passing through on their way to the motorway. People visiting the local cafes and pubs. It may look quaint, but it's not exactly your cloistered rural village.'

Murrain had gained a similar impression during his brief walks along the main street. The place had made the most of its attractive riverside location, hidden cosily among the surrounding hills and woodland, the main street lined with cafes and shops aimed at the weekend day-tripper market. Discreetly concealed off the main drag, there were rows of new-build housing—including the estate where the Dunns lived—occupied largely by commuters who were absent at work for the larger part of the week. Beyond those, towards Stockport and Manchester, there was a larger adjacent town with its own substantial population. The killer might not be a random stranger, but—in the absence of any direct link with the Dunns—the number of possible suspects could be enormous. 'I take the point,' Murrain agreed.

'All I can tell you,' Brody said, 'is that the local

community's right behind you. Whoever's behind this, they want him caught and soon.' He made the words sound like a threat. 'I head up a forum of local businesses. Just an informal thing for networking. But we've got parents of young children among the members and I can tell you they're scared to death by this. Until this guy's caught, no-one's letting their kids out of their sight.'

'Has anyone mentioned any other incidents involving children?' Murrain asked. It was a question his officers were routinely asking in their interviews. 'Attempted snatchings, approaches from strangers, that sort of thing. If Ethan Dunn was unlucky enough to be targeted randomly, it may not be a one-off. We've had reports of incidents elsewhere in the borough, which may or may not be connected, but not here.'

'I've heard of nothing like that,' Brody said. 'If there had been, I'm sure word would have got around, given what's happened now.'

Murrain nodded, keen now to end the interview, conscious he'd had no good reason for being here in the first place. 'Well, thanks for your time, Mr Brody.' He pushed himself slowly to his feet. 'I won't keep you any longer.' He paused, looking past Brody at the sunlit garden outside. Now he was standing, he could see the fencing that lined the northern border of the lawns and the meadow beyond. In the distance he could see the trees that marked the start of the woodland and Pete Tanner's farm.

In that moment, he felt something shimmering behind his eyes. Some image, blurred, ill-defined. He turned back to Brody as the moment passed and the vision, whatever it might have been, dissolved. 'Fine view.'

'Very fine,' Brody agreed. 'We're fortunate to live here, Chief Inspector.' His smile broadened, although there was no obvious warmth to it. 'Let's hope we can keep it that way, eh?'

'Let's hope so,' Murrain said, meeting Brody's gaze. Something, he thought. There's something here. But, as so often, he couldn't begin to imagine what.

CHAPTER SEVEN

Two years earlier

'Mum. Granny said we could go for a pizza! Can we go now?'

Kate Forester stood in the hallway, her jacket half off her shoulders. She gazed past Jack's bouncing figure to where her mother was watching the television news. 'That's what granny said, was it?' She pitched her voice loud enough to ensure Elizabeth could hear over the reports of some middle-eastern bombing.

Elizabeth glanced over her shoulder. 'Oh, hello, dear. You're back. What was that?'

'Jack seems to think we're going for a pizza.'

'I'm not sure where he's got that idea—'

'But, granny, you said! This afternoon. You said we could!' Jack was already adopting the uniquely shrill outrage of a child deprived of his inalienable human rights.

'I don't think that's quite what I said—'

'Don't worry, mum. If that's what Jack wants, we can go out. I don't really feel up to cooking tonight anyway.'

'Well, if that's not a problem for you, dear.'

'No, mum, it's not a problem for me. Don't worry.' Kate lowered herself wearily on to the sofa and watched as Elizabeth eased herself comfortably back into her armchair. In exchange for Kate paying a generously high rent, Elizabeth had offered to provide child-care while Kate was at work. From time to time, Kate found herself wondering whether this arrangement was quite as mutually beneficial as it had first appeared. 'Do you want to come too?'

'That's very kind of you, dear. But I might just enjoy a quiet evening to myself.'

Of course you might, Kate thought. I might, too, if the chance were ever there. She couldn't remember when she'd last had an evening to herself. Or, at least, an evening to herself when she didn't have to catch up with work.

She waved Jack out of the room. 'Get out of your school uniform, then. And we'll see about that pizza.'

'I hope that's all right, dear,' Eizabeth said, as usual expressing concern only when the die was firmly cast. 'You're looking a bit tired.'

'Always a tonic to hear that.'

'You need something to perk you up, that's all I can say.'

Kate recognised where the conversation was heading. 'Something to perk you up' was one her mother's code-phrases which could loosely be translated as 'a man'. 'I'm fine,' Kate repeated.

'I still think that you and Graeme—'

Kate took a deep breath. 'Mum. You need to get this into your head. Graeme and I are finished. Forever. We're not going to get back together. Not for you. Not for anyone.'

'It's not about me, love. I'm just thinking of what's best for you. '

'This is what's best for me. Believe me.'

Elizabeth opened her mouth and Kate knew that she was about to be treated to another lecture about the virtues of her most recent boyfriend. It was the last thing she needed right now—or ever, for that matter. 'I don't what to talk about it, mum. I'm going to have a shower and get changed.' She turned and left the room before

Elizabeth could try to have the last word.

It was her own fault, Kate supposed. She'd never shared the details of the split between her and Graeme. Better to keep it simple. She and Graeme had decided to call it a day. Nobody's fault. A pity, but there you go.

The truth was that Graeme had tainted everything, perhaps even her relationship with Jack. He'd known all along what he was doing. Step by step, inch by inch. He was subtle enough about it. Just a passing comment here or there, the occasional insinuation. It was all about gaining control. But he'd almost wrecked her memories of Ryan, inserted icy blades of suspicion into her mind, trying to destroy her image of her late husband just as if he were scribbling over a physical picture. Even later, when she knew what a bullshit merchant Graeme really was, she'd never quite been able to expunge the things he'd said. However hard she tried, the past would never be the same again.

Quite probably, even without her realising it, he'd inserted his presence between her and Jack in the same way. She couldn't see Jack without remembering what Graeme had done. What Graeme had *tried* to do, she added carefully to herself. Graeme's game-playing had always relied on its victims' ability to distort their recollections in just the ways that Graeme wanted.

Jesus. These were the kind of conversations she had with prisoners every day. Insisting they distinguish between the perpetrator and the victim. Trying to make them take responsibility for their own actions, rather than off-loading it on to those they'd chosen to harm. Jack had been the victim. No, not even that — the *potential* victim. No blame could attach to him. It was only Graeme, always fucking Graeme, who had tried to cast a cloud over that.

Kate made her way up the stairs and paused on the landing. To her surprise, she realised that there were tears in her eyes, a welling of emotion in her throat. She wasn't even sure why. Sadness for the loss of what she'd thought she'd had with Graeme? Anger at what he'd ultimately turned out to be? Or simple tiredness and frustration that life always had to be so bloody difficult?

Probably the last. She'd had a tough day, and it hadn't become any easier since she'd arrived home. Her work with Carl was still preying on her mind. Greg had been right, in part at least, that she'd allowed the case to get under her skin in a way she normally tried hard to avoid.

It wasn't healthy. She had to think about Carl only as an assignment, a set of case-notes to be completed. A file that, ultimately, she would close and pass to someone else.

She sighed and pushed open the bathroom door, looking forward to the feel of the scalding water on her skin. The pleasure of washing away the detritus of the day.

And then she'd make the most of what life was throwing at her. She'd take Jack out for a pizza. She'd have a glass or two of wine. And she'd bloody well enjoy it.

***

The next morning, Kate was halfway out the door, running late as always, when she saw it. Her head still felt slightly fogged from the previous night's wine and it took her a moment to register what she'd seen. She stopped, catching her breath, aware already of a rising emotion she couldn't define. Anger. Anxiety. Misery.

Some combination of all of those.

'Mum. What's this?' She'd raised her voice only to make herself heard above the sound of whatever cartoon Jack was engrossed in. But she couldn't disguise the emotion in her tone.

As Elizabeth emerged from the kitchen, a pan-scourer clutched firmly in one hand, Kate held up the scrap of paper. 'What's this?'

'I don't know. Is there something written on it?'

'As far as I can see, it's a phone message. From Graeme.'

Elizabeth nodded. 'That's nice.'

'Did you take it? The message.' It was an unnecessary question. The scribbled writing was clearly her mother's. Even so, Kate was struck by the queasy realisation that Jack might have answered the phone first, might have spoken directly to Graeme. Shit. How the hell did Graeme even have this number?

But that was Graeme all over. He'd have found a way to track her down. Called her friends until he found someone dumb enough to give him the information. Like her mother, none of them knew the full story anyway, even if most of them in a spirit of female solidarity were happy to accept her considered view that he was a conniving bastard.

'He called yesterday afternoon. Before you got in. We had a nice chat. He can be so charming—'

'What time did he call?' Kate interrupted.

'About four thirty. It must have been because I was watching that quiz—'

'Did he talk to Jack?'

Elizabeth frowned. 'No. He wanted to, but Jack was caught up in one of his computer games. I got a bit cross with him about it.'

Kate let out the breath she'd been holding. Thank Christ for that. But it had been nothing more than good luck. 'Why didn't you say something last night?'

'Well, I was going to, but then you started going on about how you were finished with Graeme, so I thought—'

'What did he want?'

'He wanted to talk to Jack and you, really. Said he was missing you both. He told me he was keen to patch things up.'

Kate glanced down at the scrap of paper. Nothing more than Graeme's name and a scribbled mobile number.

'I told him he shouldn't lose hope. Where there's a will there's a way, and all that.'

'I've told you, mum, it's over. There's no hope.' She screwed up the scrap of paper and walked past Elizabeth to throw it in the kitchen bin. 'If he calls again, just tell him to leave me alone.'

'But he sounded as if he really meant it. He said he regretted everything that had happened between you. I think you're being unfair—'

But he didn't tell you what happened between us, did he, Kate thought. 'I've told you, mum. It's over. I'm not letting him anywhere near me. Or Jack. If he calls again, don't let him talk to Jack.'

'But Jack needs—'

'Whatever Jack needs, it's not Graeme. He's not Jack's father. He has no claims. No rights. I don't want him anywhere near Jack.'

'He was even asking about Jack's birthday. He said that he'd wanted to get Jack a present himself, but he knew you wouldn't allow it.'

'I don't want any presents from Graeme. I don't want

him anywhere near my life.'

Elizabeth shook her head, as if she couldn't fathom this inexplicable recalcitrance. 'He didn't say whether he'd phone you back. He left the number, but I don't think he really thought you'd call him.'

Of course he fucking didn't, Kate said to herself. He knows full well I wouldn't contact him if he was the last man on earth. He has no interest in me. He just wants to spread as much poison as he can.

'Christ,' Kate said. 'I'm nearly twenty minutes late now. Nicely timed to hit the traffic.' She stomped past her mother to the front door. 'I'll say it one more time, mum. Please. If he phones again, make it clear I don't want to talk to him. And I don't want him anywhere near me or Jack. Is that clear?'

Elizabeth gazed at her, looking baffled. 'I still think—'

But Kate had already slammed the front door behind her.

***

'So how's it going, then? You got him sorted?'

For a moment, she couldn't work out where the voice was coming from. She stood in the doorway wondering what stunt Perry was working on this time. 'Some new self-effacing management style, Greg? Doesn't suit you.'

'What?' Perry's head appeared from beneath the office table. He held up a well-chewed rubber bone. 'Retrieving this.'

'Bonnie's got you doing her dirty work now?'

He climbed slowly to his feet. 'I left her at home today. Couple of HQ bods coming down this afternoon. Thought I should get the place tidied up before they arrive.'

'Very wise,' she said, looking around at the idiosyncratic decor in Perry's office, from the Preston North End poster to the supposedly authentic Native American mask he'd brought back from some conference in the US. 'Wouldn't want them to get the wrong idea.'

'That sound you hear will always be HQ barking up the wrong tree. But we do the best we can. They want to talk about your chap.'

'You mean Carl? What do they want to know?'

'Everyone's got a stake in this one. I'm told the Minister's been asking for daily briefings.' Perry was carefully stashing noxious-looking dog toys into a plastic case with a large picture of a gambolling puppy on the front.

'Hasn't he anything better to do? Like running a Ministry.'

'You might think so, but apparently not.'

'What do they want to know?'

'What do they always want to know? How we can make sure their backsides are protected.'

'Always high on my priority list. Though I don't usually notice them taking much flak when things go wrong.'

'That's why they employ people like us. Governors in charge, particularly. It's our job to resign so the big nobs don't have to. They basically want to know if he's ready for release. They want to know what actions we're taking to make sure he is. They want to know what support needs to be in place once he's out there. They want to know how we can guarantee he won't reoffend.'

She sighed. 'You know the answers to all those questions, Greg. There are procedures already in place to deal with all that. In as much as we can deal with it.

Anyway, it's not our decision. It's the Parole Board's decision.'

'Yes, I know. I imagine they know, too, if that's not giving them too much credit. It doesn't stop them repeatedly asking the questions. And it doesn't stop them taking the trouble to travel all the way up here to ask them again in person. No doubt it won't stop them sending me an e-mail tomorrow asking me to confirm all the answers yet again. Their real fear's the tabloids, of course. No matter what they do to protect his identity, it'll be a challenge to keep this under wraps.'

'Especially if there's a host of civil servants scurrying round the country like headless chickens drawing attention to it,' Forester pointed out. 'The more people get involved the greater the risk of leakage, I'd have thought. What are you planning to say to them? Your visitors, I mean.'

'I'll do my best to reassure them without actually committing to anything. And I'll remind them, yet again, that it's not our decision. Their biggest concern is still that he's never acknowledged what he did, never shown any remorse. I'll tell them about the work you've been doing. That your professional judgement is that he genuinely can't remember—'

She felt a sudden tightening of her stomach, realising she hadn't updated Perry since her previous session with Carl. 'Greg. You should know. It's probably nothing but—'

'Go on.'

She described what had happened in that last session. Her sense that a new vista might have opened up in Carl's memory.

'Those were his words?' Perry asked. '"The boy I killed." No equivocation?'

'Those were his words. It doesn't mean he did kill him. Or that he remembers doing so.'

'Doesn't it?'

'Not necessarily.'

'So what does it mean?'

'I tried to take him forward after that. Tried to get him to recall what happened next. After he met this boy. Whether they did go into the woods. What might have happened after that. But it was no good. He clammed up, told me that was all there was. That was all he could remember, and he wasn't even sure about that.'

'Did you believe him? That he couldn't remember any more.'

She paused for a long moment. Too long, she realised. 'I think I did. I'd led him further than he wanted to go. He'd acknowledged something but he couldn't cope with thinking about what it might mean.'

'But that would imply he was guilty, surely? Jesus, Kate, why didn't you tell me this before?'

'It doesn't necessarily mean that,' she protested. But, whatever the truth about the case, she already knew she'd screwed up. 'Look, he's had years of other people defining his memories. He's struggling to make his own recollections fit into that. It might just be he's shying away from finding out what's true and what isn't.' She paused. 'Do you think this throws a spanner in the works? In terms of Carl's release, I mean.'

'Christ knows, Kate. Like you say, not our decision. We're a long way down the road and these are just four words that, as you say, may mean nothing. But it certainly means I'll get a whole new lot of grief from the buggers today.'

'I suppose we have to tell them?' she said, knowing the answer before she opened her mouth.

'I think we probably do, don't you, Kate? We have to tell them. And you have to report it formally. We can't just keep these things to ourselves, you know.' He'd allowed a sharp edge of irony to enter his tone. 'I'm prepared for everyone to cover their backs up to a point, but I want to make sure they're fully aware of everything I bloody am. If something goes wrong later, I won't be taking the rap for it alone.' The last words sounded as if they were aimed at her as much as his impending visitors.

'No, obviously,' she said. 'I just don't want to rock the boat any more than we have to. Life's going to be tough enough for him.'

'It'll be even tougher if we're not fully open. Everyone has to know exactly where things stand. That way, Probation can give him the best possible help.'

'Probation will do what they can but it won't be much. You know that as well as I do. And their focus will be on public protection. Not on Carl.'

'The two aren't mutually exclusive, Kate. You should know that better than anyone.'

'Carl's not going to be helped by having the authorities breathing down his neck.' She paused, conscious of Perry's sceptical scrutiny. 'And, no, Greg, I'm not getting too involved. I'm trying to take a dispassionate view. We need to be open about Carl's position. But we don't want to overstate it, either. It's four words.'

'And a new memory. More lifting of the veil. That's right, isn't it?'

'But that could go anywhere. It's taken us months to get this far. There's no reason to think we'll get any further. I'm not expecting the dam to burst and it all to come spilling out. And if it did, we don't know what it might be. Maybe it'll confirm his guilt. Maybe it'll do the opposite. Maybe it'll bring him closure. Maybe it'll just throw him deeper into despair. Christ knows.'

'That's your professional view, is it?' His words and tone sounded, for once, close to real mockery. 'The best you can offer.'

'I'm not being flippant. It's a basic principle of my profession to get things out into the open, but you can never predict what they'll look like once they're out there.'

'You still think it's the right thing to do? Now? Just before release?'

She could almost hear the cogs turning in Perry's brain. 'What are you saying, Greg?'

'I'm asking a question. In your professional judgement, is this the right way to be handling the case? At this stage in the game, I mean. Are you confident of that?'

'Of course I'm not confident, Greg. You know that's not how this works.' She swallowed, conscious now that she was struggling to keep her emotions under control.

'He's probably only got a few weeks till release. We need to do what's in his best interests. Make best use of the time.'

She suddenly felt weary of the whole thing. It was as if, over the past couple of years, everything had been taken from her—her marriage, her future, her self-esteem. The only thing she'd had to cling on to, apart from Jack, had been her job. She'd thrown herself into work, struggled on, telling herself this was the real way forward. Now she felt as if she'd ballsed that up to. Just at the moment when Perry had most needed her professional support, she'd let him down. She could feel tears welling in her eyes, but she took a breath and continued, keeping her voice steady. 'Cards on the table, then, Greg. When we kicked this off, I thought it was the right thing to do. Help Carl get to grips with whatever's inside his head. We've made progress but it's been a bloody slow road. It's made me more confident he's not simply being manipulative. There's a genuine blind spot in his memory. We've managed to shine some light in there—'

'But?'

'But not much. And now—at this stage in the game, as you put it—well, maybe you're right. Maybe it's not a good idea to probe any more. The worst that might happen is we set off something we don't have time to deal with. Carl's not going to get serious support with these issues outside.' She was thinking through the implications as she spoke. 'If we keep trying, Carl may end up feeling like he's working to a deadline. He may even begin to manufacture memories—not consciously, but as a way of satisfying himself and the process.'

'Do you think that might be what happened today?'

'It's possible.'

She could see that Perry was taking all of this in, weighing the potential consequences. 'So?'

'So I think you're right. We should knock it on the head.'

'It's not about my being right. It's what you think best.'

'Come off it, Greg. You just want to make sure I agree with you. I've thought about it and, yes, I do. When we started this, I thought there was a chance of bringing something to the surface. And I thought it was better to do it here, where he could get proper help and support, rather than leaving it to emerge when he's out living by himself in some unfamiliar community.'

'Do you think it will? Come out on its own, I mean.'

'How the hell do I know? Maybe it'll stay buried and he'll live happy ever after. Maybe it'll pop into his head in the middle of one dark night and send him on a manic killing spree. We've not finished drafting the handbook to the human mind.' She was conscious her voice was trembling. 'If you want my best guess, it's that it will return to him slowly. It might take years, it might never be fully reliable, but eventually something will seep back. As for what that might mean — well, it depends on what he remembers, doesn't it?' Without waiting for a response, she stood up, wanting to leave before she really lost control. 'We're agreed, then, are we? We're knocking the sessions with Carl on the head. I'll hand him over to one of the team and we'll focus on the future. Get him ready for life outside.'

'If that's what you think.'

'It's what *we* think, Greg. Let's call it a joint decision, shall we?' She was already turning away, but felt she needed to make one final effort. 'Do you want me to join you this afternoon?'

He hesitated, long enough for her to know what his answer would be. 'No, Kate. I can handle it.'

CHAPTER EIGHT

Now

By the time Murrain arrived back, the MIR was already emptying for the night. They were at the stage of the investigation when the opportunities of the initial golden hours had long passed. They were facing the long grind of interviews, intelligence-gathering, working through the responses to the public appeals, generally trying to make sense of what little information they had. The first wave of calls following the media conference had tailed off, though they were expecting a further deluge when the highlights were shown on the early evening news programmes. The incoming calls were being handled by the Force Control Room with additional staffing brought in as support, and any likely leads were forwarded to a small team of officers to follow up. They were still beavering away in the far corner, headphones clamped to their ears, fingers tapping at keyboards.

'Thought you must have gone straight home,' Wanstead said lugubriously, peering up from behind his computer terminal.

'You know me better than that, Paul.' Murrain slumped down at his desk. 'This is like a second home to me.'

Wanstead snorted. 'I'd be off like a shot if I had a warm Chief Super to go home to.'

'I'll have a word with the senior officers for you. See if there are any volunteers. If Helena doesn't object.' Helena being the long-suffering Mrs Wanstead. Murrain had often wondered what she saw in her husband, given she had to share him in a quasi-bigamous relationship with his job. It might well be she preferred him in smaller doses.

'Anything useful coming out of the media conference?'

'Not so's you'd notice so far,' Wanstead said. 'Usual mix of crazies and people misguidedly trying to be helpful. One or two claiming sightings of a van that might conceivably be the one we're looking for, but nothing that's looking very promising.' He glanced at the notes on the desk in front of him. 'A couple of supposed sightings of the boy on his own, in the window between his disappearance and the likely time of death.'

'Locally? In the village, I mean?'

Wanstead shook his head. 'One up here in the town. The other in Stockport. Think we can discount the second, probably, though we'll check it out. The other — who knows?'

'But one young schoolboy looks pretty much like another?'

'Quite.'

'Anything else?'

'Three reported instances of attempted child snatching. All in South Manchester over the last couple of months.'

'But not previously reported to us?'

'Apparently not. They're all pretty trivial instances in themselves. A van pulling up and the driver trying to talk to some kids on their way home from school. Another kid claiming some van driver tried to drag him into the back of a van but he managed to slip away. Another who said he'd been approached in the street, but the guy fled because the kid's mother turned up.'

'Do they sound convincing?'

Wanstead shrugged. 'Maybe. But you know how it is. Kids—and parents—can get hysterical when something like this happens. Start imagining all kinds of stuff. Anyway, we're following them up. Alongside revisiting the other cases we've had reported over the last few months.' They both knew these kinds of reports were relatively commonplace. Sometimes they were substantiated. More often, they were left unresolved, maybe no more than the product of some child's over-active imagination.

'How are we doing with local offenders?' They were checking, as a matter of course, any local residents on the sex offenders' register, as well as any other ex-offenders who might be conceivable suspects.

'Working through them. Nothing promising so far, though.'

The more time went by, the less likely they were to make a breakthrough. At the same time, this wasn't a case that anyone—other than the killer—wanted to leave unresolved. For the Chief and his colleagues, it was too high-profile, the type of failure no-one wanted blotting their reputational copybooks. For Murrain and his team, it was too close to home. Murrain could live with the professional failure—that was part of the job sometimes—but not with the idea the killer might go unpunished or, worse still, kill again. The family and the locals would want closure—to know what had happened, to be sure the person responsible had been dealt with, to be confident they and their children could walk the streets in safety.

'What about the interviews with the schoolkids?' he asked. 'Anything new from those?' They'd been interviewing the children in Ethan's year at the primary school, beginning with those on the bus. It was a delicate process, with the child's parents or the teacher sitting in. They had to be sensitive to the children's own anxieties and emotions, and take account of the youngsters' often unreliable memories. Some of them conjured up their own imagined monsters. Others were too eager to help or over-keen to be the centre of attention, and had provided embellished accounts that were simply not credible. It had taken several days so far to work through the numbers, with little to show for their efforts. Murrain wasn't hopeful that today would have proved any more fruitful.

'Nothing new,' Wanstead said. 'None of them on the bus saw anything. A couple remember Ethan getting off but nothing after that. There was a girl got off at the same stop, but she was met by her mother and didn't register what happened to Ethan. And the mother couldn't recall anything at all. Didn't even notice that anyone else had got off the bus. Incredible, isn't it?'

It wasn't really, in Murrain's experience. It was rare to find a good, reliable witness. Most people were remarkably unobservant, too preoccupied with their own concerns and activities to notice what anyone else might be doing. 'That's children for you,' he said. 'And parents, come to that. Tied up in their own worlds. But, yes, whoever did this was smart or lucky, or a bit of both probably. Kept out of the way of CCTV. Picked the right moment. Maybe just opportunist, if Ethan did wander off after he got off the bus.' He shook his head. 'All I know is we're getting nowhere.'

He knuckled his eyes, suddenly feeling exhausted, and reached out to boot up his computer terminal. There'd be a string of e-mails from on high seeking an update. The prospect made him feel even wearier but he knew he'd have to deal with them before he left, along with whatever other correspondence had accumulated while he'd been out. Then he should head home for a break. He always felt the same awkwardness when an investigation had reached this point. The temptation was to work all hours to prove—to yourself as much as to anyone else—that you were giving it your best shot. But what the investigation needed now was rigour, attention to detail and, ideally, a dash of inspiration. At the moment, Murrain didn't feel equipped to provide any of those. 'I take it Joe's had the sense to bugger off home for the night?'

'Well, he's buggered off *somewhere*,' Wanstead responded enigmatically.

Murrain finished entering his password and waited for the network to traipse through its interminable routines. 'Go on, Paul. You're dying to tell me.'

Wanstead eased back in his chair, with the air of one about to launch into a lengthy anecdote. 'He went off with young Donovan. For a drink,' he added, as if this were the final confirmation of some long-held suspicion.

'Ah, for a *drink*,' Murrain echoed. 'Well, always good to see the team getting on.'

'I'd understood that Joe was spoken for,' Wanstead said, disapprovingly. 'Thought he was living with whatshername? Came to the Christmas do last year?'

'Gill,' Murrain confirmed. 'Yes, he is. Or was. I don't think that necessarily precludes him going for a drink with a colleague. Even I'm allowed to do that once in a blue moon, Eloise tells me.' He paused. 'Anyway, I think there might be complications with Gill.'

'That right?' Wanstead had abandoned any pretence of working on the papers he had lined up in front of him.

'None of our business, Paul. But I believe Gill's working abroad. Reading between the lines, I'm not sure how much future that relationship has. I've been meaning to have a chat with Joe about — well, how he's doing. Not so well is my guess.'

Wanstead raised an eyebrow. 'Seems fine to me.'

'Well, he keeps up the front. But I think it's hit him harder than he lets on.' As he spoke, Murrain was mentally kicking himself for not having followed matters up with Milton. They'd had a brief conversation a few weeks earlier when Murrain had detected that Milton was less than his usual enthusiastic self. With some reluctance, Milton had acknowledged that all wasn't entirely well with his domestic life. 'Gill got this terrific job,' he'd said, clearly trying hard to sound pleased about the news. 'OECD in Paris. Too good an opportunity to turn down.'

'So she's moved over there?'

'Well, temporarily. We're not sure for how long. You know.'

Murrain didn't know, but he could guess. 'You thinking of going out to join her?' He'd no desire to lose the services of his trusty deputy, but he suspected that wasn't really the issue.

Milton had smiled. 'Don't see myself as a gendarme, do you? No, it's just a temporary thing.' But he hadn't sounded as if he really believed this, and Murrain had been left with the suspicion that the split was likely to be more permanent than Milton was prepared to acknowledge. He'd not pushed the point but he'd intended to have a follow-up chat with Milton. It wasn't his place to interfere, but Milton deserved any support Murrain could provide. As always though, life — or, more accurately, Ethan Dunn's tragic death — had intervened.

'Sorry to hear that,' Wanstead responded. 'He's a decent enough lad, Joe.' That was the highest level of praise Wanstead was likely to offer about any of his colleagues.

'Don't say a word, Paul,' Murrain warned. 'If I find you've been gossiping about any of this, I'll have you back on the beat.'

Wanstead looked genuinely shocked at the suggestion. 'You know me, boss. Silent as the grave. Silent as the bloody grave.'

***

'Look, you grab a table and I'll get the drinks. What are you having?'

It was only just after six, but the place was filling up. Marie Donovan guessed the place did a brisk early evening trade with commuters popping in for a quick one on their way from the railway station to home. Most of the other customers looked as if they were returning from work, briefly relaxing after a long day in the office. She spotted a table in the far corner and, turning back to Milton, began to head towards it. 'Just something soft for me. Lime and soda?'

'If you're sure,' he said. 'I'll risk a pint.' He turned to the bustle at the bar and began gently to ease his way to the front. By the time he returned with their drinks, Donovan had secured a small table in an alcove where they could talk without being overheard. They'd decided to risk visiting the riverside pub in the village, only a few hundred yards from the spot where Ethan Dunn had been taken. She'd been hesitant when Milton had made the suggestion. It was all too easy in a case like this to find yourselves castigated for slacking on the job. Milton had persuaded her the risk was low. They'd had only limited involvement in the house-to-house interviews in the village, and no-one was likely to have any idea who they were. 'I just want to get a feel for the place,' he'd added. 'People respond artificially when you turn up as a policeman. I'd like to see what sort of community this is.'

'You're getting like Kenny,' she'd said, jokingly. 'Feelings and atmosphere. Anyway, you'll only get a feel for that part of the community that visits the pub.'

He'd shrugged. 'People are usually more truthful after a few drinks.'

Maybe that was true, she thought, looking around her now. Certainly, people were talking very volubly, the volume growing louder even in the brief time she'd been sitting there. It was a mixed crowd — youngish besuited groups on their way home from work, a few older locals propping up the bar, a couple of families sampling the decent-looking pub food.

Milton slid into the seat opposite her and pushed the glass of lime and soda towards her. 'Busy old place.'

'Doesn't look as if people are locking themselves away in fear of our killer.'

'Don't suppose they feel personally threatened.' Milton glanced at a family seated at a nearby table — a pleasant-looking young mother and father, two primary-school aged children munching away at their burgers. 'Imagine they're keeping their kids close at hand, though. I hope we get this bastard soon.'

'If he's not already passed through on his way to somewhere else,' Donovan said. 'Assuming it is a he.'

'That's the nightmare thought, isn't it?' Milton agreed. 'That this is just some passing stranger. Someone we'll only catch years down the road. If at all.' He stared gloomily at his pint, then took a deep swallow. 'Christ.'

'Let's hope not.'

They sat in silence for a few minutes. Donovan was wondering whether this had been a good idea after all. Milton seemed lost in his own thoughts, oblivious to her and everything around them.

'You OK?' she asked, finally.

'Sorry. I'm being lousy company,' he said. 'Things on my mind.'

'Apart from the case?'

'Well, including the case. But yes.'

'Want to talk about any of them?'

He took a swallow of his beer. 'You don't want to listen to me boring on,' he said.

'I don't mind. If it'll help.'

'Shit. I don't know. It's just that everything at home—' He stopped and took a breath. 'I was living with my girlfriend. Gill. Well, maybe I still am. Living with her, I mean.' He trailed off, conscious how little sense he was making. 'We were doing OK, you know. I thought we were in it for the long haul. Then she applied for this job in Paris.'

'Ah.' Donovan sipped at her own drink. She'd been wondering where this was heading.

'She's an academic,' Milton went on. 'A labour economist. She'd completed her PhD and was lucky enough to find herself a job at Manchester Met. Junior lecturer. Even that's like gold-dust these days. Then this opportunity came up at the OECD.'

'In Paris?'

'In Paris. Initially just a six month contract so a bit of a risk because the uni wasn't likely to hold the job open for her. But, well, it was the OECD. Good for the CV, all that. Chance to live in Paris for a while. And the prospect of the contract being extended. So we both thought she should give it a go.'

'You as well?'

'I couldn't stand in her way, could I? Not with that kind of opportunity. But—well, I never really believed it was going to happen, I suppose. Then it did, and she'd gone and I was left stuck in our house in Sale by myself.'

'Only temporarily, though. She must be due back soon.'

'That's the thing. They extended the original contract, and then she found out last week they want to offer her a further extension. With the prospect of making it permanent, if she wants.'

'Right.' Donovan took another sip of her drink, wondering what was the right thing to say. Across the room, a heavily-built man was holding court among a diverse bunch of drinkers, regaling them with some extended anecdote as laughter rippled across the room. Life went on, whatever might be happening outside. 'What does she want?'

'She wants to stay on, obviously. But she's not quite saying it. Keeps asking me what I want. And, of course, I have to say I want what's best for her.'

'Is that what you want?'

'Oh, Christ knows. I mean, yes, of course it is. But if I'm honest—with myself, with her—I think we're finished.' He stopped abruptly, and took another large mouthful of beer.

'Have you been going out there to see her?'

'We had a plan to do it monthly. You know, alternating between us. But it starts to get expensive and she's got other things going on and I end up working all hours, so we've let it slip the last month or two. You know how it is.'

She knew only too well. She'd found herself drifting apart from her late partner, Liam, when she'd been working undercover. She'd come up with excuses not to make the trip home, even when she'd known Liam was ill and needed her. She was only too aware how easily an apparently solid relationship could melt into nothing. Even now, with Liam long gone, she still sometimes woke in the night, the guilt gnawing at her.

'What about you moving out there? Is that an option?'

'What would I do? I've a good career here. I'd have nothing there.' He shook his head. 'Even if I did, I can't see our relationship surviving. We had something good, but I think it's already gone. She's got a new life.'

'You think there might be someone else?' The question sounded too blunt, but she couldn't unsay it.

'I don't know. She's got new friends. I don't think there's anyone serious. But it's only a matter of time.'

'You don't know that.'

'I don't know anything. But I'm beginning to think it's over.' He sat staring at his beer then looked up and laughed. 'You must wish you hadn't come. I'm not normally this gloomy. I know things will sort themselves out, one way or another.' He gestured towards the room in general. 'Then we've got this to deal with. Makes my domestic problems seem pretty trivial.'

'I know. I keep thinking about the parents,' Donovan said. 'I mean, they're not to blame. But how would you feel if you were the mother. The one day you didn't keep an eye out and something like that happens.'

'I think it's getting to Kenny as well,' Milton said.

'You reckon?' She didn't yet know Murrain well enough to guess what he might be thinking or feeling, but she knew enough about his past to understand that the loss of a child would be close to home.

'It's always difficult to tell with Kenny. He tries to keep it all under control, so people don't think he's completely away with the fairies. Everything neat and in its place, including his emotions. Especially his emotions.'

'From what you told me, I can understand why he might worry.' They both knew that the one blot of Murrain's record was an attack on the father of a boy Murrain had believed responsible for his own son's death. It had nearly ended his career, but—much more devastatingly for Murrain—it had prevented his son's killers from ever being brought to justice. 'That's why he's so punctilious about everything?'

'Punctilious bordering on obsessive sometimes,' Milton agreed. 'You've seen him lining stuff up on his desk. Even the way he parks his car. That's part of it. That—and, you know, his feelings.' She knew now this was something no-one in the team liked to acknowledge openly. Milton had taken her aside when she'd first joined and explained that Murrain's approach could be, well, distinctive—that he sometimes relied on sensations or instincts that seemed more than straightforwardly rational. At the time, she'd been unsure how to take the comments, but now she believed Murrain's unique insights had helped save her life. 'He can't control those. When they happen, what they mean. How significant they are. That gnaws away at him. Particularly when he's faced with a case like this. He wants to *know* and he can't.'

'You think he's OK, though?'

'For the moment. But he won't want to fail. Not on this one.'

'None of us does,' she agreed. 'On that note, it might

be time to make ourselves scarce.'

Milton could see she was looking thoughtfully over his shoulder, but he resisted the urge to turn his head. 'What is it?'

'There's a guy over there who's clearly keen to be the centre of attention. No idea who he is, but I recognise a couple of his acolytes.' The group around the large bearded man had been expanding as she'd watched, and two women — one roughly Donovan's own age, the other a little older — had just finished buying drinks from the bar. 'One of them runs a stationery shop up the high street here. Can't quite place the other one. But I interviewed them both a couple of days ago.'

'OK. Let's slip out discreetly before we find ourselves facing a lynch mob.' He smiled. 'Not sure this was quite what either of us had in mind when I asked you for a drink, was it?'

'It's been fine.'

'Not sure it has. I'll try to do better next time.'

'Next time?' She could see his face reddening. 'Of course you will.' She glanced over his shoulder at the laughing crowd of drinkers. 'Though maybe somewhere else, eh?'

'Definitely somewhere else.' He led them through the thickening crowd, keeping as far from the bar as possible. It wasn't until they were outside that he turned back. 'And, well, thanks.'

'For what?'

'For coming.' He stopped, fumbling for his car keys and then looked her in the eye for the first time since they'd left the pub. 'And for listening. I needed it.'

CHAPTER NINE

Two years earlier

She stepped out of the main doors of the administrative block into the warm summer afternoon. They'd had a week or so of cloud and rain, but the sun had finally reappeared. For the first time it had begun to feel like summer. Her own office was a few doors along from Greg Perry's but all she wanted to do was get out into the open air. She gazed out across the well-tended prison estate. Rows of neat housing, closely-cut lawns, flowerbeds blossoming in the sunshine. More like an upmarket holiday camp than a prison. But that was the intention. To allow prisoners to grow accustomed to something resembling the real world. The security levels were low, designed primarily to keep the curious out rather than the prisoners in.

As she made her way down the steps, she saw Carl sitting on one of the park benches. Her first instinct was to turn away but she forced herself to walk over to him.

'I've just been talking to the Governor,' she said slowly. 'I'm going to call a halt now. In our sessions, I mean.'

She couldn't read his expression. It might have been disappointment or relief. 'You think that's the right thing to do?'

'I'm sure it is. You need to concentrate on the future.'

For a moment, she was certain he was going to disagree. But, finally, he nodded. 'You're probably right.

I needed to try but, well—'

'We haven't got very far?'

'I don't know.' His gaze had shifted away from her. 'What I said the other day. What I remembered—' He stopped. 'What I thought I remembered.'

'You're not certain?'

'It comes and goes. For a moment, it seems vivid. That morning, just as I described it to you. Then it's like some dream I can barely remember at all. And what I said—'

'Go on.'

'I don't know what that means.' He shook his head, and she could sense some anger there now. Directed not at her but at himself. 'It's so bloody frustrating. I felt we were getting somewhere.'

'And now I'm saying we should stop.'

'I just wish we had more time. Christ, I've been inside for twenty years and just when we start to make some progress—'

'You get released? Don't you want that?'

'I can't imagine what it's going to be like out there.'

'That's why you need to focus on that now. That's what matters. Not what did or didn't happen in the past.'

'You're the expert,' he said. 'Is this it, then? The last time I see you?'

'No, of course not. We'll help you work with probation. There's plenty of stuff still to do.'

'I'll see you around then.'

It felt almost like an awkward lovers' farewell, she thought. 'Yes,' she said. 'I'll see you around.'

Feeling her emotions welling up, she turned hurriedly towards the car-park. Behind her, she could hear Carl humming to himself, semi-tunefully. The sound of someone feigning unconcern, she thought.

Tell him to buy me an acre of land...

***

She knew as soon as she entered the house that something felt strange. Even when she thought about it later — much later — she could never pin down the source of her unease in that moment. Something in the air, something that felt different. Some missing sound she'd never noticed before and would never be able to recognise again. A familiar scent.

Perhaps nothing more than a mother's instincts.

She could hear the familiar sound of the television from the sitting room. The unfailingly cheery tones of some game-show host mouthing the same pat phrases he trotted out every evening at this time. The same shepherded audience applause.

But something made Kate stop in the hallway and take a breath. Something felt like a cold hand clutched around her stomach. Something told her that, however miserable she might be feeling after her dealings with Greg Perry and with Carl, the fates weren't finished with her yet.

Elizabeth was in front of the TV, her eyes fixed on the flickering screen. Nothing was out of place. The sofa and the carpet and the table-top were clear. The room had been tidied, recently. Her mother fussing round as she always did.

But the resulting order didn't usually survive untouched for more than a few minutes.

'Where's Jack?' Her voice louder and sharper than she'd intended.

Elizabeth looked up in surprise. 'What?'

Don't jump to conclusions, she told herself. Don't be

stupid. There are a thousand and one possible explanations.

'I said: where's Jack?'

'I wasn't expecting you back yet,' Elizabeth said. 'I thought—'

'For Christ's sake,' she said, her voice rising, 'where's Jack?'

Her mother's mouth dropped open, her expression a mixture of puzzlement and concern. 'Well, I thought—'

'Just tell me,' Kate said. 'Tell me!'

'He told me he was meeting you. He said it was all arranged—'

'Who did? Who told you that?'

'Well, Graeme. He took me by surprise, turning up like that out of the blue. He said you were giving it another go and you'd arranged it together. A treat for Jack. For his birthday—'

Kate could feel the panic welling up again. 'What fucking treat? Tell me.'

Elizabeth looked bewildered now. 'You were taking him to the cinema and then for a meal. He said it was an early showing so you'd asked him to pick Jack up so you could meet them straight from work —'

But Kate was no longer listening. She'd already left the room. She crossed the hallway, picked up the phone and, scarcely aware of what she was doing, began to dial 999.

Somewhere, in the back of her mind, she could heart the tune repeating and repeating.

And he shall be a true lover of mine...

Then suddenly the fear and the despair overwhelmed her and she felt herself folding, crouching, the telephone still clutched unnoticed in her hands, as she began to scream and scream.

PART TWO

Now

CHAPTER TEN

'Where'd you want this?'

Kate Forester stared at the cardboard box for a few seconds, feeling as if the question was impossible to answer. Most of the boxes had been clearly, if not always helpfully, labelled. It had all seemed to make sense back at her mother's. She'd confidently scrawled a destination on each of the boxes. Bedroom. Kitchen. Living Room. Everything in its place and a place for everything.

Except that some of the labels were just plain wrong, or at least only partially accurate. Kitchen utensils had ended up in the living room boxes, and there was bedroom stuff apparently destined for the kitchen. And because this place was significantly smaller than Elizabeth's, there wasn't a perfect match between the two houses. She hadn't been consciously aware of it at the time, but she realised now that, faced with any difficult choices about where to allocate items, she'd simply stuffed them into the nearest available box. Sufficient unto the day, and all that. Except that now the day was here.

The box in front of her didn't seem to be labelled at all. She couldn't understand that. She could have sworn she'd labelled all the bloody boxes, however tentatively.

'Oh, God, I don't know,' she said. 'If they're not labelled, stick them in the sitting room and I'll go through them later.'

'Right you are. Nearly done now, anyway.'

There were two removal men, both young. Younger than she was, anyway, though that seemed increasingly common. Even the bloody prison governors were getting younger. Tim Hulse, her new boss, looked like a teenager. But that just made her wonder what she was looking like these day, after everything she'd been though.

The main thing was to get a grip. That was what this was all about. Making a new start. Remembering what it was like to be alive. Keeping control.

'What about this one, love?' The removal men were unfailingly cheerful, undaunted by a day of lugging her possessions on and off the lorry parked outside. This one was brandishing a large standard lamp, as if about to deploy it as a weapon.

'In the living room again, I guess,' she said. Jesus, he'd called her 'love'. That was what you called middle-aged housewives, wasn't it? She knew she was already long past the age when she might have registered on these lads' sexual radar.

He disappeared down the hallway past her. His colleague appeared in the doorway a moment later carrying another large cardboard box. 'Bedroom,' he said, nodding down towards the label. 'Last one.'

'That's good,' she said, sincerely. 'Do you want a drink before you head back?'

'Suppose a beer's out of the question? No, seriously, wouldn't say no to a cuppa, love.'

She watched his tightly-bejeaned backside as he lifted the box carefully up the narrow stairway. Not in a lustful way, she told herself. Just with a slight wistfulness for a past that seemed to be receding with increasing rapidity.

She'd made sure to bring the kettle and associated tea-making items with her in the car rather than trusting them to the vagaries of the removal firm. While she waited for the kettle to boil, she gazed out of the kitchen window. It wasn't much of a view — just a small postage-stamp of a garden, flanked by battered wooden fences, with a rough-hewn stone wall along the bottom end.

The real views were at the front. There was a larger front garden and, beyond that, a road and the canal. On the far side of the canal, past another row of houses, the land fell away towards the river valley. From the sitting room and front bedroom, there were views of the hills and then, in the distance, another valley and some far off Pennine town she couldn't even name.

In a few months she'd no doubt come to appreciate the real value of the location. For the moment, she felt barely able to think beyond today. She had another couple of days' leave before she was due to go back to work, and she intended to fill those with unpacking and sorting through this stuff.

The main thing was to keep moving. It was the routine she needed. She went through the familiar ritual of dropping teabags into clean mugs, pouring on the boiling water. Even that mundane activity felt strangely satisfying after all these months.

'Right. All done.' The removal men were standing at the kitchen door, one holding a clipboard. 'Just need you to confirm we've not stolen all your worldly goods.'

She handed over the two mugs of tea and took the paperwork in return, signing it in the places he'd marked.

'Nice place,' the lead removal man said. 'On your own here, are you?'

'It's a long story.'

'Ah.' He took a deep swallow of his tea, clearly recognising this wasn't a topic to pursue. 'Wouldn't mind a place like this. Me and the girlfriend are saving, but almost everything seems out of our price range.

Thanks for the tea. Thirsty work.'

'Thanks for all your help. Makes a big difference having a couple of cheerful types like you.'

'Stressful business, moving. Still, you can get properly settled in now.'

'I hope so,' she said. She gazed out of the window at the small sunlit garden. She could imagine a child running about out there, playing securely in that confined space. 'I really hope so.'

CHAPTER ELEVEN

Murrain finally managed to escape the MIR just after eight. He'd sent the other lingering members of the team home an hour or so before, even finally managing to prise Paul Wanstead away from his desk. There was always a temptation in this kind of investigation to believe that, if you carried on for just another five minutes, something would turn up—the key fact, some critical connection, the clue that would finally open up the case. Well, it might happen, Murrain thought, but most likely if it did we'd all be too tired to spot it.

Murrain himself had spent the last thirty minutes on the phone to the Head of Communications. She had at least left the office, but, in Murrain's experience, never actually seemed to stop working. In the past, he'd received e-mails from her timed in the small hours of the morning. It wasn't healthy, but he had to acknowledge that she was always ahead of the game. Now, she was preparing to draft a statement for release to the media over the weekend.

'We've nothing to tell them,' he'd pointed out.

'All the more reason why we need to tell them something,' she'd said, with her usual irresistible logic.

The truth was that all they could really say was that the investigation was proceeding, that they were pursuing various avenues of enquiry, and that they were making satisfactory progress. At least two-thirds of that was true, Murrain reflected. That had been the gist of several previous statements they'd released, but the Comms Team were adept at finding new ways of saying essentially the same thing. And that, by and large, had been the outcome of their telephone conversation this evening.

At that time in the evening, the traffic was relatively light heading west. As Murrain pulled up at the lights at the junction with the A6, his phone buzzed on the seat beside him. He activated the hands-free.

'Kenny? It's Joe. Sorry to disturb you. Just thought I'd call for a quick catch-up as I missed you earlier.'

'I hear you've been out on the town,' Murrain said. 'Had a good evening?'

There was a moment's silence and Murrain recognised that his words had emerged more ironically than he'd intended. And he'd been the one warning Wanstead to keep his mouth shut. No doubt Milton was aware that others might be gossiping.

'Just a quick one,' Milton said, finally. 'Place down in the village. Thought it might be good to get a feel for the place.' He sounded defensive.

'Good idea. Anyway, we all need a break, Joe. You're putting in the hours on this one.'

'We all are. Sounds like you're only just on your way back.'

'I got stuck with Comms,' Murrain said. 'Yet another content-free statement to the media tomorrow.'

'If it helps keep them off our backs, I won't be sorry.'

'Too right. How was the pub, anyway?'

'Busy. People don't seem too fazed what's happened. Not yet, anyway.' He paused. 'We left in a bit of a hurry. Was a bit afraid we might be recognised.'

'Can't imagine it,' Murrain said. 'One flatfoot looks pretty much like another to the general public.' The lights changed, and he pulled away left into the main road.

'There was a little cluster of people I recognised.

Couple of the local shop owners—people I'd interviewed. There was some large guy with a beard who seemed to be running things. I'd seen him before but couldn't think where. Just came to me that he was in the care home near where the body of found. I didn't interview him myself, but I saw some of his staff.'

'Finlan Brody,' Murrain confirmed. 'Yes, I met him. Heart of the community type.'

'Didn't seem short of an ego, anyway. Seemed to be a bunch of people gathering round him. More coming in even as we slipped out.'

Murrain felt a sharp stab of pain just behind his eyes. For the briefest of seconds, he caught an image, crystal clear. A face. But then it was gone, and he could scarcely remember anything about it. The car behind him sounded its horn and he realised that, momentarily, he'd allowed the car to slip out of its lane. He blinked, shocked by the unaccustomed intensity of what he'd felt.

'You okay, boss?'

'Sorry. Yes, Joe. Fine. Somebody tried to cut me up.' He wasn't sure why he didn't just tell Milton the truth. But he needed to come to grips with what he'd just felt.

'Won't keep you talking, then,' Milton said. 'Any other news?'

"Nothing to speak of. Did you know any of the people who were coming in? With Brody, I mean?'

'Not really.' Milton sounded surprised that Murrain had reverted to the previous topic. 'Seemed a very mixed bunch, though.'

'Must be this Business Forum thing he runs. Maybe we should find out a bit more about that.'

'You think? Is it likely to be relevant?'

'Can't see how,' Murrain acknowledged. 'But there might be a network there we can tap into.'

There was another moment's silence. 'You got some sort of feeling about this, boss?'

'I don't know. Maybe.'

'Might be worth a shot, then. Look, I'll leave you to get back to Eloise safely. I'm assuming you're planning to be in tomorrow?'

'What do you think? But you don't have to do the same.'

'You reckon I'm likely to do anything else? It's not like I've much to keep me at home at the moment.'

That would have been the moment, Murrain thought, to bring up Milton's domestic situation. But he couldn't bring himself to do it. He was still feeling shaken by the sensations he just experienced, and he couldn't face the thought of trying to engage in a sensitive discussion at that moment. Instead, he said: 'No pressure, though, Joe. Like I said, we all need a break.'

'I've already had a beer,' Milton laughed. 'I'll have another couple this evening. I'll be fine.'

'See you in the morning, then.'

Murrain was just turning into his drive when the phone rang again.

'Murrain.'

'Kenny. Gerry Winters.' A long-serving Sergeant, Murrain recalled. One of the Stockport East team. Murrain didn't know him well but their paths had crossed at various points and Murrain had always found him helpful and likeable. 'Sorry to bother you after hours.'

'No worries, Gerry. Only just getting back anyway. What can I do for you?'

'You've got the Dunn case, haven't you? You'll pick this up on the system but thought you'd want to know ASAP. Looks like we might have had another attempted snatching.'

He pulled to a halt and turned off the engine. A magpie was hopping across the lawn, looking for food. One for sorrow. 'Go on.'

'Not too far away,' Winters went on. 'Hazel Grove. Yesterday afternoon, but the parents didn't report it till later yesterday evening.' He paused and sighed. 'And, yes, I know we should have got the news to you earlier, but you know how it is. Whoever took the call in the FCR didn't register the significance, so it just got allocated to one of the local PCs to follow up. He was caught up with something else so didn't get on to it until I spotted it in the log and—well, you know. Sorry.'

'Not your fault, Gerry. We're all struggling to keep on top of things. Thanks for the heads-up now. Have you got the details?'

'Yeah. I assumed you'd want to interview them yourselves?'

'In the circumstances, definitely. I'm planning to be in tomorrow so I'll pick it up first thing. Might be nothing, but could be the lead we've been waiting for. ' As he spoke, Murrain tried to assess his own feelings. Something, he thought. But not much, not yet.

'I'll confirm on the system that we've referred it to you,' Winters said. 'You say you're going to be in tomorrow? I'll e-mail all the info over so it's waiting for you.'

'Thanks, Gerry, you're a gem. Need all the luck and help we can get on this one.'

He ended the call and sat for a moment longer in the car, still reflecting on the sensation that had hit him while Milton had been talking. What had Milton been saying? Something about more people coming in to join Finlan Brody. Was it something about someone in that group?

Maybe. Maybe not.

That was the maddening part. The feelings, whatever they were, came and went. Usually they meant something, but that something wasn't always what you expected. Sometimes, occasionally, they meant nothing—or at least nothing that made itself apparent. And sometimes, mostly, he just didn't know.

Finally, he pushed open the car door and climbed out into the night. The magpie had hopped away, and night was beginning to fall. Time enough tomorrow, he thought, to worry about what kind of trouble the bird might have been portending.

CHAPTER TWELVE

From the corner of the bar, Sue Myers watched as Ged effusively greeted the nervous-looking man who had just joined him. 'You reckon that's him, then?' she said to the woman standing next to her. 'This bloke Ged's bringing along?'

'Looks like it,' Joanna said. 'He's not bad. He'd do for you, Sue.'

'Oh, piss off.'

'You could do worse.'

'No, really. Piss off, Jo. Piss right off.' Both women were laughing now. They watched as Ged led the man towards them. Ged was balancing a tray of drinks. The man was awkwardly clutching a pint of lager.

Sue wondered quite what the man had been expecting. The truth was that it was a motley crew gathered at the corner of the bar. There were couple of youngish men who were part of Ged's extended network of trades-people. Jo and Sue were both in their early thirties, and there were two older women, smartly turned-out, conveying an air of slight daring at being out with a younger crowd on a Friday night. Finally, in the heart of the group, there was a single older man, an avuncular-looking figure, with a neat goatee and a self-consciously arty air.

Ged jerked a thumb over his shoulder. 'You'll have guessed that this is our new member, Kev. Just bought a place up the hill. Met him while I was repointing his brickwork. Psychologist, would you believe? So he's already sizing you all up. Working out who's the maddest.'

'He's already met you, Ged,' Sue said. 'So the question's answered.' She patted the top of the bar next to her invitingly. 'Come and join us, Kev. So you're a psychologist. Just what we all need. Someone who can help us get our heads examined. I'm Sue, by the way,' she added as an afterthought. 'Run the stationery shop on the main street.'

'Pleased to meet you. Kevin Wickham.'

Sue gestured around the group. 'This is Joanna. Runs the new hairdressers down the main road. Liz. She manages the florists in the village. Julie. She's got the cafe next door.' She waved a hand towards the two young men. 'Pete and Andy. Mates of Ged. And the leader of our little gang, Finlan Brody.'

Brody leaned across the table to shake Wickham's hand firmly. 'Good afternoon to you,' he said. He had a deep sonorous voice, the voice of a man all too accustomed to public speaking. 'Delighted you were able to join us. Though we're all a little nervous that you know exactly what we're thinking.' He leaned back against the bar, chuckling ostentatiously at his own joke.

Wickham smiled amiably back. 'I wish I did. I feel rather a fraud to be here, to be honest.'

'Why so?'

'You're a local business forum. Networking, from what Ged tells me. I'm not sure I can contribute much.'

'You run your own business, don't you? That's what Ged said.' Sue asked. 'So you've as much right to be here as any of us.'

'I suppose. But I'm not really working locally. I'm doing some work for people in Manchester and in London. Just contacts and word of mouth, as well as stuff through bigger consultancies. I'm not sure I bring much to the local scene, the way the rest of you do.'

Brody threw his arms wide in a gesture of welcome. 'We're a social club more than anything else, Kevin. We do a bit of networking, and we put business in each other's direction when we can. And we've got members who give advice—you know, accountants, financial advisors, that sort of thing.'

'But mainly,' Jo interrupted, 'we meet up to get mildly pissed on a Friday night.'

Brody nodded sagely. 'Or, in my case, not so mildly. You're thinking we're a rather disparate bunch for that? Well, it depends who turns up—I'm the only real constant. We have a drink or two here, then the various groups peel off and go their separate ways. The younger ones might get the train into Manchester for a raucous night out. We older ones might stay here or head off to grab a bite at the local Chinese.'

'And some of us head home for a quiet night in with a DVD,' Sue said. 'Your choice really.' She smiled, noting his so far untouched glass. 'You don't get out of paying your way by drinking slowly, you know. We've set up a kitty.' She gestured towards a pile of ten pound notes on the bar. 'Ten pounds each. If it's not used, we carry it forward. Finlan keeps the records. We don't trust him an inch but no-one else can be bothered to do it.'

'Sorry—miles away.' Wickham took a swig of his beer, then reached into his pocket to add his own note to the pile. 'Been a long day.'

'And it's not over yet,' Sue said. 'OK, Kevin, tell me something about yourself. Ged says you've just moved in. What brings you to these Godforsaken parts?'

'It's a long story,' he said, after a pause, 'and not a very interesting one. Just had a few problems. You know, personal stuff. Decided to make a new start.'

'We've all been there, haven't we?' Sue said. 'Everything always happens at once. Some sort of relationship thing, I'm guessing?'

'Like I say, it's a long story. You really don't want to know.'

Sue's expression suggested that, actually, she very much did, but it seemed Wickham wasn't inclined to take the conversation any further. 'So why come here?'

'Just somewhere fresh. I decided to get myself an education, finally, and came up to Manchester to do that at first. Then I decided to stay. Trawled round the estate agents and ended up here.'

'You were lucky to be able to afford anything,' Sue said. 'I know lots of people struggling to get on the ladder.'

'Had a bit of a legacy, helped me along in the first place.' Wickham took another mouthful of beer. 'What about you? Do you live nearby?' He spoke hurriedly, as if trying to move the conversation on.

'Been here about five years. Cosy little place along in the village. You'll have to come and see it sometime.' Sue realised that, unintentionally, she'd already begun to flirt with him. She could feel Jo watching her, amused, and tried to avoid catching her eye. 'Divorced,' she added, as if he'd asked her directly. 'I like reading. Cinema. Go for a run every other morning. Anything else you need to know?' She held up her now empty glass. 'Oh, and I prefer red to white.'

Wickham seemed to take the hint. 'Shall I get another round in?' he offered to the table at large.

Brody boomed back: 'I see that Ged's judgement is sound and that you're the right man for us. Anyone who goes to get a round is welcome here. I'll give you a hand. I know what these reprobates drink.' He moved along the bar to stand beside Wickham. 'I hope you're enjoying the evening so far. Young Sue's good company, and she could do with a chap like you.' He paused, noticing and relishing Wickham's blushing face. 'Don't tell me the thought hadn't occurred to you?'

'I—'

Brody was already ploughing on, oblivious to any response. 'We'll move on to the formal stuff in a second, but we don't spend too long on that. Then we can get down to some serious drinking. The young blokes will head off to town to get properly rat-arsed.' He tipped his head and smiled at Wickham. 'Don't see that as your scene, though. You might prefer to stay here with us fogies. Which usually includes all the women of whatever age, if that's any incentive.'

Wickham blinked, as if unsure how to respond. 'You run a retirement home?' he asked, after a moment.

Brody arched his back, momentarily reminiscent of some jungle animal preparing to defend its territory. 'Care home for the elderly. Keeps the wolf from the door. But I do all sorts round here. Local busybody. You know the sort.'

'You've lived here a long time?' Wickham said.

'You're a newcomer in these parts unless you were born here,' Brody said. 'Always lived in and around the north west. Been down here in the village a few years.' He waved his arms expansively. 'Glorious part of the world. Wouldn't live anywhere else. Trick is to get yourself involved.' He patted Wickham heartily on the back. 'So there you are. You've made the first step tonight. Joined our happy and soon-to-be-inebriated little band. You won't regret it. Anyway,' Brody continued, now apparently talking to the group at large, 'we all need a bit of cheering up after that awful business up the road. I had yet another visit from the plods today.'

Wickham was still standing on the fringe watching the others, three glasses of wine balanced awkwardly in his hands.

'I hope they get the bugger,' Ged offered. 'Hanging's too good for a bastard like that.'

'I think few would disagree with you on that,' Brody said.

Wickham handed out the wine-glasses. He turned to face Brody who was now standing in front of him, offering a brimming glass of beer. 'Here you go. You'd agree, wouldn't you, Kevin? It's the one thing that's really beyond the pale. ' He paused while Wickham took the pint. 'The deliberate harming of a child. No-one can forgive that. Can they, Kevin?'

CHAPTER THIRTEEN

Murrain woke early, as he usually did, and lay as the room gradually grew light, the first pale sunlight creeping round the edges of the curtains. He usually enjoyed these first minutes in the morning, a chance to gather his own thoughts, to prepare himself for whatever the day might have to offer. So much of the time he felt as if he were just charging from crisis to crisis, struggling with a case-load that was always too large, battling with the bureaucracy increasingly at the heart of modern policing, fighting for time and resources. This was a moment to catch his breath. To get his head together. And Christ knew his head was more fragmented than most.

He could hear the soft sound of Eloise breathing beside him, the faint clicks of the radiators warming.

Eloise rolled over and pressed her body against his. 'Assume you're going in today?' she mumbled.

'I thought I might,' he said, as if the question had ever been in doubt. 'Just to keep on top of things.'

'No-one will thank you,' she said.

She was right in a way. Officers of Murrain's rank were not eligible for overtime payments, and the overtime budget for lower ranks was always under pressure. By turning into work on a rest-day, Murrain was setting an example his team might feel obliged to follow. If he authorised their overtime, the divisional commander would be on his back. If he didn't, he'd feel he was exploiting their good-will. On the other hand, the divisional commander was already on his back because of their lack of progress, and Murrain knew he was constantly taking advantage of his team's commitment. One more day wouldn't make much difference, and he couldn't sit at home doing nothing.

'The parents might, if we make a breakthrough,' he said. 'Anyway, you know that's not the point.'

'I know that's not the point,' she agreed. 'You go and be a hero and I'll enjoy a lie-in. Then we're both happy.' She released him and turned away. 'And good luck,' she added, her voice muffled by the duvet.

By the time he'd showered, dressed and grabbed a reviving coffee, it was nearly eight. There'd be no traffic to speak of on a Saturday morning, so he'd be at the MIR in fifteen minutes or so.

As he'd been driving in, he had been wondering whether he should conduct the Hazel Grove interview by himself or disturb one of his colleagues, but the question was answered on his arrival at the MIR. Joe Milton's car was parked in front of the station entrance, and Joe himself was sitting at his desk tapping at his computer.

'Assume you have actually been home, Joe?'

Milton yawned. 'Yeah. Got an earlyish night too, by my standards. Not that I slept brilliantly. Too busy fretting away at this stuff.'

'Tell me about it.' Murrain sat at his own desk and booted up his PC. 'You keep thinking you've missed something obvious. That there's some straightforward line we should be pursuing.'

'Had that this morning. Managed to doze off for a bit. Then woke up convinced—you know, absolutely convinced in those seconds before you're fully awake—that there was some major lead in one of yesterday's interviews I'd overlooked. So obvious I couldn't imagine how I'd not seen it.' He smiled. 'Then woke up properly and hadn't a clue what it might have been.'

'The good news is,' Murrain said, 'that we do have another lead. Probably nothing, but you never know.' He recounted the conversation he'd had with Gerry Winters, then looked at his watch. 'Still a bit early to disturb them on a Saturday, but I'll give them a call as soon as it's decent and we can head over there.'

'What do you reckon?' Milton asked. 'Something in it?'

It wasn't a casual question, Murrain realised. 'There's enough there to make me feel it's worth following up — not that we wouldn't in any case. But not enough to make me feel confident it'll take us anywhere.' He shrugged, feeling oddly embarrassed. Milton was one of the few fellow officers he could even begin to talk to like this, but it was never easy. 'But that doesn't prove much. The whole case has felt like that so far. Maybe I'm losing my touch.'

Milton regarded him curiously. 'Is that possible? I mean, with these feelings of yours.'

'Who knows? Sometimes I think I just imagine the whole thing. Though Christ knows why I would.'

'I've seen enough to believe there's something there,' Milton said. 'Whatever it might be.' He paused, unsure how much to say. 'And I've seen enough to suspect that you might not be entirely sorry if it were to disappear.'

'If there is something, it's so much a part of me that I can't think about it objectively.' Murrain pushed himself to his feet, heading towards the small kitchen at the back of the station. 'Coffee?'

'Why not? Need something to keep me alert.'

Murrain had been wondering whether this might be the time to discuss Milton's domestic circumstances but he already felt as if they'd intruded too far into personal territory. He needed a few moments to himself. 'I'll see if there's any milk left.'

Milton took the hint and busied himself with some paperwork while Murrain made for the kitchen. He didn't know, even now, why he found it so difficult to talk about these issues. Even with Joe. Even, for Christ's sake, with Eloise. Maybe it was just habit. He'd grown accustomed to keeping all this to himself for fear of what others might think. But it felt more than that. Almost as if it might bring ill-luck to focus on it too directly.

He carried the coffees back into the MIR and placed one beside Joe, who nodded his thanks. Murrain settled himself at his desk and continued working through the stack of e-mails that had accumulated over the previous twenty-four hours. He'd picked up and responded to all the urgent ones—mainly from various senior officers seeking yet more content-free updates—the previous night. But there were numerous others relating to other live cases or past cases progressing through the judicial pipelines, or just to the interminable administration that went with his line management role. He spent a productive half hour or so working through them, responding to some, deferring others and deleting the rest.

As the clock passed nine, he dialled the number Winters had forwarded on to him. A female voice answered.

'Mrs Morrison? DCI Murrain from Greater Manchester Police. I'm calling in response to the incident you reported yesterday.'

There was a pause. 'Oh, yes. Charlie.'

'Your son?'

'Yes. Look, I don't know if we should have bothered

you, really. It was my husband— Charlie's a very imaginative child. I don't know...' She trailed off.

'I think we should come and talk to you anyway, Mrs Morrison. And to Charlie. It won't take long.' He'd encountered this kind of reluctance before though the reasons varied. Often, it was nothing more than a desire not to get involved or not to waste police time. In this kind of case, it sometimes felt like a form of denial, magical thinking to ward off possible harm. As if by pretending nothing had happened, she might protect her child.

'I'm not sure that there was anything really —'

'Quite possibly not,' Murrain said gently. 'But I think we need to be sure. Would you be available for us to come and talk to you, and to Charlie, this morning?'

'Well, I don't know. My husband works on a Saturday morning.'

'Was your husband present when the incident occurred?'

'No. He was still at work. But I didn't really see —'

'In that case, we probably don't need to speak to your husband. If you could just spare us a few minutes, that would be marvellous.'

'If you think it's necessary.'

'It would be very helpful to us, Mrs Morrison. My apologies for any inconvenience.'

They agreed a time and Murrain ended the call. He sat for a moment with the phone still clutched in his hands, staring at nothing. He felt for a moment as if an image were coalescing in his mind, but it refused to take shape. Something half-familiar.

'You OK?' Milton asked.

'Yes. But that call. It was odd. She seemed keen to avoid talking to us.'

'Most people are,' Milton observed. 'For one reason or another.'

'That's what I thought. But—I don't know. Just as I ended the call. I got something. Something quite strong. Not just a feeling but—well, almost an image.'

'Go on.'

'You know how it is. Well, you don't, but I've told you. It's like waking from a dream. A minute ago it was clear. Now it's fading. But it was a sense of—I don't know—of Mrs Morrison. And someone else. Someone with her. Someone who matters.'

***

The drive to Hazel Grove took them only about fifteen minutes in the early Saturday morning traffic. Murrain drove past the Morrisons' house and pulled in further down the street, wanting to get some sense of the place before they met Mrs Morrison and her son.

Hazel Grove was a sprawling residential area surrounding the busy A6 south of Stockport, much more suburban than its name suggested. Away from the A6 itself, it was the sort of area that would be attractive to young families. Neat estates of detached and semi-detached houses, decent-sized gardens, wide streets. No doubt there were well-regarded schools and good transport links. Not the sort of place that appealed to Murrain, who liked to feel closer to open countryside, but he could see the attractions.

The street itself was quiet, though there was a steady stream of traffic along the road beyond, heading up towards the main artery of the A6. That was presumably where, according to the account Winters had provided, the school bus had dropped young Charlie. Charlie was accustomed to walking the last fifty or so yards by himself. It might be no more than coincidence, but the circumstances were very similar to those surrounding Ethan Dunn's killing. A school bus. A child walking alone for only a few minutes. A waiting van.

'What do you think?' Milton said from behind him.

'Who knows? Let's go and see what young Charlie has to say.' He led the way up the Morrisons' driveway, past a parked Ford Fiesta, and pressed the doorbell. The house and garden looked tidy, but without the obsessive neatness that had characterised the Dunns' home. This place looked lived in. There was a half-deflated football at the edge of the lawn, a child's bicycle visible behind the gate at the side of the house.

It was a few moments before the door opened and a woman in her mid-thirties peered back at the them. Murrain held out his warrant card, but the woman was already opening the door to invite them in. She looked keen to get this over with.

'Thanks for sparing the time, Mrs Morrison. We won't keep you any longer than necessary.' Murrain followed her into the house.

'If you think it's really worthwhile.' She gestured for them to enter the sitting room. 'Take a seat. Can I get you a tea or coffee?'

Murrain would normally have refused, but instinct told him they'd benefit from giving Mrs Morrison a few moments to calm herself. She seemed unexpectedly on edge. 'That would be nice. A coffee, please, if it's no trouble. Just white without.'

'Same for me, please,' Milton said.

Once he could hear the sound of the kettle being filled in the kitchen, Milton said: 'I think she was hoping we wouldn't stay long enough to drink a coffee.'

'Seems a bit jumpy.' Murrain looked around. Like the exterior of the house, the room looked neat but far from sterile. There was a pile of toys in one corner, a stack of children's books on the low coffee-table, a scattering of unsorted DVDs under the television.

After a few minutes, Mrs Morrison returned with a tray topped with three coffee mugs. Murrain and Milton rose to take their coffees and waited as Mrs Morrison took hers and sat down facing them.

'I really hope we're not wasting your time,' she said. She was a short, slim woman with blonde hair. Good-looking, Murrain thought. The sort who'd have been able to have her pick of the men when she was a little younger.

'Definitely not, Mrs Morrison,' Murrain said. 'You'll be aware of our ongoing murder investigation?'

'That poor child. A bit too close to home.' She looked up and peered at Murrain. 'I saw you on the local news. With the parents.'

'You can see why we need to talk to you. Even if this incident turns out to be nothing. We need to check. Any possible lead could be helpful to us.'

'I don't know if Charlie was exaggerating. You know what children are like. I think he might have heard about the other case while we were watching the news. You think they're not listening but they take it all in.'

She was talking too quickly, Murrain thought. 'Is Charlie prone to exaggeration?'

'He's just a child. And he's more imaginative than most.' She gestured towards the pile of books. 'He reads a lot.' She made it sound like a vice.

'You think it's possible he just made up this story?'

'It's not that he lies. Maybe something happened. There was something that scared him. I just don't know if it's quite what he says. His story—well, there are parts of it that don't really make sense...' She trailed off.

'Are you OK for us to speak to Charlie? We'll be careful not to frighten him.'

'I told him you were coming. He was quite excited by the idea of talking to police officers.'

'He'll probably be disappointed we're not in uniform,' Milton observed.

Mrs Morrison rose and poked her head around the living room door. 'Charlie. The gentlemen are here to talk to you.'

They heard a clattering of feet on the stairs. A moment later, a small head peered around the door. 'Are you really policemen?'

Murrain nodded solemnly and held out his warrant card. Charlie came tentatively into the room and peered at the document. He jabbed a finger at the photograph. 'Is that you?'

'It doesn't look much like me,' Murrain acknowledged. 'But yes. I'm a detective. Do you know what one of those is?'

'Like Sherlock Holmes.'

'Exactly. We're hoping you might be able to help us in our investigation.'

'Will I get a reward?'

'I'll see what I can do,' Murrain said. He'd had plenty of experience in interviewing children and, during the short drive over, had asked Milton to stop at a newsagents so he could purchase a couple of bars of chocolate. 'We just need to know about what happened yesterday. When you got off the school bus. Can you tell us?'

'Think so.' Charlie lowered himself down on the carpet in front of Murrain, with a serious look on his face.

'Where does the bus stop?'

'Just at the end of the road. Then I walk the last bit by myself.'

'You must be a big boy, then,' Murrain said. 'Do you usually walk by yourself or are there other friends who walk with you?'

'Mostly on my own. There's a girl who sometimes gets off there. But she's younger and with her mum.'

'But they weren't there yesterday?'

'No. They don't always get the bus.'

'I know Pam, the mother,' Mrs Morrison offered from across the room. 'She usually picks up Lizzie in the car on her way back from work. But she doesn't work Fridays so she often walks up to the school then gets the bus back.'

Murrain nodded. It was possible that someone could have noted that routine, known that Charlie would be by himself. 'So you walked up the street on your own. Then what happened?'

'Then he grabbed me.'

'Right. Where was this, Charlie?'

Charlie waved his hand towards the window. 'Just outside.'

'How did he grab you?'

'He grabbed my arm and he pulled me—' Charlie stopped as if the reality of what he was describing had just hit him. 'Do you think he wanted to kidnap me?'

'That's what we want to find out, Charlie. Where was he pulling you? Did he have a car?'

'There was a van. With its back doors open.'

Murrain glanced across at Milton. He'd been feeling a low-level pulse through his skin all the time that Charlie had been talking. It grew no stronger now. 'Do you think he was trying to pull you into the van?'

'That's what I thought,' Charlie said earnestly. Then he smiled. 'But I managed to pull away. He hadn't got my arm properly because I had my anorak on. So I got free and then I ran home. Mum always leaves the front door a bit open so I just ran inside.'

'That was clever of you, Charlie,' Murrain said. 'Did the man try to follow you?'

'I don't know.' For the first time, Charlie looked slightly shamefaced. 'I was too scared to look back.'

'You did the right thing,' Murrain said. 'You were very clever and brave. Can you tell me anything about the man? Did you see what he looked like.'

Charlie rubbed his eyes, presumably to signal that he was thinking hard. 'I don't know. He had a—thing around his face.'

'What, like a mask?'

'Not really. Like a sort of hat.' He looked across at his mother. 'I used to have one when I was little. That granny knitted for me.'

'A balaclava?' she offered.

'Yes. One of those. So I couldn't see much of his face. But I thought I knew him.'

Murrain leaned forward, keeping eye contact with the boy. 'You thought you knew him? How did you know him?' He sensed that Charlie wanted to look away, to seek some guidance from his mother, but he stared back at Murrain as if mesmerised.

'I don't know,' Charlie said, finally. 'I thought he was a friend of mum's—'

'I told you the story didn't make sense,' Mrs Morrison interrupted. 'How could it have been anyone I knew?'

Murrain looked up at her. Suddenly, momentarily, he'd felt the same sensation he'd felt back in the MIR.

123

Something, some image. Some figure. 'I don't know, Mrs Morrison,' he said. 'How could it have been?'

'Well, it couldn't, could it? That's the point.'

Murrain turned back to Charlie. 'Why did you think it might be a friend of your mum's, Charlie?'

'Well—' Now Charlie had looked to his mum, as if hoping that she might interrupt again. 'I don't know really. I thought he looked like someone I'd seen coming out of the house once.'

'Is that possible, Mrs Morrison?' Murrain asked. 'Can you think of anyone? I mean, not necessarily a friend. But someone who might have been to the house for some reason?'

The image in Murrain's head had faded almost as quickly as it had appeared, but he felt surer than ever that there was something here worth pursuing.

'Off the top of my head, I really can't think of anyone. I mean, I suppose it's possible that this person's been hanging around and Charlie's seen him. I can't say that I've noticed anything though.'

'Is there anything else you can tell us, Charlie?' Murrain asked. 'How big was this man? As tall as me?' He pushed himself to his feet. Murrain was a large, heavily-built man. 'Or was he trim and fit like Detective Sergeant Milton?'

Charlie shuffled back on the carpet and regarded the two men carefully. After a moment, he pointed to Murrain and said: 'More like you. But not as tall.'

'That's very helpful,' Murrain said. 'Anything else you can remember? What was he wearing?'

'I don't know, really,' Charlie said, apologetically. 'A coat, I think. Maybe an anorak.'

'OK. And what about the van. Did you notice anything about that? What colour was it?'

'Blue, I think, dark blue. I noticed because that's my favourite colour.' Charlie smiled.

'That's really good, Charlie.' Murrain had sat himself down again. 'You were very brave yesterday. And very clever. And you've been very helpful to us in our investigation.' He reached into his case and produced the chocolate bars. 'You definitely deserve a reward.' He smiled at Mrs Morrison. 'Hope that's all right, Mrs Morrison. Given how helpful Charlie's been to us.'

'You shouldn't really—'

'No, I know. But Charlie deserves our thanks.'

Charlie was gazing at the chocolate as if he'd been handed a vault-load of treasure. He looked up at Murrain. 'Are you going to catch him?'

'With help like yours, I'm sure we're going to, Charlie. Thanks again.' He looked back at Mrs Morrison. 'We won't take up any more of your time, then, Mrs Morrison. Thanks for all your help.'

'I just hope we haven't been wasting your time,' she said.

'I'm sure you haven't. I don't know if what happened to Charlie's connected to our case, but every possible lead is worth following up.' Murrain followed her towards the front door, Milton lingering behind them. Charlie had already disappeared upstairs, clutching his new-found treasures.

'I don't even know whether anything really happened,' Mrs Morrison said, opening the front door. It was clear that now they'd finished speaking to Charlie she just wanted them out of the house as quickly as possible. 'All that stuff about it being someone I knew.'

'You really can't think of anyone that might be?'

'No, it's nonsense. Why would I know anyone like that?'

'I'm not suggesting you do, Mrs Morrison. But it could be it's someone who visited the house. Someone working on the house, maybe? A builder? Plumber? Someone delivering something. There are lots of possibilities.'

'I can't think of anyone.' She was almost ushering them out of the door. Murrain could sense she was looking over his shoulder, peering down the street. Looking for what?

Murrain handed her a business card. 'If anything occurs to you, you'll give us a call, won't you?'

'Yes, of course.' It was obvious that the card would be dropped in the bin the moment they'd left.

'And thanks again for your time. Thank Charlie again for us.'

'Yes, no problem. Thank you for coming out.'

The door was almost slammed behind them. Murrain stood gazing round the front garden, almost reluctant to leave, as if he were walking away from something important. Milton was already halfway down the drive, heading for the car.

There was definitely something here, Murrain thought. Not necessarily anything straightforward. Maybe not even something directly relevant to their case. But something to pursue.

He hurried after Milton, catching up with him as they reached the street. 'She was lying, wasn't she?' Milton said. 'I don't need your gifts to know that.'

'I think so,' Murrain said. He was trying to make sense of the impressions forming and fading somewhere just beyond his conscious mind. 'What puzzles me is quite what she was lying about.'

CHAPTER FOURTEEN

'Are you OK?' Sue sat up and watched in the dim light as Kevin Wickham opened his eyes. 'You OK, Kev? You were making strange noises. Even stranger than last night, I mean.' She laughed faintly and pressed her warm, soft body against his.

She still felt half hungover, but it was coming back, like an image resolving itself on a computer screen, an abstract scattering of pixels coalescing into a clear picture. The night before. She had no idea whether they'd done the right thing but, looking back, she thought it had been inevitable from the moment they left the pub together. If she'd been more sober, she'd have registered it in Brody's parting words and expression. 'Have a good evening, you two. Nothing I wouldn't do.' Brody's intonation had implied that this injunction involve no serious constraint.

Sue's house was along the street at the far end of the village, tucked away in a quaint courtyard behind a small cluster of shops, including her own stationer's. 'I can just fall out of bed into the shop in the mornings,' she'd said to Wickham as she led him into the house. 'Just as well—I'm not a morning person. Don't open till ten. If I'm feeling lazy, I grab a coffee and a bacon sarnie in the cafe on the way past.' She paused and laughed. 'It's not a bad life down here, you know.'

She'd been in this place for a few years now. It was just a small cottage, furnished in a homely way, with ornaments and pictures that she'd intended to reflect every aspect and moment of her current and past life.

She felt cocooned each time she stepped in through the front door.

She'd settled him down in the living room and returned with an opened bottle of red wine, which she emptied into two glasses. Wickham was already looking slightly the worse for wear, although she thought he'd only knocked back two or three pints across the evening. Sue was several glasses ahead of him, and felt cheerful and boisterous but otherwise unaffected. 'It won't be anything special,' she said. 'Just what's in the fridge. Pasta OK? You're not vegetarian or anything, are you?'

Wickham shook his head. 'Pasta's fine.'

As it turned out, it was more than fine. They'd eaten in Sue's dining room and then returned to the living room to polish off the rest of the wine. Sue had wondered whether to continue her gentle interrogation about his past, but she'd sensed he was reluctant to talk and she was happy to let that lie for the moment. Instead, she talked about the village and the larger town up the hill—some of the local characters, the best shops, where to eat.

They ended up slumped on Sue's cavernous sofa, working their way through the wine while Sue picked out a DVD for them to watch. She grabbed a handful of cases from the shelves by the TV. 'What do you fancy?'

'Up to you.'

Sue gazed at the boxes as though she'd never seen them before either. 'Dunno,' she said. 'They're all a bit girly. Do you mind?'

'Whichever you think's best.'

Sue picked out a recent British rom-com. She'd seen it a couple of times before so wasn't too worried about paying it much attention. She was becoming increasingly focused on the proximity of Wickham's body to her own.

She'd moved herself so that she was resting against him in a manner that, for the moment, she hoped suggested comfort rather than anything overtly sexual.

During a lull in the movie, she poured the final dregs of the wine into their glasses, taking the opportunity to press herself even more openly against him. He moved himself away slightly, looking uncomfortable, and Sue glanced up at him, quizzically. 'Am I being too forward again?'

'No. Of course not. It's just—'

She sat more upright. 'I'm very straightforward,' she said 'And, frankly, too old and single to spend time going round the houses.' She laughed, as if a thought had just struck her. 'Or beating about the bush. As it were. Sorry—bit tipsy.' She took a mouthful of wine as if it were an antidote to that condition. 'The thing is, you're an attractive man. I hope you find me an attractive woman.' She didn't allow him time even to think about responding to that. 'I won't be offended if you say no, but I was wondering whether you'd like to stay the night?'

He'd responded with apparent surprise and some hesitation, but she had the impression, thinking about it later, that he'd never been likely to say no. She could already sense his arousal. After a while, they swallowed the last of the wine, watched the final few minutes of the movie—where everything ended happily, more or less, at least for the lead characters—and, with the awkward ease of the semi-drunk, made their way up to Sue's bedroom.

Wickham hadn't been the best lover she'd ever had, not that the competition was very extensive. At first, he'd seemed gauche and clumsy, as if he hadn't had much of an idea what he was doing. But, in fairness, Sue had thought that about most of the men she'd been with. At least Wickham seemed willing to listen and learn. In the end, they'd had a pretty enjoyable time. Even so, she thought, the best part wasn't the sex itself, but the aftermath — the point where, exhausted and still woozy from the wine, they'd nestled together under Sue's weighty duvet and, after only a few moments, had fallen deeply asleep.

It was the same now, waking in the half-light the early morning, feeling the pressure of his body against hers. It was something she'd missed more than she'd realised.

'What sort of noises?' he asked finally.

She wrapped herself around him, and pressed the weighty curve of her breasts against his chest. 'Last night or just now?'

'Just now,' he smiled.

'I wasn't very awake myself. But you sounded — I don't know — breathless. Scared. As if you were afraid of something.'

'Just a dream, I suppose.'

'I can put up with you dreaming, as long as you do it quietly. At least you don't snore.' Again, in her experience of men, Wickham was close to being unique in this respect.

'I do my best to please.'

'Your best was pretty good. At least once I'd licked you into shape.' She paused, then gave a winey giggle. 'As it were. God, I'm going to feel so hungover in the morning.'

'What time is it?'

She pulled away from him and sat up to peer at the luminous face of the alarm clock by the bed. 'It's only four-thirty. If we get up at nine, we can grab a quick breakfast in the cafe before I open up.' She lay back down and rolled over to face him. 'That is, if you can still bear my company by the morning.'

There was a moment's pause. 'I ought to go back really,' he said. 'I wasn't expecting to be away all night.'

She sat up in bed, suddenly feeling anxious. 'You're not about to tell me you've someone waiting for you back at home?'

'No. No, of course not. Nothing like that.' He was silent for a second, as if he couldn't think how to explain. 'I'm just a bit of a creature of habit, you know?'

'Well, I reckon in that case it's about time you picked up a few new habits, then.' She lay back down and moved her body against his, more purposefully this time. 'Tell you what,' she said. 'Give me a few minutes and then see how you feel about going home.'

CHAPTER FIFTEEN

'Why would she lie?' Milton had asked on the way back to the MIR.

'Who knows?' Murrain said. 'Most likely nothing to do with anything we're interested in. That's what makes this job so difficult. As you say, everyone has their secrets.'

'You don't think that, though, do you? I know you. You think it's relevant.'

'I don't know. I'm pretty certain young Charlie was telling us the truth, as best he could. Someone tried to grab him yesterday. He thought he recognised the man's face, for whatever reason. And there's something the mother doesn't want us to know, which may or may not be significant. That's all.' He paused for a moment, staring out of the car window, trying without success to recapture those sensations.

Milton felt there was more, but there was no point in challenging Murrain further. He'd say more when he felt able to. 'So what next?'

'I'm nervous about deflecting effort from the murder,' Murrain said. 'But I think we can justify some door-to-doors among the Morrisons' immediate neighbours. Just in case there were any other witnesses to what happened to Charlie—someone watching from a window or someone further down the street who might have seen the van drive off.'

'With the odd discreet question about the Morrisons' thrown in?'

'You've got the idea. But very discreet. Make sure we

use someone with some sense. Bert Wallace, maybe. She's good at extracting information without you really noticing.' DC Roberta Wallace was a young member of Murrain's team whom he regarded with increasing respect. 'She does it to me all the time.'

'Fair enough. And I'll get all the usual CCTV checks and suchlike in train,' Milton said. 'If the van went on to the A6, there's a chance we might have got the reg on one of the ANPR cameras. Bit more likelihood here than where Ethan Dunn was snatched.'

Back at the MIR, the desks had already begun to fill up. DCs Bert Wallace and Will Sparrow were in on authorised overtime, heading out to complete door to door interviews with neighbours who had been unavailable during the working week. Dave Wanstead was at his desk carrying out some unfathomable bot no doubt essential case administration task on his computer. Marie Donovan was apparently entering data into the system, working painstakingly through pages of notes. Murrain noticed the smile she gave Milton on their return, and forced himself not to exchange a knowing glance with Wanstead.

'Christ,' Murrain said as he sat down. 'Don't any of you lot have homes to go to? I can't afford to pay you all overtime, you know.'

'Lots to do, boss,' Wanstead said. 'And we all want to catch this bastard, don't we?'

There was no shortage of work, even discounting the countless other competing cases that members of the team would still be juggling. But the murder was the priority—making progress while there was still progress to be made.

Murrain felt distracted—one of those all-too-frequent days when his sensitivity felt more like a curse than a gift—but managed to use the day productively. Around lunchtime, he called an impromptu meeting with those present to discuss where they were up to. Not very far, was the honest answer. Masses of data but precious little intelligence. Calls were still trickling in following the television appeal. A handful were worth following up, but most were going nowhere. The forensics were still being processed, but nothing looked promising.

By mid-afternoon, Murrain was in the mood to call it a day. Wanstead was still beavering away at something that only he understood. Wallace and Sparrow had long ago left the building to kick off their interview schedule. Milton and Donovan were reviewing interview notes together. Murrain himself had fielded four calls from senior officers, including the Chief, seeking updates, knowing he'd left each caller more dissatisfied than the last, for all their words of encouragement. Something was buzzing behind his eyes, as irritating as an errant bluebottle. He couldn't tell whether it was something significant or an incipient migraine.

He was about to call Eloise to say that he was on his way back, when he saw Wanstead, talking on the phone, suddenly sit up and gesture to him. The expression on Wanstead's face indicated some significant development. As Murrain rose, Wanstead finished the call.

'Something from the TV appeal?'

Wanstead was stony-faced. 'Wish to hell it was.'

'So what then?' Though Murrain hardly needed to ask.

'That was the control room. We've another one. Another bloody missing child.'

***

The rain had arrived unexpectedly. It had been a fine early autumn day, with the promise of clear skies and the threat of a first frost before dawn. But late in the afternoon the clouds had rolled steadily in from the west. Dark, heavy clouds with the scent of thunder. Sitting in Sue's immaculate front room, waiting for the phone to ring, they heard the first scatterings of rain against the window.

'We should be out there,' she said. 'Doing something.'

She'd called Wickham without really thinking. She wasn't really thinking clearly about anything, and she'd dialled his number in panic almost before she knew what she was doing.

'Kevin?' She felt barely in control of her words.

There was a long pause and, for a moment, she thought she hadn't recognised her voice. 'Sue? Are you OK?'

'Can you come round? You need to come round. Shit—'

'Sue, what is it?'

'Oh, Jesus, Kevin. You need to come round. It's Luke.'

'What's the problem, Sue? What is it?'

'He's gone missing. They can't find him.'

Another silence. 'Who's gone missing? Who are we talking about?'

'Christ, Kevin. It's Luke. He's gone missing.'

'Luke?'

It had taken her another moment to realise that Wickham had no idea what she was talking about. 'Oh, God, Kevin. I didn't tell you. I'm sorry.' Her head was struggling to try to find the right words, but in the end all she said was: 'He's gone missing, Kevin. Luke. My son. My little boy—'

Wickham turned up at the house ten minutes later,

shortly before the two uniformed police officers arrived. The officers' initial words, at least, had been reassuring. The disappearance of a child was always a concern, they said, and particularly so at the moment, but so far Luke had been missing for scarcely two hours. There could be countless reasons for his absence. Nevertheless, it had been clear to Sue that they were taking this very seriously indeed.

'The fucking idiot,' Sue spat. 'This is just bloody typical.'

This was her ex-husband. She'd already told Wickham that she was divorced. She hadn't deliberately withheld the information that she also had a young son from the marriage, but she supposed she hadn't wanted to raise the topic until she was sure that something more serious might be developing between the two of them. Nine year old Luke divided his time between Sue and the ex-husband, Tony and his new wife, Caitlin. In practice, in recent months the boy had been spending more and more time with Tony and Caitlin.

'That's Tony,' Sue said. 'He's engineered it, step by step, slowly but surely. Stretching it a little each time so you seem petty if you object. That's the way he is. Devious but irresponsible. Typical man. Nothing personal.' She was conscious that she sounded more bitter than she'd intended.

However devious Tony might be, it seemed his irresponsible side had been to the fore that afternoon. 'I can't believe even he'd be that stupid,' she said. 'He was due to drop Luke off tomorrow night, so he'd be here for the week. But it always has to be what's most convenient to Tony.'

Wickham had sat and listened patiently since the police had left. Sue knew she was coping with her anxiety by venting her spleen against her ex but couldn't stop herself talking. 'So, of course, bloody typical, this afternoon he phones to say it's not convenient to come over Sunday so he wants to drop him off Saturday. I told him I'd arranged so go out, so he starts up with the "well, if you've not got time for Luke..." stuff. It was going nowhere, and in the end I told him to do what he bloody well wanted.' She paused and took a breath, realising she was talking too much. 'I didn't expect him to take that literally.'

'But you weren't here?' Wickham asked.

'That was the thing. Tony dropped him off at the end of the road like he usually does. Anything to avoid having to come into contact with me. He just assumed I'd be in the shop. But I'd shut early to get my hair done, because—' She stopped and, for the first time since he'd arrived, met Wickham's eyes. 'Well, because I was supposed to be meeting you later.'

His face showed no expression. 'So what happened to Luke?'

'We don't know. Tony dropped him off and saw him walking along the road to the shop. I got back half an hour later, and a bit after that Tony phoned to say Luke had left his coat in the car. It was only then I realised he was supposed to be here.'

'There's nowhere he might have gone?'

'He's got a few friends locally he might have gone to, but I've tried all those. The cafe was already closed. The post office was still open, and I thought he might have gone there, but they hadn't seen him. The police have been talking to the others along the street but no-one has any recollection of seeing him. Oh, *Jesus*, Kevin. What's happened to him?'

Wickham shifted awkwardly across the sofa and

placed an arm around her shoulders. 'He'll be fine, Sue,' he said, though she thought he sounded unconvinced himself. 'He'll have found his way somewhere. Probably won't even have realised we're missing him. You know how kids are. They get caught up in something and don't think about anyone else.'

She lacked the energy or the will to respond. She lay back for a moment on the sofa, feeling the weight of his arm around her. Then, unable to keep still, she rose and stamped over to the window. She pulled back the curtain and peered out into the wet gloom, as if Luke might be waiting in the street outside. It was still only early evening, but the rain was coming down harder now, lashing at the glass, and it was barely possible to see over the road.

Wickham had moved to stand behind her, resting a comforting hand on her arm. On the opposite side of the street, beyond a substantial stone wall, the River Goyt flowed through the village, sandwiched into a narrow gully as it passed below the road bridge before widening in the open land beyond. His face was blank but, for a moment, he grasped her arm more tightly as if he'd been struck by a sudden anxiety. Sue glanced up at him, accepting the gesture as a sign of his concern. 'I'm glad you're here,' she said. 'It's the one thing keeping me sane.' She'd thought at first that she'd made a mistake in calling him—she'd have been better calling one of her girl friends—but now she felt reassured by his presence.

She was about to say something more when they were both startled by the loud buzz of the mobile on the table. A moment later it was followed by the shriek of the ringtone, some 1980s pop-hit, grotesquely out of the place in the circumstances. She jumped across the room and clumsily thumbed the call button. 'Yes? Yes, of course. Oh, thank Christ—' She looked up at Wickham and mouthed: 'He's all right.'

Wickham nodded, smiling, and offered her a silent thumbs up.

Sue was still gabbling into the phone. 'Yes, Tony called to say he'd dropped him off and I didn't know what— No, God, no, not your fault at all. Bloody Tony's fault. Thanks for taking care of him—I'll get up to you straightaway. Thanks again.' She ended the call and, in the same movement, threw herself into Wickham's arms, sobbing against his shoulder. He held her awkwardly, as she felt the emotion and tension draining from her body. Eventually, she calmed herself and lifted her head. Her face was blotched and tear-stained but she was smiling. 'Oh, Jesus. Maybe I'm not an atheist any longer. If that's what praying can do.'

'He's all right?'

'He's fine, apparently. Doesn't even know he's been missed.'

'Where is he?'

'Would you believe at bloody Finlan's?' She moved herself away from Wickham and sat herself down on the sofa, feet curled under her. She felt vulnerable and child-like, scarcely old enough herself to be out on her own.

'Finlan's? How?'

'He was walking home through the village when he saw Luke hiding in a doorway a few houses up, apparently. Luke had been waiting outside the house, but got scared because he thought someone was following him. He can be a bit like that. Full of bravado one minute, scared of his own shadow the next.' She took a breath. 'He knows Finlan a bit—seen him in the shop a few times—so Finlan offered to take him back to his place until I got back. Just as well, I suppose. It started raining after that.' She paused, as the significance of all this hit her once again. 'I'm going to have Tony on toast for this. Stupid fucking bastard.'

'Why didn't Finlan call earlier? He must have known you'd be worried.'

'He didn't. That was the thing. Luke told Finlan I hadn't been expecting him tonight.' She smiled, weakly. 'Even a nine year-old's smart enough to work out that that might be an issue. Unlike his idiot father. Finlan didn't have my mobile number. He tried the shop a couple of times, but there was no answer and he'd assumed I wouldn't be going back there tonight. In the end, he managed to get hold of the number from one of the others from the Forum. Thank Christ for that. And for Finlan. Most people wouldn't have even noticed he was there.'

'All's well that ends well, then,' Wickham said. 'You'd better let the police know.'

'God, they'll think I'm a total numpty, won't they?'

'They'll think you're a mother who cares about her son, that's all.'

'Just not enough to actually be here when he turns up.'

'Not your fault, was it? You did the right thing. Anyway, might be useful ammunition if you want to make sure Tony doesn't take advantage of you on the custody front.'

'If I have my way, he'll never have custody again.' She stopped, the adrenaline seeping away so she could finally think more clearly. 'You don't mind, do you? About Luke, I mean.'

She could see that he hesitated a moment too long before responding. 'Oh, shit. I'm taking things too fast, aren't I?' she said, before he could answer. 'I keep forgetting we only met last night. It's been a bit of a rollercoaster, hasn't it? You only find out I've got a kid because he goes missing—' She realised she was talking too much again. 'Sorry. I'm just hoping that this might get more serious. You and me, I mean.'

'No, that's fine,' he said, finally. He was smiling fully now. 'No. Me, too. And of course Luke's not a problem. It's just been a lot to take in. Like I told you, I'm a bit of a creature of habit.'

'You think we should take it a bit more slowly, though. Step-by-step. Is that what you're saying?'

'Well—'

'Is this just a kind way of telling me to bugger off?'

'No, no. It really isn't. I want to see you. I want to be with you. But, you know, it's all new. Let's keep going.'

She nodded. 'Yes, you're right. You're obviously right. As long as you're not just finding a polite way to say goodbye.'

'I'm really not. I'm saying hello.' His smile was unwavering.

'But cautiously.' She laughed to show she was joking though she knew he could read the anxiety in her eyes. He put his arms around her and held her close. They were still standing by the uncurtained window, rain pouring down the glass in a steady stream.

'OK,' she said. 'I'd better brave the police before they waste any more public money on my behalf. Then I'll get up to Finlan's to pick up Luke. Do you want to come with me?'

Another hesitation. 'I think I should leave you and Luke to each other tonight. He probably needs you and you definitely need him.'

Her head was still buried in his shoulder, so she couldn't read his expression. 'You're probably right,' she

said. 'Will I see you tomorrow?'
 'Yes,' he said. 'Tomorrow.'

CHAPTER SIXTEEN

Kate Forester slowly pushed open the door of the living room. For a strange moment, as she'd entered the house, she'd been certain it wasn't empty. That she wasn't alone. In her head, she could already see Graeme sitting there in the armchair facing the door. Perfectly positioned so that he could wait for her with that familiar mocking smile on his face.

The chair was empty.

Of course it was. The room was, as far as she could see, the same as she'd left it that morning. Nothing disturbed. Nothing moved. It had begun to rain outside, and she could hear nothing but the dull patter on the window. She couldn't imagine now why the thought of an intruder had even entered her head. Something as she'd entered the house, she thought. Some familiar scent. Some unexpected echo of Graeme.

It was partly because she so desperately wanted this place to be a sanctuary. She needed it to be somewhere safe, somewhere she could live with Jack without any fear that Graeme might turn up unexpectedly on the doorstep. She'd shared her address here with almost no-one beyond the necessary authorities and utilities, and her mail was still being forwarded from her mother's. She suspected that some of her older friends might be offended by her apparent secrecy, but she knew that, if he chose to, Graeme would be adept at worming information out of even her most loyal confidante. For the moment, she preferred to remain off the grid.

The result, though, was a continuing paranoia that

somehow Graeme might track her down. Every evening, she returned from work with the same half-formed anxiety — that he'd be waiting on the doorstep or even, as she'd feared tonight, somewhere in the house. In reality, she knew he'd be more careful. He wasn't going to give her the excuse to involve the police or the courts to keep him away. He'd managed to talk himself out of trouble when he'd taken Jack away, claiming it had all been a misunderstanding. That he'd understood she'd agreed to the trip. That he couldn't imagine why she'd become so hysterical. After all, he'd had a long friendly chat with Kate's mother when he'd come to pick up Jack. She'd obviously seen nothing untoward in his visit. But, well, he'd have told the police, Kate sees herself as a wronged woman in their relationship and you know what they say about a woman scorned.

She could imagine all too vividly how that conversation with the two police officers would have gone. Her own mental state at the point would have served only to confirm what he was telling them. By the time they finished with him, they would have seen Graeme as the victim and herself as the wrong-doer, at best hysterical and at worst malicious, with young Jack stuck in the no-man's land between two antagonistic exes. The officers had told her they'd advised Graeme not to bother her again but she suspected they'd said it with the air of warning him to avoid a killer-shark or a mountain lion.

She'd been back at work a couple of weeks now, heading up the Psychology Team in a nearby women's prison. She liked her colleagues and her new team, and she'd been impressed by Tim Hulse, the young Governor-in-Charge. But it was a different type of establishment from anywhere she'd worked previously, and she'd already found the work more demanding that she'd expected. She'd wanted a complete change, a new role, a new location.

But now she found herself worrying that it was too much for her. Perhaps she'd returned to work too soon. She wasn't ready for it. She wasn't ready to take control of a team. She wasn't ready for the workload. Above all, she wasn't ready to deal with the lives and concerns of prisoners who, after all, had far worse problems than anything she'd ever have to face. She had found herself thinking that it was irresponsible even to think she was in a state to take all that on.

Just at that moment, arriving home at the start of another week, she was tempted just to pick up the phone and tell Hulse she'd had enough. She could put herself back on long-term sick, another victim of the stresses of the job. In practice, it would probably mean the end of her career — if not immediately, then before too long. Word would get around. But that might be for the best.

She opened the freezer door and stared inside, as if the solution might lie among the stacks of dinners-for-one. The closest she could see was a pepperoni pizza. Scarcely conscious of what she was doing, she tore off the packaging, switched on the oven, and thrust the pizza inside. Another healthy meal, then.

She poured herself a glass of wine and took it into the living room. When she'd first visited the house with the estate agent, she'd found this room light and airy, with its view out over the garden to the canal, the valley and the open sky beyond. Now, it felt bleak and impersonal and the vista outside simply left her feeling exposed. She pulled the curtains firmly shut before slumping lifelessly on to the sofa.

She flicked aimlessly through the TV channels, but

nothing caught her attention. Eventually, she left it playing silently on a news channel and booted up her laptop instead. Sipping her wine, she began to check her e-mails in the vague hope that it might help her feel more connected to the outside world. For the most part, the contents of her inbox had the opposite effect. Endless spam messages generated automatically in some back room in who-knew-where. Equally unengaging marketing bumf from companies who'd at some point got hold of her details. A couple of relevant but anonymous bulletins from the British Psychological Society.

Only a couple of the e-mails were actually personal, and one of those only marginally so. A e-mail alert that someone called Kevin Wickham wanted to friend her on a social media page. She idly clicked the link through to the Facebook page. The name rang no bells. The avatar showed a faded image of a child—presumably said Kevin Wickham at a younger age. The picture looked as if it had been taken on a holiday, with slightly too much sun in the frame. The boy was little more than a toddler, and the clothes suggested the picture had been taken sometime in the late 1980s or early 1990s. There were no other clues. Wickham's page contained no other public information that might help her identify how she knew him.

She'd occasionally been advised not to accept friend requests from strangers, but she'd never really seen the harm, even given her line of work. It wasn't as if she actually used social media much or ever posted anything personal herself. It was just a way of keeping in contact with old acquaintances she was unlikely to see face-to-face. Once in a while, she'd stumbled upon some old friend or colleague who'd vanished out of her life years before, sometimes all but forgotten. She'd generally been pleased to make the contact, even when it led nowhere but to a desultory exchange of good wishes. After a moment's hesitation, she clicked on the accept button and returned to scanning through her e-mails.

There was one other e-mail that caught her eye. A note from Greg Perry. She'd received a brief friendly note from him at her work address earlier in the week, wishing her well and promising to find an excuse to visit her new establishment before too long. It had been typical of him, she supposed. He'd remembered, or more likely had noted, when she was due to start the new job, and had taken the trouble to send his good wishes. The note had been short and business-like, but the sentiments had seemed sincere.

The e-mail was simply headed 'News'. It was unusual for Perry to contact her on her personal address, though he'd sent one or two messages of encouragement and support when she'd been unwell. Intrigued, she opened up the message.

Characteristically, it was short and to the point.
'*Hi Kate*

Still confidential so don't go blabbing yet. Especially not to Tim. Got promotion to Area Manager or whatever they're calling it these days. Thought you'd want to know you haven't got rid of me just yet. Sorry about that. Official announcement in next few days so remember to look surprised.

Best

Greg.'

She'd always assumed that Perry was destined for the top, or somewhere close to it. But she hadn't expected he'd progress quite so quickly. He'd been one of the youngest Governors-in-Charge when he'd first been appointed, and the expectation—his, as well as others, or so he'd said — was that he'd have to earn his spurs across various types of prisons before having any chance of progressing further. But after a couple of years running a relatively small Local, a year at a Cat A High Security, and then a similar period in charge of an admittedly high-profile Open, here he was slithering his way further up the greasy pole.

She could imagine that Tim Hulse, who was a similar age and had already held down a couple of challenging Governor postings, wouldn't necessarily take kindly to having Perry leapfrog past him.

She could also imagine it might make her own life even more difficult. Hulse knew that Perry had rated her and that they'd had a relatively close relationship in her last posting. He might see her as Perry's spy in the camp. The message from Perry, however well-intentioned, just made her feel awkward. She'd have to be careful how she handled the situation.

She tapped out a quick return note of congratulations, promising Perry she'd say nothing before the official announcement. She ended with a question: 'Are they going to allow you to take Bonnie to the Area Office?'

She suspected that Bonnie had already served her canine purpose. For a Governor in Change, the dog in the office was a mild eccentricity. It ensured Perry was noticed and talked about. People remembered that character who ducked out of meetings to feed his favourite pooch.

But Area Manager, or Deputy Director, or whatever they'd decided to call it this week, was a whole different animal. You spent your time bandying words with the Director-General and the top team, with local MPs and Councils across the region. You were much less operational and much more of a desk-driver. Above all, you were expected to be *serious*. Her guess was that poor old Bonnie wouldn't make the transition to Area Office, and that Perry would be putting her out to grass.

Swallowing the last of her glass of wine, she made her way back into the kitchen, rescuing the pizza just before it was incinerated. Something was nagging at her mind. It took her a few moments to work out what it was.

The friend request. From—what was that name again?—Kevin Wickham. The name still rang no bells. But something about it had caught in her brain. Still chewing her pizza, she went to retrieve her laptop from the sitting room and opened it up on the table in front of her.

She clicked on Kevin Wickham's avatar and peered at the image, zooming in to try to see more details. At this magnification, it was blurred and unclear, a haze of pixels. A young child, holding the hand of an adult, as if seeking protection from the camera lens, though it was impossible to read the child's expression with any certainty. The adult hand and bare arm appeared to belong to a woman—the child's mother? The background was largely obscured, although the visible patches of green suggested it was a garden or a park.

The image, or something about it, seemed familiar. She was fairly sure she hadn't seen this specific picture before, but she felt she'd seen something similar. She stared at it for several minutes, trying to imagine why the image made her feel so uneasy. There was some memory there she couldn't quite grasp.

She hesitated then she began tapping out a direct message to Kevin Wickham. 'Hi. Thanks for the friend request. Have we met somewhere?' She kept the note as short and impersonal as possible. No point in offering any kind of familiarity to someone she might well prefer to avoid.

She pushed the laptop away and helped herself to another slice of the pizza. Her next task would be to call her mother, have a pre-bedtime chat with Jack. That was the other thing that had kept her going. Half-term was only a week away, and then she'd be bringing Jack up here to join her. He even seemed excited by the prospect of a new school, a new life, new friends. She hoped that he was still young enough to make the transition without any undue trauma.

She poured another glass of wine and went back into the living room. She still felt anxious, but the thought of finally being back with Jack made her feel more optimistic. This was all new, she thought. It was bound to be frightening. But it was also an opportunity to start again, to do things differently. Perhaps everything would finally begin to work out after all.

CHAPTER SEVENTEEN

DC Roberta Wallace gazed at him for a moment as if weighing up his right to be there. After a moment she said: 'Yes, of course, that's fine. Mr—?'

'Wickham,' he said. 'Kevin.'

Wallace held his gazed for a moment longer and then turned her attention back to Sue who was sitting coiled in a corner of the sofa. She looked, Wallace thought, as if she were about to be physically attacked. 'I can appreciate that this is stressful, Mrs Myers, especially after last night. But it's nothing to worry about. Just a couple of things we need to check.' She turned and smiled at Wickham. 'And, of course, absolutely no problem in Mr Wickham sitting in if that makes you feel more comfortable.'

Wallace was only in her late twenties, but she carried herself with an air of confidence and authority. As Paul Wanstead had noted approvingly, her manner and tone of voice managed to blend compassion with an undeniable implication that she'd suffer no nonsense. 'DC Wallace, but call me Roberta,' she'd said in her introductions, emphasising the informality of the discussion. 'It's an awful name, but it's better than Bert, which is what my colleagues call me.'

Sitting next to DC Wallace was DC Will Sparrow. He was a chunky, heavily built young man with short-cropped light brown hair. He was a year or two older than Wallace but generally seemed content to defer to her leadership. They were all sitting awkwardly in Sue Myers's small living room. The previous night's rain had long passed, and the late morning sunshine was streaming in.

Wallace pulled out her notebook, gesturing apologetically with her pen. 'Sorry. Just need to make a few notes. Memory like a sieve.' That was far from true, but Wallace liked to ensure that she had a written note of any interview she was conducting, however supposedly informal. She noted that Sue's eyes were fixed on the notepad as if it posed some kind of threat. For his part, Wickham was sitting motionless, his face blank.

'I'm sorry we're having to take you through all this again, but you'll appreciate that, given what happened up the road, we're keen to see if there's anything in Luke's experience that might help us with our investigation.'

'But nothing happened to Luke,' Sue said.

'No, of course not. But there are one or two points that seemed worth following up. Just to make sure we've got the facts straight. Luke, your son, arrived here what time yesterday afternoon?'

'I didn't know he was coming,' Sue said. 'That was Tony—'

Wallace held up her hand, as if reliving her days on traffic duty. 'You don't need to explain all that, Mrs Myers. We've already had a conversation with your ex-husband.'

'You have?'

'We had a chat with him this morning.' It had been a routine conversation, but they'd wanted to ensure that the two stories tallied. It sounded as if the ex-husband had simply been irresponsible, but the fact was that, whatever the circumstances, a young child had effectively been abandoned alone, in the late afternoon and in bad weather, only days after a child murder in the same neighbourhood. On the face of it, it didn't look good.

'What did he say?'

Wallace smiled, though no warmth reached her eyes. 'He admitted it was his fault. Well, *largely* his fault, I think were his exact words.'

Sue bridled. '*Largely?* There was nothing I could have done to—'

Another raised hand. 'Yes, I know. We pressed him on it. At first, he claimed there'd been some misunderstanding, that you'd said it was all right to drop Luke off. So we asked him to explain just how that misunderstanding had arisen. Eventually, he acknowledged you were expecting him to bring Luke tonight.'

'So why the hell did he bring him yesterday?'

'Reckoned he was annoyed with you. That you'd been pressing him to increase your time with Luke. And then he got an opportunity to go out with his—'

'Mistress,' Sue said. 'Well, not now, I suppose. But she was.'

Wallace blinked, for the first time appearing momentarily disconcerted. 'Well, yes, quite. He'd got hold of a couple of tickets to some band at the Arena, so thought he'd call your bluff—as he put it—and let you have Luke anyway.'

'So why didn't he phone me?'

Wallace smiled again, this time with something approaching sincerity. 'If you'd like my considered opinion on that one, Mrs Myers, I'd say it's because he's an idiot. He told us he didn't phone you because he knew you'd be difficult. That you'd decide you couldn't take Luke after all, just to spite him.'

'Well, I've no intention of jumping to his whims. Yes, I'd have made it difficult. But I'd have taken Luke in the end, because I want to spend time with Luke. He knows that.'

'I'm sure he does. So that was why he decided to cut to the chase and just leave Luke with you. He says he's normally just dropped Luke at the end of the road anyway.'

'He does,' Sue said. 'So he doesn't have to face me. But normally he knows I'm going to be here. Last night he hadn't even bothered to check.'

'He'd just assumed the shop would be open and you'd be there.' Wallace paused, checking her notebook. 'He said he assumed you'd be professional enough to keep to your advertised opening hours—'

'Christ. The arrogant, pompous little—' Sue stopped, struggling to find a noun appropriate to Tony's character.

'Like I say, Mrs Myers.' By now, the smile seemed actually to have permeated Wallace's whole face. 'We made it clear to Mr Myers that, if there was any repetition of this kind of incident, we could be looking at a charge of child neglect. And that if you were considering an application to change the custody arrangements, we'd be happy to provide a statement. I hope that puts your mind at rest.'

Sue nodded. 'Thank you.'

'To go back to my original question, Mrs Myers, what time do you think your son arrived here yesterday? I mean, what time do you think he was dropped off?'

'I thought you'd spoken to Tony.'

'We have. But, as we've agreed, Mrs Myers, he's not necessarily the most reliable of witnesses. I just wanted to be sure of the timing.'

'But I don't—' Sue stopped. Wallace's smile hadn't altered in any obvious way, but her expression somehow conveyed that her patience was wearing thin. 'Well, I normally close at five on a Saturday. It's not usually worth staying open much later at the weekend. In the week, I open a bit later to catch the rail commuters coming back through the village. Anyway, I'd made an appointment to get my hair done after work and she could only fit me in at four, so I shut just before that. Five to, I guess. It's a five minute walk over there.'

'What time did you get back?'

'I don't know exactly. Around five, maybe? It was about quarter to six when Tony phoned to tell me that Luke had left his coat in the car. I was watching the local news on TV.'

'So Mr Myers must have dropped Luke off sometime between four and five, or thereabouts?'

'I suppose so.'

'That ties in with what Mr Myers thought. He reckoned it was probably just after four, so he must have just missed you. He wasn't keeping an eye on the time, but he'd left home at about three-fifteen and had a slow drive out of Manchester. Traffic was heavier than usual because of the rain, I imagine.' Wallace sounded as if she was thinking aloud. 'Can you remember what you told us when you called last night, Mrs Myers? About what Luke said to you about what happened when your husband—sorry, your ex-husband—dropped him off.'

Wickham leaned forward and spoke for the first time since the interview had begun. 'I'm sorry, I don't see where these questions are going. Is there something you're concerned about?'

Wallace turned to him, and for a second looked as if she were about to give him a tongue-lashing. The painted smile was back now. 'I just want to check the timings, Mr Wickham. I've no concerns about what Mrs Myers is saying.' Her tone of voice, more clearly than her words, told him to mind his own business. 'I just want to make sure we've got the sequence clear,' she said to Sue. 'You left at around four. It sounds as if your ex dropped Luke off just a few minutes later. Mr Brody—'

'You've spoken to Finlan?'

'Just briefly, this morning. To complete the picture. He reckons he spotted Luke probably around quarter to five. He'd been in Manchester and got the train out just after four. So by the time he'd got here and walked down from the station, that sounds about right.'

'So you're saying Luke was on his own in the rain for forty-five minutes?' Sue said. 'I hadn't realised it was that long. Finlan said he'd given him a dressing-gown and dried his clothes. The poor kid must have been absolutely soaked.' Wallace could see that she was already beginning to plan her retribution against Tony.

'What did he say to you about what happened after he was dropped off?' Wallace said.

'He said he came along to the shop. Luke thought I must be in the back, even though the door was locked. He banged on the door a few times but obviously there was no answer. After a while he realised I couldn't be there. So he made his way up here and rang the doorbell. But of course I wasn't here either.'

'He doesn't have a mobile?' Wallace said. 'I thought every kid had one these days.'

'It was in the coat he'd left in Tony's car. Sod's law.'

'So what did he say happened after that?'

'He's a sensible kid,' Sue said. 'He didn't worry too much at first. It hadn't started raining yet. He saw that the lights were on in the house so he guessed I wasn't far away.'

Sparrow leaned forward and spoke for the first time. 'What about Mr Wickham? Does he live locally? Wouldn't Luke have thought you might be there?'

'It's—well, quite a new thing, me and Kevin—Mr Wickham,' Sue said, after an awkward pause. She glanced at Wickham who gave no response. 'Luke doesn't really know him yet.'

Wallace nodded, as if this had confirmed something in her mind. 'What about neighbours? Doesn't Luke know any of your neighbours?'

'Not really. Not as people he could turn to in that situation. Most of the people here work in Manchester or Stockport, so we don't see much of them except at weekends.'

'So his plan was just to wait for you to turn up?'

'It was the only option, really,' Sue said. 'My front door's tucked away off the main street so he was OK at first. Even the rain wasn't a major problem as the doorway's quite sheltered.'

'But that wasn't where Mr Brody found him?'

'He got spooked, apparently. Reckoned there was someone watching.'

'That's what Mr Brody told me. But he didn't want to go into it with Luke last night. Did Luke say any more to you?'

'Not much. He's not the most forthcoming boy. He's at that age.'

'Did he mention a van?'

Sue looked up. 'A van?'

'That's what he told Mr Brody. That he'd been waiting in your doorway, and a van had pulled up. Parked on the road opposite, by the river.'

'He just said he thought someone was watching him.

He didn't mention a van.' Sue paused. 'I didn't think much about it. I was just glad he was OK.'

'He told Mr Brody the van pulled up and stopped there. He thought there was just one person inside it. They turned down the window and were watching him. That's what he thought. He didn't say any of this to you?'

'I didn't press him on it,' Sue said. 'I thought he'd been through enough. I'm sorry, like Kevin said, I don't really see where this is going. Luke's fine. Nothing happened to him. Even if there was a van out there, it was probably nothing. People stop along here all the time.'

'Just making sure we've tied up all the loose ends, that's all.' Wallace flicked back a few pages in her notebook. 'We've had a few other reports. Since the murder.'

'Reports?'

'At least one other attempted child snatching. Driver of a van. And a couple of other reports of cars and vans parked by schools, drivers behaving suspiciously. You know the kind of thing.' Her tone was off-hand.

Wickham leaned forward and exchanged a glance with Sue. 'You really think this might have been the same person? The person who snatched the boy up the road, I mean.'

'I don't want to sound alarmist. We get a lot of this stuff, as you can imagine. Kids get spooked easily, like you said about Luke. A lot of it's urban myth stuff. Children have seen the news reports. Then they see a van pull up and convince themselves it's something threatening. Word gets around and they all think they've seen it. We had a spate of reports a couple of years back with no real cause. A black van supposedly trawling the backstreets of Stockport snatching kids off the street. Even had a couple of parents reckoning they'd seen it.'

'But there was nothing in it?'

'As far as we could tell. None of the incidents amounted to anything. But of course this is different. We're dealing with a murder. We have to be sure.' Wallace snapped shut her notebook, as if she'd just acquired the final clinching piece of evidence. 'All's well that ends well, anyway,' she said to Sue. 'I'm sure you and your ex will make sure nothing like this happens again.' Sue blinked, clearly registering that, whatever Wallace might have said earlier, she was now implicitly implicating both parents in what had happened to Luke.

Wallace turned her attention back to Wickham. 'Good to meet you, Mr Wickham. I hope you're settling in round here. I understand from Mr Brody that you're a newcomer to the area.'

Wickham shifted awkwardly in his seat at the unexpected attention. 'Well, I've been here a couple of months now,' he said. 'Beginning to find my feet.'

'I've been here twenty years,' Sue said. 'And some of them still treat me like a new arrival.'

'That's the countryside for you,' Wallace said. 'Still, I'm sure everyone's been very welcoming.' She turned to Sue. 'I'd wondered whether I ought to interview Luke. See whether he remembered any more about last night. Anything about that van.'

Sue looked across at Wickham for support. 'Well, I can get him if you think it's necessary. He's upstairs playing some computer game.'

Wallace paused as if considering this offer, then smiled. 'I don't think we need to bother him for the moment. Must have been traumatic enough for the poor little chap. I don't imagine he'll be able to tell us anything we haven't already heard. But if he says anything else significant, you'll let us know, won't you?'

'Yes, of course.'

'And if you think of anything else, you'll do the same?'

'Anything else?'

Wallace shrugged, as if she had no idea of what she might have had in mind. 'When you were returning to the house, you didn't see any other vehicles? Anything that looked suspicious?'

'No. There were probably a few cars went by as I was walking down the main road, but nothing that struck me.'

'What about you, Mr Wickham? You didn't see anything last night?'

'I wasn't here,' he said. 'Not till Sue called. I'd been working at home all afternoon.'

'No, of course. I wasn't thinking. By the time you got down here, it was too late, obviously.' The smile hadn't changed. 'Oh, well, if anything does occur to either of you—' She left the sentence hanging. 'Thanks for your help, both of you. We'll try not to bother you again.'

Wallace glanced back as she and Sparrow made their way back to the car they'd left parked further down the street. Sue Myers and Kevin Wickham were still watching from the open doorway. 'That felt a bit odd,' Wallace said. 'What did you make of that guy Wickham?'

Sparrow shrugged. 'Not sure,' he said. 'He looked uncomfortable enough, but then so did she. Maybe not surprising in the circumstances. Didn't exactly get the sense that it was a well established relationship.'

'No, me neither,' Wallace said. 'Almost like they hardly knew each other. And there was something about

Wickham—' She stopped as they reached the car.

'You don't think he could be our man?'

'I don't know. He just struck me as a bit—well, odd, I suppose. As if he's not used to being with other people. The type who seems like a natural loner.' She waited while Sparrow fumbled with the car keys, then added: 'Which makes me wonder quite what he's doing with Mrs Myers.'

CHAPTER EIGHTEEN

Murrain had sat in silence after she'd finished speaking, and it occurred to Wallace, just for a moment, that he might think she was taking the piss.' Well, not instinct, exactly,' she'd added, after a moment. 'But, you know, intuition.' Oh Christ, she thought, I need to stop digging.

But Murrain's smile was genuine enough. 'Whatever it is, Bert, I'm happy to go with it. If you think there's something worth looking at.' He didn't often bring himself to call her Bert. Wallace usually saw it as a mark of his approval.

She glanced at Will Sparrow. He was looking as if he might rather be anywhere else just at that moment. 'I don't think I was imagining it. Will felt it too. Didn't you, Will?'

Will shuffled awkwardly. Murrain had come to the conclusion that Sparrow was a capable enough young officer, but that he lacked the spark of intelligence and fresh thinking that distinguished Bert Wallace. On the other hand, he displayed a caution and, from time to time, a political nous that suggested he'd probably go far. Murrain knew from his own experiences that those qualities were generally more highly valued than any signs of uniqueness. 'I think Bert's right,' Sparrow said after a pause than suggested he'd been weighing up his response. 'Something felt a bit off. The whole relationship felt strange. And Wickham seemed—I don't know—on edge.'

'A lot of people are on edge when they're being

interviewed by the police,' Murrain observed, thinking back to his own interview with Mrs Morrison.

'Maybe,' Wallace said. 'But it felt more than that. My impression was that he was wary. Nervous about what we had to say.'

'You think he had something to hide?'

Murrain had articulated the question more bluntly than she'd expressed it to herself. 'If you put it like that,' she said, 'then, yes. That was my impression.'

'Have you checked him out?'

'I looked him up on the PNC. He was on there, as it turns out. But nothing significant. He received a caution for a public order offence at the Iraq war demos in 2003. Some fracas in Trafalgar Square.' She sounded as if she were describing a prehistoric event.

'I remember it well,' Murrain said. 'Of course, that might explain why he's so wary around the police. We may not have treated him as gently as he might have liked.'

Wallace had thought at first that that comment was intended as a dismissal. But an hour later she found herself standing on Kevin Wickham's doorstep, this time with Murrain hovering silently behind her. They'd tracked down Wickham's address easily enough. There was no record of him in any of the on-line directories but his name had been recently added to the electoral roll.

At first, there was no response to the bell. Wallace pressed again, this time holding it down. A moment later, they heard the rattling of the lock as the door opened. Wickham stood in front of them, with another male figure standing just behind him. 'Oh my Gawd, it's the rozzers. I'd better scarper pronto,' the second figure said in a thick mock Cockney accent.

It took Murrain, peering past Wallace, a moment to

recognise the man who had spoken. 'Mr Brody,' he said. 'Good to see you again.'

Finlan Brody edged his way past Wickham out on to the doorstep. 'I'll leave Kevin to your tender mercies,' he said. 'Just been putting a bit of business his way, so hope you've not got him bang to rights.'

'Just routine enquiries, like my discussion with you,' Murrain said, pointedly. He didn't want Brody spreading any rumours about the reasons why they might be visiting Kevin Wickham, 'By the way, thank you for taking care of Luke Myers. I'm sure his mother was relieved he was in safe hands.'

Brody shrugged. 'Anyone would have done the same. I only wish I'd been able to call her earlier. All I can say is she's well rid of that idiotic ex of hers.' He glanced meaningfully at Wickham. 'Hope she makes a better choice next time. Well, I'll leave you to continue your enquiries with young Kevin here. And if I can be of any further assistance, please do call in anytime.' He smiled and, waving a theatrical farewell, headed off down towards the village.

Murrain turned to Wickham. 'Friend of yours?'

'Not really.' Wickham was watching them warily. 'I met him through the local business forum. He was asking me about supporting them at the home with recruiting some care assistants. Doing some psychometric tests. Couple of days' work for me, I hope.'

Murrain held out his hand. 'I'm sorry to trouble you. DCI Murrain. I think you already know my colleague DC Wallace. Would you mind if we came in for a minute? There are a couple more questions we'd like to ask.' He could see that Wickham had registered his rank.

Wickham nodded and ushered them into the house. After a moment's thought, he led them down the hallway to the kitchen. Murrain had the sense, somehow, that he didn't want them entering the more personal areas of the house.

Wickham was looking a little more confident now than when he'd first opened the door. He gestured for them to take a seat at the kitchen table, and sat himself down opposite. 'How can I help you?'

'We just wanted to follow up DC Wallace's conversation with you and Mrs Myers.'

'How do you mean?' He shifted in his seat. 'I don't think there's anything I can add.'

Murrain was sitting in silence, gazing down at the table. After a moment, he looked up and gazed squarely at Wickham. 'You're aware we're investigating a murder in the village, Mr Wickham?'

'Yes, of course. That little boy. It's a dreadful business.'

'What time did you visit Mrs Myers on Saturday night?'

'Well, I got there while the police officers were still talking to her. I don't know — about six, maybe?'

'You hadn't tried to visit her earlier in the afternoon?'

'No. We'd originally arranged for me to come around about half-eight to go for a drink and a meal. Then she phoned me about Luke. By the time I got there the police had arrived.' He'd stiffened defensively in his seat. 'Why are you asking?'

'As you heard, Mr Brody said Luke thought he was being watched by someone in a van. Do you own a van, Mr Wickham?'

Wickham's eyes darted from Murrain to Wallace and then back again. 'No.'

'Any kind of vehicle?'

'Yes, a Fiesta.'

'A saloon?'

'An estate. I don't see—'

'What colour is it?'

'Dark blue. I—'

'Do you think someone could mistake it for a van? In the dark? In the rain?'

Wickham sat up his seat, looking alarmed now. 'How would I know? The point is I wasn't there.'

'No, of course not.' Murrain picked up his coffee, as if he'd suddenly lost interest in the conversation. 'You'll appreciate we have to be sure, Mr Wickham. How long have you known Mrs Myers?'

'Well, not long. A week or two.'

'You're fairly new to the area, I understand?' Murrain's tone had changed, as if he were engaging in nothing more than idle chat.

'Well, a couple of months here. I've lived up in the north-west for a while, though. Did my postgrad in Manchester. Look, I really don't see where this is going.'

'You'll appreciate, Mr Wickham, that in the circumstances we have to explore all the avenues. Were you aware Mrs Myers had a son? When you started a relationship with her, I mean?'

'I'm not sure we have "started a relationship" as you put it. We've been out together a couple of times, that's all. I knew she was divorced. We're neither of us exactly teenagers. But, no, I didn't know about Luke, not really.'

'Not really?'

'Not at all. Till Saturday night.'

Murrain raised an eyebrow. 'So the first you knew about Luke was that he'd gone missing?'

'Well, yes. I guess Sue had been picking her moment to tell me.'

'Indeed.' Murrain paused. 'But you're happy with the

father figure role?'

Wickham was silent for a moment. 'Like I say, it's early days. We're not really thinking in those terms yet. Look, I don't want to seem difficult, but I'm still not clear why you're here. What you want from me.'

'It's all routine, Mr Wickham,' Murrain said. 'We have to follow up every avenue. Thank you for your assistance.' He turned to Wallace. 'Is there anything else you'd like to ask, DC Wallace?'

She caught his eye. 'Just one thing, Mr Wickham. We took the liberty of seeing if there was any reference to you on the Police National Computer.'

As she spoke, she registered that Murrain had suddenly sat back in his seat, almost as if he'd been physically struck. For her own part, she'd noticed Wickham's fingers whitening as they pressed down harder on the table.

'I'm sure you did,' he said. 'Did you find anything?'

'Nothing of significance. Just a small incident at a protest in London.'

He blinked. 'I was given a caution, that's all. Frankly, it was your lot who should have been prosecuted. It was just a peaceful protest.'

'I'm sure, Mr Wickham,' Murrain said, placidly. 'I'm sorry, we've taken up far too much of your time.' He pushed himself to his feet. 'We're very grateful for your assistance. I take it you'll be happy to talk to us again. Should the need arise.'

Wickham had also jumped up, seemingly keen to get them off the premises. Wallace remained seated for a moment, painstakingly writing something in her notebook. Then she rose and followed the two men out into the hallway. Wickham already had the front door open.

Outside, after the previous days' rain, it was a fine afternoon. 'Is this your car?' Murrain asked, gesturing towards a Fiesta Estate parked at the roadside.

'That's it,' Wickham said. 'I don't think you'd mistake it for a van, would you?'

Murrain walked closer and regarded the vehicle. 'Thanks again for your time. I hope we won't need to disturb you further.'

He stood, still gazing at the vehicle, while Wickham disappeared back into the house, closing the front door firmly behind him. Then he turned to Wallace. 'Well, you wouldn't mistake it for a van on a day like today, anyway. And not close up. But a child? In the distance? At night? In the rain? Who knows? I guess it's possible.'

'What did you think?' she said.

'I thought,' he said, 'that there was something odd about Mr Wickham. Something not quite right. Something in particular about his entry on the PNC.' He paused. 'I don't know what it is. But I've an odd feeling we might be about to find out.'

'Feeling?' Wallace echoed.

'Yes,' Murrain said. 'A definite feeling.'

CHAPTER NINETEEN

'Afternoon, people,' Tim Hulse said. It was difficult to read his expression. 'Apologies for missing the daily meeting this morning, but it sounds as if John held the fort admirably as always. And apologies also for interrupting your afternoon, but I wanted to give you the opportunity to say hello to our new Regional Director.' He waved his hand in Greg Perry's direction, in the manner of a compere introducing the top of the bill. 'I imagine many of you will have come across Greg previously.' He glanced over at Kate Forester. 'Some more recently than others, I guess, Kate?'

'I thought I'd escaped from him.'

'You can run, but you can't hide,' Perry said. He was looking his usual relaxed, genial self. 'Afternoon, ladies and gents,' he said. 'I just wanted to say hello while I was on site. I've literally only taken up the job today, so not really even got my feet under the table.' He looked slowly around the room as if appraising them all individually. 'I spent most of my time as Governor wondering what the hell it is that the Regional Director actually does. I suppose I'm about to find out. Any advice gratefully received.'

John Hodges, the Deputy Governor, was sitting at the far end of the table, intent on completing some intricate doodle in his notepad. 'Good of you to spare us the time so soon, Greg,' he said, without looking up. 'Why are we so high on your priority list?'

'You've been in the Service too long, John. Breeds paranoia. Just luck of the draw, I'm afraid. I'm planning to get round the whole patch over the next couple of weeks.'

'Question is,' Hodges said, 'are we the short straw or the long one?'

'Oh, definitely the long one as far as I'm concerned.' Perry gave a smile that revealed nothing. 'I couldn't imagine meeting a more delightful group of people on a Monday afternoon.'

Hodges snorted. 'I can see how you got promotion,' he said. 'You were never this smooth when you were working for me.'

'I worked as a Head of Ops under John,' Perry explained to the others. 'Learned everything I know from him.' He laughed. 'So Christ knows how I ever got this job.'

This was it, Kate thought. Greg Perry working his magic. When they'd been called to this meeting, the mood among her colleagues had been a mix of cynicism and anxiety. The old hands, like Hodges, claimed to have seen it all before. 'He's just pissing up the wall,' he said, characteristically. 'Marking his territory so we all know where we stand.' Sharon Barnes, the Head of Residence, was newer to the game and, in career terms, had much more to lose. In the few hours before this meeting, she'd worked herself up to an almost supersonic pitch of worry. She'd appeared three times at the doorway to Kate's office for what she described as an 'all girls together' chat, presumably because she thought Kate might have some inside track to Perry's mind. 'But *why* would he come here on his first day?' she'd asked repeatedly. 'There must be some reason he's chosen to do that. It can't just be coincidence.'

But now, in the meeting, he was winning them over. That was Perry's great skill. Not everybody liked him but most people ended up respecting him. He knew which buttons to press, how to get people supporting him, without ever seeming manipulative. Before long, he had them all contributing to the discussion. Even Sharon Barnes seemed to have lost her anxieties and was explaining various aspects of the regime to him with enthusiasm.

Perry was smiling at Kate, as if he knew exactly what she'd been thinking. 'You haven't said much so far, Kate.'

'I'm just the new girl,' she said. 'I don't know there's much I can add.'

'Fresh pair of eyes and all that. Just wondered what your impressions were.'

'I'm still getting used to the place,' she said. 'It's a whole different set of challenges from anything I'm used to. But I've been impressed so far. The psychology team are really excellent.'

Perry nodded, as if she'd offered a genuinely profound insight. 'That's good to hear.' He smiled amiably around the table. 'Well, this has all been really interesting. Thanks for taking the time to update me. If everyone's as forthcoming as this, I might even get the hang of the job sometime before I retire.' He looked at his watch. 'I really don't want to take up any more of your collective time. If it's OK with Tim, what I might do is have a wander round afterwards, and grab a few more minutes with one or two of you. Just to explore a few more specific issues. That all right with you, Tim?'

'Well, if you're sure you've got time—'

'Might as well do things properly while I'm here.' Perry pushed himself slowly to his feet. 'Thank you very much, ladies and gentlemen. Very much appreciated. I'll leave you to get on with some real work.'

***

'I may owe you an apology.'

Kate glanced up from her computer monitor. She'd been in the middle of a risk assessment report and had lost track of the time. 'Really? I thought it was the other way round.'

Perry was leaning against the door. There was no sign of Tim Hulse. 'That wasn't your fault. Just one of those things.'

'That's what you're supposed to say. Mental illness counts as a disability these days, so you have to demonstrate you're not being discriminatory. But I let you down, and you must have been mightily pissed off.'

Perry closed the door behind him and lowered himself into the chair opposite Kate's desk.

'They already think I'm your spy in the camp,' she pointed out. 'It won't help if they think we're having secret confabs in my office.'

'Are you?' he said. 'My spy in the camp, I mean.'

She saved the file she was working on, and turned to face him. 'You wouldn't want me to be,' she said. 'That's not the way you work.'

'If I want information, I get it for myself.'

'So I'd noticed.'

'Hope it wasn't too obvious.'

'Only to those of us who've studied your methods, Holmes,' she said. 'I hope you found out what you needed.'

'Getting there.' He stretched out in the chair and looked curiously around her office. She'd never been one for introducing home comforts into her working environment, and so far she'd done nothing to personalise her new work-space. 'Not even a coffee machine,' he commented.

'There's plenty of instant in the kitchen down the corridor,' she said. 'If you're thirsty.'

'Tim's been feeding me coffee by intravenous drip.' He paused. 'I'm not just being PC, you know.'

'Well, there'd be a first time for everything. How do you mean?'

'About your illness. That's what it was. I wouldn't have been pissed off if you'd taken time off because you had cancer or been in a car accident. And I wasn't pissed off because you took time off for the reasons you did. You were ill.'

'It caused you some problems.'

'It wasn't ideal timing,' he admitted. 'But these things never are. I'm paid to cope with them.'

'But it doesn't help if your Head of Psychology goes doolally at the point when you're trying to reassure the powers-that-be about the release of a high profile prisoner?'

'Doolally? That the technical term, then? Well, no, it wasn't the most convenient moment.'

'They were convinced he'd confessed something to me, you know? Something I wasn't revealing. Something I hadn't put in the Parole Board report.'

'I know,' he said. 'They kept asking me the same question. As if I'd have kept something like that to myself.'

'They really didn't get it,' she said. 'They kept going on to me about patient confidentiality, and about how public safety had to override all those considerations.' She shook her head at the memory of a series of encounters that, up to now, she'd successfully shoved to the back of her mind. 'I kept telling them I knew what my job was. That I wouldn't do anything to jeopardise public safety. And that, no, Carl hadn't confessed anything to me I hadn't already shared with them.'

'They're HQ wallahs,' Perry said. 'You can't win with them, by definition. It would have been easier not to report what he'd said in that final session. "The boy I killed". That complicated things just at the wrong time. But if we hadn't told them, and it had somehow come to light—'

'Yes, I know,' she said. 'But it wasn't a confession. That's what I kept trying to tell them. Not in any meaningful sense. It's possible it might have led to a confession in the longer term, if there'd been a longer term.' She shook her head. 'But I didn't help you. I was a mess by that point. In tears half the time. Had lost all perspective. I can't really even remember what I was thinking. But it was clear they didn't trust my judgement.'

'Not sure that lot ever trust anybody's judgement,' Perry said. 'Except their own, however ill-founded that might be. But they thought you'd got too close to the case. They even thought that maybe it was something Carl had told you that drove you over the edge in—well, you know—'

'In throwing those wild accusations at Graeme?' she said. 'That was the phrase they used to me. "Wild accusations". They knew nothing about me or Graeme or anything that had happened. They only knew about it in the first place because they wanted to know why I'd been taking time off. Then they seized on it as if it proved their point. There was nothing coherent about their arguments. They couldn't decide whether I was being hysterical in accusing Graeme or whether there really was something in what I was saying. In which case if I'd been taken in by Graeme, maybe I'd also been taken in by Carl.'

'Coherence has never been HQ's strong point. They just keep asking random questions until they hear an answer they like. Which is generally that they won't be held responsible for anything that might subsequently go wrong.'

'Mind you,' she said, 'you're not so far from being an HQ wallah yourself these days.'

His expression changed to one of mock outrage. 'How dare you?' he said. 'I'm still one of the people. One of the more senior people now, admittedly. But I'm still the same little old Greg, deep inside.'

She smiled. 'No-one's ever got that deep inside. But if you say so. Not sure that everyone here believes that.'

'No, well, if I'm honest, one or two people here perhaps have some reason to be anxious on that score.'

'Are you sure you want to share these thoughts, Greg?'

'I wouldn't expect you to tell me anything. Even if you were in a position to. But, like I say, I do owe you an apology.'

'Go on.'

'I pointed you towards this job. I encouraged you to apply. Wrote a damned good reference for you, too. It's largely my fault you're here.'

'What do you mean, "fault"?' she said. 'What's going on?'

Perry looked about him, as if appraising the fabric of Kate's office. 'This place has problems,' he said. 'Serious problems.'

'Really? I mean, there are challenges—'

'You knew it'd had a couple of really crap inspection reports?'

To her embarrassment, Kate realised that, in her eagerness to move on, she'd not even carried out that basic level of due diligence before taking the job. She'd asked one or two colleagues their opinions of the place, that was all, and had heard nothing bad. 'Tim said the last one had some criticisms, but only what you'd expect.'

'The last two inspections were bad. Not just the kinds of things you might expect, but a litany of criticisms — bullying, victimisation, physical violence, rampant drug taking. And not just among the prisoners, either. We've had five Officers suspended and ultimately dismissed from here in the last couple of years. Again, all kinds of things — physical violence, inappropriate behaviour, sexual assault, corruption. You name it. And those five were just the tip of the iceberg.'

'I've seen no signs of that.'

'You wouldn't, would you? They'd be very careful not to wash any dirty linen till they were sure you were elbow deep in suds as well.'

'You said two inspections. The first of those would have been before Tim's time here, surely?'

'Has Tim worked his charms on you, then? Not surprised. He's got himself a long way on charm, has Tim. Too many people keen to protect him. But you're right. The first of the inspection reports was completed before he arrived here. It was damning enough, and that was why Tim was brought over here — to try to sort it out.'

'Is that his reputation?' she asked. 'The troubleshooter type?'

'Not particularly,' Perry said. 'He was under a cloud, already. He'd been highly regarded when he joined the Service — graduate high-flyer, like yours truly — but too many things went wrong. Not all his fault, but enough to get him noticed for the wrong reasons. And some of it definitely was his fault—like being caught with inappropriate material on his laptop. He got a formal warning for that. Lucky to escape dismissal.'

She frowned. 'So as punishment they made him responsible for a failing prison? I suppose that does sound like the logic we'd expect from the Service.'

'Nobody doubted Tim had ability. It was made clear to him this was his last chance. If he turned the place round, it would be one of those career-making moments. If he failed, the best he could hope for was some harmless back room role in HQ. The second inspection report was, if anything, worse than the first. Tim was given some benefit of the doubt as he hadn't been in post for long at that point but it didn't look good.'

'And now?'

'Now it's looking even worse. There's another inspection due in a couple of months. The view from on high is that the outcomes still won't be satisfactory. Maybe some improvements but nothing like what's needed. Tim won't talk his way out of this one.'

'Bit tough, isn't it? If he's taking things in the right direction?'

'I've no axe to grind, Kate. I've been one of Tim's supporters over the years. I thought he had real potential. I stuck my neck out for him when some people would have happily seen him canned. He's a bright guy, an able guy. Maybe just over-promoted. A great Dep, but not up to the top job. There are plenty like that.'

'John Hodges?'

'I'd say so, wouldn't you? John's a great guy. Just the person you want standing behind you when things get tough. But maybe not the person you'd want standing in front of you leading the charge. The difference is that John knew it and found his level. I'd love to think that Tim was different, that he's up to it. But the signs are that he isn't. That's why I wanted your opinion. Not to badmouth him, but because I trust your judgement.'

'I thought I'd pretty much forfeited that trust,' she said.

'We've been through that, Kate.' He paused. 'Anyway, you were right.'

'Was I?'

'About Carl. You said there was no reason not to release him. The HQ wallahs got jittery and took further soundings, but they could find no substantive grounds to challenge our reports. The Parole Board were happy enough. As far as I know, the decision's been vindicated.'

'As far as you know?'

'You know how it is with those cases. It's all hush-hush. But the word on the grapevine is that Carl's OK. That he's integrated better than anyone might have feared. New life, all that.'

'He deserved that. Whatever he did or didn't do, he'd paid the price.'

'Not sure the tabloids would agree with you. It was a notorious case in its day. But, yes, everyone deserves a second chance. Which brings us back to Tim.'

'And that's why you're here? Because of Tim?'

'The senior bods are getting the jitters about this place and want it sorted as quickly as possible.'

'They think it's that serious?'

'They think anything's serious if it has the potential to reflect badly on them. There've been a lot of problems here. The view is that this place is a powder keg and that something's going to kick off before too long. Either some major incident—a riot, a major escape—or some sort of media exposé. There are too many problems to brush under the carpet.'

'So what's going to happen?'

'That's what I'm here to decide.'

'And what have you decided?'

'I haven't entirely, yet. But you know me, Kate. I'm not one to mess about. Tim's got to be replaced. But I think it'll need more than that. The politicians are already getting interested in this place. We need, not just to sort it out, but to be seen to be sorting it out. That probably means a complete overhaul of the management team and a root and branch investigation of the staff generally. A complete clear-out.'

She pushed herself away from the window and sat back down in the chair facing Perry. 'That's why you owe me an apology, is it? Because I'm going to be collateral damage in Tim's downfall?'

'I'm just trying to be honest with you. Giving you a heads-up.'

'Which is more than you're doing with any of my colleagues here.' She could feel herself growing angry.

'I'll be equally honest with them, Kate, when the time comes. I don't want any of you to end up as "collateral damage" as you put it. Like I say, it's a good team here.'

'But they'll—we'll—all be replaced? That's what you said.'

'That's probably what'll happen. You might be OK because you've only just arrived. You're not tainted with the old regime.' She was on the point of interrupting, but he held up his hand. 'I just don't know, Kate. I can make recommendations on how it should be handled but I don't know how much weight that will carry. When the politicos get involved, they tend to throw the baby out with the bathwater.'

'So my career gets wrecked just because I joined the wrong prison at the wrong time?'

'You'll be OK. You'll all be OK. Whatever noises are made, everyone will understand the reality. They'll all know it wasn't really your fault.'

'You reckon? First, they see me crack up almost in front of their eyes. Then they see me ousted in disgrace from the first job I come back to. How much doubt do you reckon they'll give me the benefit of?'

Perry gazed back at her impassively. 'That's not the way it'll be seen. I'm sure.'

'And what about Tim?'

'Who knows? Maybe some sort of pay-off. Maybe some innocuous HQ job.'

She dropped her head into her hands, exhausted by the whole thing. 'Jesus, it's a brutal business, isn't it?'

'Less brutal here than many places, Kate. It's tough, but we've got to make sure the job's being done properly. You know how important it is we get things right. We can't just play at it.'

'It still leaves me halfway up the creek. I'm trying to start a new life up here, moving Jack over during the holiday. Now you throw this at me.'

He was still gazing back at her, his expression unchanged. There was something in his eyes, some emotion, she couldn't read. 'I never expected that it would work out like this.' He paused. 'But I'll do what I can. You know me.'

She forced herself to smile. 'Yes, of course.' But that was just it, she thought. She wasn't sure that she did know him. Not any more.

CHAPTER TWENTY

On his return, Murrain was struck by an air of depression in the MIR. They were all working hard. Many of the team were still out pounding the streets, conducting door-to-door interviews or following up possible leads. Others were reviewing endless minutes of CCTV footage or collating interview notes. On the surface, it looked busy and productive. But he could feel they were going through the motions. The energy had drained. Murrain knew this was a critical period. If they didn't make a breakthrough soon, things would start to slip. It wasn't that the team would stop trying. It was simply that they'd stop believing they could succeed. Then, almost inevitably, they wouldn't.

Wanstead looked up. 'Chief Super dropped in earlier.'

'Told you to keep up the good work?'

'That sort of thing. Still, seems a decent bloke.'

The previous head of the Serious Crimes Division had spent two years coasting down to retirement and for most of that time had adopted an approach that was hands-off to the point of invisibility. His successor, CS Marty Winston, had been promoted from CID in North Manchester and, apart from a few informal encounters, had been an unknown quantity down here. So far Murrain had found him personable, supportive and reliable, which was the most he ever asked for in a superior officer. 'That's my impression.'

'Asked if you could give him a call when you got in.'

'Thanks, Paul. Will do.'

No doubt Winston would be seeking an update,

hoping for some good news. Unlike some of his superiors, Winston had refrained from seeking two-hourly briefings but he'd be getting more jittery with every day that went by.

'Marty? It's Kenny Murrain. You wanted me to call.'

'Kenny. Thanks. How's it going?'

'Well, you know. It's going. But nothing new so far, I'm afraid. Still chasing shadows.'

'Hear this latest one turned out to be a false alarm?'

'Thankfully.'

'Yes, thankfully.' Behind Winston's despondent tone lurked the truth that both of them understood: that a second snatching might at least have opened up some new leads. 'Anything else?'

'Not to speak of. We're following up this supposed case in Hazel Grove. Checking for sightings of this dark van. But it feels like a long shot.'

'Well, good luck. We just need one breakthrough.'

Just the one, Murrain thought. Any suggestions gratefully received. 'It's only a matter of time,' he said. 'It always is.' Though both of them knew that, day by day, time was running out.

'Something will turn up. Actually, Kenny, the main reason I dropped by was something else. Bit of an odd one, actually. Have you or your team had some dealings with a guy called Kevin Wickham?'

Murrain felt it then, almost like an electrical jolt through the phone. 'Wickham?' he said. 'Funnily enough, I've just got back from seeing him. Why?'

There was a moment's silence at the other end. 'You've been to see him? In what context?'

'The false alarm you mentioned. A couple of the team interviewed the mother. Wickham was there. Partner or boyfriend or whatever you want to call him.'

'And you went to talk to Wickham?' There was a faint emphasis on the name.

'My officer thought there was something—well, not quite right about the way he behaved. In the circumstances we thought it best to have another chat with him.'

'You wanted to see the whites of his eyes, Kenny?'

No doubt the gossip about Murrain's methods had long ago reached north Manchester. 'We're desperate for any kind of lead, Marty. I don't want anything significant to slip through the net.'

'No, quite right. So what did you think?'

'There's something odd about him, certainly. Whether it's pertinent to this case, I don't know yet. But I think he's worth checking out a bit further.' He paused. 'What's this about, Marty?'

'To be honest, I'm not entirely sure. I had a call this morning.'

'Go on.'

'They'd been in touch with the Chief. Who'd passed it down to me. Some bod from the Ministry of Justice.'

Murrain could feel it more strongly now, that familiar steady pulse through his skin. The sense of some meaning coalescing he couldn't quite apprehend. Almost as if there were a voice calling to him, just out of earshot. 'What's this to do with Wickham?'

'That's the thing. The first question he asked was whether we were investigating a Kevin Wickham. I said the name meant nothing to me, but I'd find out.'

'How the hell did they know?'

'That was the first question *I* asked, if a little more circumspectly. Or, at least, why they had reason to think we might be. They said they'd received notification that someone had accessed his records on the PNC.' There was a pause and the sound of rustling papers. 'A DC Wallace. She's one of yours, isn't she?'

'She is. And, yes, she checked him out on the PNC. There was some trivial offence recorded but nothing relevant to what we're interesting in. What's this all about?' It wasn't news to Murrain that use of the PNC could be monitored in this way, but the MoJ's involvement was more than intriguing. Generally, if the file was significant for some reason—typically because the individual in question was an undercover officer or subject to a Witness Protection order—it was another force that was alerted.

'They weren't very forthcoming. Just asked if I could look into it and get someone to call them back asap. Which is what I'm doing.'

'You want me to give them a call?'

'Better you than me, Kenny. Christ knows what questions they might ask. You'll have all the answers. You'll keep me posted if it's anything important?'

'Of course.' He finished chatting to Winston and sat for a moment with the phone still in his hand, feeling that familiar repetitive pulse and wondering what it might be telling him. Finally, he tapped in the number that Winston had given him.

'Hello. John Barker.'

'Mr Barker. This is DCI Murrain from Greater Manchester Police. I was asked to give you a call. In connection with a Mr Kevin Wickham, I believe?'

'Ah, yes. Thanks for calling back—' There was a pause and the sound of Barker rustling through papers. 'Right, yes. We understand one of your officers has accessed Mr Wickham's file on the PNC. Is that right?'

'We access a lot of files on the PNC, Mr Barker. Can I ask what—?'

'Yes, but Wickham's file. That's been accessed?' Barker's voice was mild, but he had the air of someone unaccustomed to being questioned.

'I believe so, but—'

'Can I ask why your officer was interested in Mr Wickham?'

Murrain was generally a patient man, but he could already feel himself being rubbed up the wrong way. 'With respect, Mr Barker, can I ask why *you're* interested?'

There was a pause. 'I'm not playing games here, DCI Murrain. I want to know why your officer was interested in Wickham.'

'I'm not playing games, either, Mr Barker. You'll appreciate I can't simply provide potentially sensitive information to anyone who enquires. Even if they're from the MoJ. I don't wish to be uncooperative, but I don't know who you are, what your roles is or why you're making this enquiry. Without more information I'm afraid I'm not in a position to assist you.'

There was another silence, presumably while Barker processed this. Murrain had a feeling the outcome might be the termination of this conversation and another call to the Chief. Well, fair enough. If Barker presented his bona fides to the Chief, they might start to make some progress.

'My role, DCI Murrain, is concerned with public protection. I need to know the reasons why your force is interested in Kevin Wickham.'

Murrain mentally counted up to five before responding. 'OK, Mr Barker. We don't seem to be getting very far. Perhaps we need to try a different approach. I'm really not being difficult. But I do have certain responsibilities. Which, as you'll appreciate, also involve public protection. As well as the protection of potentially sensitive public data. I can think of several reasons why accessing the PNC might trigger an alert—'

'DCI Murrain—'

'First,' Murrain ploughed on, 'because the individual concerned is an undercover officer. That would normally trigger an alert with another force or maybe with the NCA. Second, because the individual is on a witness protection programme. Again, that might trigger an alert with another force. But I suppose in a very sensitive or high profile case, I could see yourselves or the Home Office being involved. Do stop me if I'm getting close, by the way.'

'DCI Murrain—'

'The third reason, I suppose, would be if the individual in question was a high-profile ex-offender who had been given a new identity. The Mary Bell kind of case. How am I doing?' Murrain had been working out the logic of this as he was speaking, but the rising electrical buzz through his veins was already telling him he was on the right lines.

'You're not to be underestimated, are you, DCI Murrain?' Barker conceded grudgingly. 'Well, if we were to say that your assumption is not a million miles wide of the mark, would that persuade you to provide me with the information I'm seeking?'

'Of course,' Murrain said, 'as long as the process is mutual. As you say, we're both in the business of public protection. If there's anything about Wickham that's relevant to my investigation, I need to know about it.'

'So you accessed Wickham's file in connection with an investigation?'

'That's the nature of our business, Mr Barker.' Murrain decided he'd had enough of the sparring. 'Yes, one of my team accessed Wickham's PNC file in the course of a current investigation. But I should say that, at present, Wickham isn't material to our enquiries. His was just one of numerous files we've accessed. You'll appreciate that any major investigation involves countless routine enquiries, most of which go nowhere.'

'May I enquire about the nature of this major investigation?'

'You'll have seen the reports in the media,' Murrain said. 'A child murder. Ethan Dunn.'

There was another pause, much longer this time. Finally Barker said: 'I see. In that case, DCI Murrain, I think we really do need to meet. And as soon as possible. I'll make the arrangements.'

***

Barker was as good as his word. Four o'clock that afternoon found Murrain in a one of the meeting rooms in Fred Perry House facing an array of important-looking individuals. CS Winston was sitting beside him, looking as if he'd much rather be anywhere else.

Barker himself appeared the epitome of a Whitehall mandarin, with an expensive-looking suit and an air of unchallengeable authority. From the moment of his arrival, he'd taken charge as if no other arrangement were possible. That was fine by Murrain, but he could see that Winston was beginning to bridle.

'Thank you, gentlemen,' Barker began. 'I'm grateful that you were all able to make yourselves available at such short notice.'

'And we're delighted to welcome you,' Winston said, pointedly. 'We're obviously keen to gain some understanding of the situation here.'

'Of course.' Barker nodded in the manner of a teacher congratulating a well-intentioned pupil. 'Perhaps we should begin with some introductions. As you know, I'm John Barker. MoJ.' Murrain noted that Barker had given no indication of his job title or role.

Barker gestured to the man on his left. 'Colin?'

'Colin Ashworth. Assistant Chief Probation Officer. Greater Manchester.' Ashworth was a tall, skinny man who blinked at the world through thick spectacles. He nodded towards the third visitor, a thick-set man with short-cropped grey hair.

'Robin Kennedy, Protected Persons Unit, National Crime Agency.'

'DS Martin Winston,' Winston said, adopting the same formal tone. 'My colleague, DCI Kenneth Murrain. DCI Murrain is leading the investigation into the murder of Ethan Dunn.'

Murrain couldn't recall the last time anyone had referred to him as Kenneth. It would have been his late mother, probably, in those final days before the Alzheimer's swallowed her entirely. 'We understand you can tell us something about Kevin Wickham?'

Barker nodded. 'I don't know whether either of you gentlemen recall the Ben Wallasey case?'

Winston leaned forward. 'A child killing, wasn't it? Mid-nineties sometime? Pretty big deal at the time, if I remember correctly.'

Murrain remembered it only too well. He'd been a young DC at the time, had only recently made the move over into CID. He sometimes cringed now to think of the young man he'd been — brash, over-confident, expecting that he could eventually knock some sense into his complacent superiors. Unlike some, he'd been bright enough to realise, before it was too late, how little he really knew and how easily he could make himself unpopular. But in those days he'd had little time to waste on sentiment or emotion. He'd been surprised, therefore, by how hard the reports of the Wallasey case had hit him.

'You remember the details?' Barker prompted.

'It was another child,' Murrain said. 'Another child who apparently tortured and then strangled Wallasey.' He frowned, racking his brain to think of the name. For a few weeks, the case had gained the notoriety of the James Bulger or Mary Bell cases, the name plastered across the newspapers. 'Hancock?' he said, finally. 'Carl Hancock?'

'You've a good memory,' Barker said approvingly. 'Carl Hancock.'

Murrain exchanged a glance with Winston. Both of them understood where this was heading now, even if extracting the information was feeling like a bout of twenty questions. 'You're telling us Wickham is Carl Hancock?'

'On his release from prison some eighteen months ago,' Barker said, 'Mr Wickham was given a new identity and support to set up a new life in the north-west.'

Murrain noted again Barker's reluctance to answer a direct question. 'No-one thought to advise us he was arriving on our patch?'

'Only a small group of individuals—most of whom are gathered round this table—are aware of Hancock's new identity. You'll appreciate the sensitivity and the risk of leaks to the media. There was considerable— hysteria about the case.' Barker's expression momentarily indicated distaste, though it was unclear whether it was the murder itself or its media coverage that had aroused his disapproval.

'I appreciate that we apparently have a murdered child and a convicted child killer in close proximity,' Winston said. 'It might have been helpful for us to be aware of that.'

Barker tapped his fingernails on the table in a manner that suggested he was becoming slightly bored with the discussion. 'Our first priority, of course, is to ensure no hint of this reaches the media.'

Murrain opened his mouth but Winston was ahead of him. 'With respect,' he said, 'our first priority is to apprehend Ethan Dunn's killer.'

Barker nodded. 'I understand your concerns, Chief Superintendent. However—'

'There is no "however",' Winston said. 'We have a murdered child. We have a killer still on the loose. That's the priority.'

'There's no evidence that Hancock is responsible for Dunn's death,' Ashworth said. Barker shot him a cold look, suggesting he'd spoken out of turn.

'And there won't be, if we don't investigate him,' Murrain pointed out. 'No-one is saying that Hancock's the killer. But, given his history, it's a line of enquiry we have to pursue.' He looked back at Barker. 'I can imagine how the media would react if they discovered the authorities were aware of this and chose to ignore it.'

Barker met his gaze. 'I trust that's not a threat, Chief Inspector.'

'We have a job to do,' Murrain said. 'That job is to protect the public.'

'Then we're on the same side.' Barker smiled 'But, for our part, we have a duty to ensure these things are handled sensitively. We don't want to risk causing undue alarm.'

Murrain mentally translated that as: we don't want to

risk any embarrassment in Whitehall. 'So what are you suggesting?'

'I've consulted with my colleagues here,' Barker said in a tone which indicated that the consultation had been largely one-sided. 'Our considered view is that Hancock is unlikely to be your perpetrator.'

'I don't see—' Winston intervened.

'But of course we understand you need to investigate the possibility. All we ask is that you do so discreetly, and that you work with our support.'

'Now that we're aware of the possibility,' Winston pointed out, 'we have an obligation to investigate, with or without your support.'

'I assure you that you'll find it much harder to do so without,' Barker said.

'I trust that's not a threat, either, Mr Barker,' Winston said.

It was clear to Murrain that Winston was approaching the limits of his patience. 'In practical terms,' Murrain said to Barker, 'what are you offering? As Martin said, we have an obligation to act—legal, professional and moral. If you can help us meet that obligation more effectively, well and good. If you're simply going to be a barrier, then frankly—'

'Understood, Chief Inspector. We only wish to help. It's in none of our interests that this story hits the media until we know where we stand. It wouldn't help you to have some kind of media circus up here.'

That was true enough. If the media got hold of this story, they wouldn't be inclined to look beyond Hancock as a potential suspect. Senior officers would become increasingly defensive and jittery, and Murrain's task would probably become impossible. 'What are you suggesting?'

Barker leaned back in his chair and regarded Murrain as if he were weighing up his capability or perhaps his trustworthiness. Murrain had a suspicion this was a technique Barker had practised on his underlings in the Ministry, a way of implying that the listener was privileged even to be allowed access to Barker's invaluable insights. Another minute of it, Murrain thought, and Winston might actually explode.

'As I say, my own considered view.' Barker said, finally, 'having studied the background and discussed the case at length with my colleagues here, is that Hancock is very unlikely to be your killer.' It was clear that Winston was about to intervene again, but Barker continued smoothly on. 'But, as I say, I appreciate that we can't discount the possibility. He clearly needs to be investigated thoroughly but discreetly at this stage, at least until we know whether there are genuine grounds to consider him a suspect. My proposal therefore is that Chief Inspector Murrain conducts the investigation in conjunction with Mr Ashworth here, with Mr Kennedy available to provide advice as required. Mr Ashworth will be responsible for ensuring that Hancock's interests are protected.'

'You mean that the Ministry's interests are protected,' Winston said.

Barker nodded and smiled. 'There is a certain congruity between those objectives. But Hancock's well-being in our priority. It's critical that we keep this knowledge solely among ourselves.'

'I can't agree to anything without informing the Chief,' Winston said. 'He can't be kept in the dark about something like this.'

'I'll ensure that the Chief Constable is informed.'

'And I need at least one other member of my team

involved,' Murrain said.

Barker looked sharply up at him. 'Why's that, Chief Inspector?'

'Because we're conducting an investigation of a serious, high profile crime. We have to do everything by the book and be seen to do so. Whoever the killer is, whether it's Hancock or anyone else, I don't want them escaping justice because we messed up on the procedural side. If we're interviewing Hancock, I want two officers present.'

'Who did you have in mind?'

'My deputy. DI Milton.'

'Is he trustworthy?' Barker addressed the question to Winston. Which, Murrain reflected, was probably a mistake.

'Oh, for Christ's sake,' Winston said, 'of course he's bloody trustworthy. More so than some jumped-up Whitehall pen-pusher—'

Barker's smiled remained fixed. 'Of course. I'll happily defer to your judgement, Chief Superintendent.' He looked back at Murrain. 'But this goes no further than you and your deputy, Chief Inspector. If this story were to leak, the consequences could be severe.'

That certainly sounded close enough to a threat, Murrain thought. 'I think we appreciate the gravity of the matter.'

Barker pushed himself to his feet. 'We've taken enough of your time, gentlemen. Perhaps we can leave you with Mr Ashworth to discuss the logistics.' He smiled at Winston. 'I'll ask the Permanent Secretary to give the Chief Constable a call. Just so we're all clear where we stand.'

Winston exchanged a glance with Murrain. 'I think we're all very clear where we stand, Mr Barker. Thank you for your time.'

CHAPTER TWENTY-ONE

Tim Hulse had booked a back room in the local pub for the farewell do. It was the Friday before half-term and Kate was still planning to drive back to her mother's, but felt she ought to show her face. Whether she'd be welcome was another question entirely.

In fairness, Greg Perry had been as good as his word. Not a word had leaked, even on the notoriously sensitive Service grapevine, about Perry's report on the prison. When Hulse's move was announced, only a few days later, it had been presented as a promotion. He'd been selected by the Regional Director, at the instigation of the Director-General, to carry out strategic project work on the future of public sector prisons in an age of reducing costs, or some such nonsense. It was an honour and a privilege to be selected personally to carry out this critical assignment, he'd been reported as saying in the in-house newsletter. Kate knew from Hulse himself that he'd never uttered those words, and that his real response when the offer was first made had been heavily laden with expletives.

In any case, the announcement had fooled no-one. Everybody recognised a sideways move when they saw one, and it was an accepted truth that an operational governor wouldn't move into a backroom role voluntarily. A move like that meant at least one of three things — you'd burnt out, you'd offended the wrong person, or you'd failed. Quite often, all three.

Hulse had borne up pretty well. He'd toed the party

line in talking to the wider world, but made it clear to the powers-that-be that he was going through the motions. He was no doubt already looking round for an alternative job with some private-sector prison provider. Well, good luck to him, Kate thought.

This wasn't strictly speaking goodbye, in that Hulse was expected to be around for another few weeks yet. Perhaps he wasn't sure how long the rest of the team would be around. The current expectation was that John Hodges would hold the fort for a month or so till a permanent replacement was identified. Hodges seemed happy enough with that but only on condition he was then given the early retirement deal he'd been angling for. Others on the senior team had concluded that, once a new broom arrived, their days would be numbered and most were actively looking for transfers.

Kate hadn't decided about her own future. This was supposed to have been a new start—a new job, a new house, a new life. She was still due to bring Jack up to join her during the holiday so he was ready to start his new school at the beginning of the next half term. That was all going ahead, but she felt as if the rest of her life was once more on hold.

She knew she was viewed with some suspicion within the prison. She was seen as Perry's lackey even though she'd had barely any contact with him, other than a couple of phone calls, since the meeting in her office. Hodges seemed fine with her—he'd been around the block enough times not to be fazed by corporate politics—but there was a frisson in her relations with the other members of the senior team.

Tonight Hodges was as welcoming as ever. 'Come in, lass. Fill your glass and join the wake.' He was sitting at the bar, apparently content not to join any of the chatting groups around the room.

'Is that what it is, then?'

He took a sip from his pint of beer. The pint was barely touched and she guessed it was still his first. Hodges gave the impression of being one of the lads but maintained a degree of detachment from their more boisterous behaviour. 'I'm not sure what else you'd call it. That's what usually follows a death, isn't it?'

'Who's died?'

He raised his glass. 'To the memory of Tim Hulse's career.'

'He'll bounce back, won't he?'

'Once your card's marked, it stays marked. People have long memories.' He looked up at her. 'Your friend Greg Perry might do well to remember that.'

'He's not a friend. Just someone who used to be my boss.' The words felt oddly like a betrayal, but they were true. 'What did you mean about long memories?'

He took another almost imperceptible sip of his beer. 'You pass a lot of people on your way up. And some of them remember you.' He smiled. 'I go back a long way. Mine and Greg's paths crossed a few times over the years. I know where a few of the bodies are buried.' He smiled, but it wasn't clear whether he was entirely joking.

'Is that right?' She felt that Hodges was inviting her to enquire further but she had little inclination to do so. 'Where's Tim? I ought to have a chat with him. I can't stay too long.'

'I'm not planning on staying much longer myself. Leave that kind of thing to the youngsters.' He swivelled on his bar stool and gestured towards the far corner of the room. 'Tim's over there. Might be glad of being rescued.'

Hulse was in the corner of the room, being talked at by Sharon Barnes. Kate had no great desire to engage in any conversation with the latter, though she hoped insufficient drink had been taken to fuel any conflict. She smiled her thanks at Hodges and eased her way to where Hulse was standing.

He caught her eye over Sharon's shoulder with ill-disguised relief. 'Kate! Glad you could make it.'

Sharon regarded Kate coolly. 'Good you could spare the time, Kate. You're usually in such a hurry.'

'I'm heading back to my mother's tonight,' she said, 'so I can't stay long.' She held up her Coke. 'Can't even drink.'

'Better keep your wits about you,' Sharon said. 'I'll leave you to Tim's tender mercies.' She pushed her way, perhaps more brusquely than she intended, back towards the bar.

'She's not happy,' Kate observed.

'Just anxious,' Hulse said. 'Who can blame her?' He had an almost empty pint glass in his hand. Kate guessed it wasn't his first, and probably not his second.

'Not me,' Kate said. 'Can I get you another?'

'You certainly can. Follow me.' Hulse led her in Sharon's wake towards the bar. Sharon was already apparently deep in conversation with John Hodges. Hulse caught the barman's eye with practised ease and ordered a pint for himself and another Coke for Kate. 'I put £100 behind the bar. Reckon that'll last fifteen minutes or so with this bunch.' He waved his hand towards the door. 'You mind going outside for a few minutes? Could do with a cigarette.'

She'd never seen him smoking before. He wasn't one of those who'd cluster, regardless of the weather, in the allocated smoking area outside the administrative block.

'Given it up for years,' he said, reading her thoughts. 'Till a few days ago.'

She followed him into the pub car park. It was a decent enough evening, still light, though the low sun was stretching shadows across the tarmac. Hulse avoided the smoking shelter and walked over to the small garden area at the side of the pub. He slumped down at one of the tables and fumbled with his cigarettes and lighter. 'Is he really a friend of yours, then?'

She perched on the bench next to him, conscious of the damp wood beneath her pale skirt. Hulse was already halfway through his pint. 'Who?'

'Greg Perry. You seemed to be buddies. More than I'd realised.'

'I'm not sure Greg even has any friends.'

'No, well, that figures.'

'I want to get one thing straight, Tim,' she said. 'Whatever Greg might have done, whatever decisions he might have made, they're nothing to do with me. I'm not his grass.' She thought back to that last meeting with Greg, and wondered whether this was strictly true.

'I know that,' he said. 'I'm not a fool, Kate. Greg Perry's reputation goes before him. And, by and large, it's a good one. He's professional, gets the job done. Treats people fairly. Blah, blah.'

'But?'

He took a deep swallow of the beer. 'But I don't think he's treated me fairly. He's shafted me.'

'I don't think I'm in a position to—'

'No, I don't expect you are. Nobody is where Perry's concerned.'

'You've lost me, Tim.'

'Sorry.' He held up his glass and peered into the

amber contents. 'Look, Kate, I know you didn't have anything to do with what's happened. I imagine Perry asked your views of me and of the prison. I imagine you were honest with him. People usually are. That's one of his gifts. He makes you trust him.'

'I didn't—'

'I don't really care whether you did or didn't, to be honest. It wouldn't have made any real difference. He'd already made up his mind. He was just looking for ammunition.'

She could see where this was going. Hulse had persuaded himself that Perry had acted unreasonably, and that was no doubt the version of events he was sharing with everyone. It was one way of preserving a shred of dignity.

'It doesn't stack up, Kate. Everyone knows this place has had its share of problems. That's why they offered me the job in the first place. I had a reputation of my own, you know.'

She did know, or at least she knew what Perry had told her. 'So it was your job to turn the place around?'

'Exactly. I'd had been a success at my previous place. Same kind of issues. The place was a mess. I'd joined as the Dep without really knowing what I was letting myself in for. Within a few weeks the Governor disappeared with a supposedly stress-related illness which rapidly turned into an early retirement. I kept the show on the road and they offered me the job on a permanent basis. Within six months, I'd got the place back on track. So they knew I could do it.'

'But this place must have been a big challenge?'

'It was. It is. That's what's so frustrating. I mean, the inspection report before I came was dire. Everything was wrong. And now—'

'You think it's improved?'

'We're in a different league. I'm not saying we're perfect. There's still some way to go, but I've done everything that could reasonably have been asked and more. All the performance measures are there. We've sorted the drugs issues. We've got rid of all the bad apples among the Officers. We've built up a great management team, present company included.' He took another swallow and finished the pint. 'The really frustrating thing is that whichever bugger is here when the next inspection takes place will receive all the plaudits.'

'I'm really sorry, Tim,' she said, after a pause. 'I don't know what to say. If you think Greg's shafted you — well, what reason would he have to do that?'

'You really *don't* know him, do you?'

'What do you mean?'

'Everyone admires Greg Perry. Good manager. Decent chap. Builds a good team under him. Attracts a lot of loyalty from his staff.' He smiled at her, meaningfully. 'That sound familiar?'

'It sounds like my impression of him, more or less. And?'

'And he's a ruthless bastard. If you get in his way, he'll destroy you.'

'That's not been my experience,' she said. 'Almost the opposite.'

Hulse nodded slowly, as if considering this point-of-view. 'Yes, you had your problems, didn't you? And he was supportive. Put in a very good word for you with me.'

'Doesn't sound very ruthless,' she said. 'Given I hadn't made life easy for him.'

'Doesn't, does it? Generous of him to recommend you

for a move to a place that he proceeds to shaft only a few weeks later.'

'But—'

'It's not my place to influence what you think of him. All I know is what I think of him. We go a long way back. We joined at the same time on the graduate scheme. Fairly parallel careers, though he's generally been a step or two ahead of me. I spent a couple of years working for him when he was Dep in a Young Offenders'. That was a long time ago, but it was when I first realised what he was like. I'm not going to dish any dirt, but I caught him doing one or two things he shouldn't have. I wasn't intending to shop him, as it happens. That's not my style. But he knew I knew. Next thing, it was *my* career going down the toilet. Inappropriate material discovered on my work laptop.'

She stared at him. 'And you didn't put it there?'

'Well, Christ, no. Nothing to do with me.'

'You're saying—'

'Draw your own conclusions. The fact was that he'd had access to the machine a couple of weeks before. He'd borrowed it a couple of times while his was supposedly out of action. I couldn't think of anyone else who'd been in a position to do it. But there was nothing I could do. I'd no evidence he'd even borrowed the laptop, let alone that he was responsible. It was perfectly pitched. The stuff wasn't extreme enough for them to dismiss me, but serious enough that they had to do something. A formal warning in the end. Just enough to slow down my career when it was about to take off. And enough to destroy any credibility I might have had in blowing the whistle on Greg Perry, if I'd been so inclined. The man who's now our Regional Director.' He stopped, as if he'd run out of things to say, and gestured towards her glass. 'Let me get you another. Same again?'

'No, bugger it,' she said. 'I'll risk a white wine. I feel like I need a drink.'

She watched as he disappeared back into the pub. It was beginning to grow dark and the lights had come on around the pub, with a row of spotlights casting a spectral glare over the garden where she was sitting. Kate was struck by a sudden feeling that, by staying out here, by continuing this conversation with Hulse, she was taking a risk, though she couldn't fathom what kind of risk that might be.

He was back quicker than she expected. As he ambled out of the pub doorway, she found herself unexpectedly relieved to see him. Even in the few minutes he'd been away, her anxiety had been growing. Every movement in the shadows had felt oddly threatening. A sudden sweep of light from a pair of headlights across the far side of the car-park had almost sent her scurrying inside.

'Thought you might have buggered off,' Hulse said. He placed the two drinks on the table and slid the glass of wine in her direction. 'I went for the Sauvignon Blanc,' he said, 'on the basis that they'd just opened the bottle. The Chardonnay looked like it'd been sitting there a while.'

'Wise move. Though anything winey and alcoholic's fine by me.'

'I'm your man then.'

She laughed, wondering how much he was really joking. 'You weren't long in there. I thought you'd get waylaid. People wanting to know why you'd gone missing at your own party.'

'I kept out of the back,' he said. 'Guess who's just arrived?'

'Who?'

'Your friend and his, Greg Perry.'

'I didn't see him go past.'

'Must have gone in the other way. From the main car park. I just saw him heading into the back. Not that I invited the bastard.'

She remembered the sweep of headlights and how unreasonably startled she'd been by the sudden glare. 'You really think this is personal?'

'He screwed me over once before. I don't see why he wouldn't do it again.'

'But if what you told me was true—'

'It was true, right enough. I'll never be able to prove it, but I know what happened.'

'OK, but then he had a reason to shaft you. Why would he do it here? Why now?'

'I've no idea how that bastard's mind works. Maybe he's just been waiting for the opportunity. You'd have to ask him.'

'You don't think you're being paranoid?'

'No, I don't. I've not been allowed to see it, but I'm told he's written a confidential report on this place that paints us blacker than black. He's said I'm not up to the job. A lack of leadership, was the phrase.'

She hesitated momentarily then said: 'You don't think there might be any substance in what he's saying? Shit, that sounded wrong. I know you're a good manager, Tim. I suppose what I mean is, isn't it possible that Greg's just got it wrong? Or—I don't know—that's he's just trying to make an impression in his new role by showing how tough he is?'

'You mean, am I just deluding myself?'

'That's not what I meant—'

'It's a fair question. Nobody wants to be on the end of something like this. We all try to paint ourselves in the best light. But I think I'm being realistic. I'm not perfect. The prison's not a hundred percent yet. But I think I—we have made all the progress that could reasonably have been asked of us, given the state the place was in when I took over. I know that whoever comes in won't make any significant changes but will get all the plaudits when the Inspection goes well.'

'Isn't there any way you can appeal?'

'Against what? The official line is I'm being given a—what's their phrase?—a "lateral opportunity for development and operational purposes". Some bullshit like that. I haven't seen the report he prepared. I'm not even officially supposed to know it exists. I only found out because an old mate at HQ tipped me off. It's full of total bollocks, apparently. Even implies I've been fiddling the performance stats.'

'But why would he do it?'

'You still haven't got it, have you? He's a vicious, ruthless bastard. Part of it will be what you said. He wants to make an impression. He'll pretend he's taking a hands-on role in sorting out the mess I've supposedly left behind. He'll probably be the one who takes the credit when the Inspectorate gives us the thumbs up, along with whoever he appoints here. But that won't be the main reason. The main reason is that he wants to destroy me.'

It all sounded too melodramatic to Kate. She was beginning to buy some of what Hulse was saying, but she still couldn't see Perry as a pantomime villain. 'Why would he want to do that?'

'Like I say, who knows how his mind works. Maybe because he thinks I'm still a threat. Maybe because I'm the only person who really knows what he was up to at that YOI. He pulled the rug from under me then. But he might still think I've got something over him.'

'After all these years?'

'I don't know. It's the first time he's had any real authority over me. Maybe it's the first time he's had the chance to do it.' He paused. 'But it feels to me like there's something more. Some reason he's done this now.'

'Such as?' She took a first small sip of the wine. Hulse's pint was already half gone.

'That's why I wanted to talk to you. You know him better than I do—or at least you know what he's like now.'

'I hardly know him at all,' she said. 'That's what I'm realising. He gives nothing away. All you ever get's what's on the surface.'

'Your partner did,' Hulse said, quietly. 'He knew him very well.'

She looked up, baffled. 'Ryan knew him?'

'Ryan?' Hulse looked equally baffled for a moment. 'Oh, Christ. Of course. Jesus, that was stupid of me. Look, I'm sorry—'

She took a much larger mouthful of the wine. 'What are you talking about, Tim?'

'I'd forgotten. I saw a reference in your file, but I wasn't thinking.' He shook his head. 'About your husband. God, I'm sorry.'

'It's in the past. I wouldn't say I'm over it, exactly, but—well, you know.' It was always like this when she talked about Ryan. She was the one who ended up giving reassurance to others. She'd grown sick of that in the months after it had happened, having to be mindful of others' feelings while she was struggling to make it through the day.

'I didn't mean your husband,' Hulse said, finally. 'I meant—'

She suddenly understood. 'Graeme,' she said. 'You meant Graeme. Of course. It's always fucking Graeme.'

'I'm sorry,' he repeated. 'Yeah, Graeme Ellis. That guy.'

'How'd you know about Graeme?' She'd been confused by the apparent reference to Ryan, but at least Ryan had been in the Service. It was likely that Hulse would have come across him.

He frowned. 'It was on your file.'

'Really?' She was beginning to feel as if the world was shifting slightly but continually under her feet. 'I mean, we were hardly together. Only a couple of months. I hardly told anyone about it. Especially at work.'

'Look, I probably shouldn't really say this. But there was stuff on the file about—well, about why you were off sick.'

'There was bound to be some stuff,' she said. 'There were reports from my GP to human resources. That kind of thing.'

'Not just that. There was a file note about accusations you made. Against Graeme Ellis. There was an implication that—well, that your judgement had been impaired at that point. That it might have implications for your professional work.'

'But that was nothing to do with—' she began, then stopped. 'Who wrote that note?'

'Guess who. Your loyal boss. I only saw the note after you'd started down here and the full personal file was sent over.'

She frowned, trying to make sense of all this. 'You said Graeme knew Greg. But why did Graeme's name mean anything to you in the first place?'

Hulse seemed as puzzled as she was by the way the conversation was unfolding. 'Well, I knew him. Graeme.

We both did, me and Perry. From his days in the Service.'

This time it really did feel as if the ground had been pulled from under her. 'Graeme? In the Service?'

'You didn't know? Jeez. He was an officer at the YOI I was talking about. Worked for Greg.'

'I didn't know. He never said. He never bloody mentioned it. He knew where I worked, and he never bloody mentioned it.' She took another mouthful of wine. 'Why the hell would he never have bloody mentioned it?'

'He and Greg Perry were thick as thieves in those days,' Hulse said. 'Ellis left the Service unexpectedly after a couple of years. While we were still at the YOI. There were rumours he left under a cloud, but I never heard anything definite. When I saw his name in the file, I assumed you must have met him through Perry.'

'No, not at all.' She was trying to remember exactly how she had met Graeme. He'd slid into her life with such smoothness she'd barely recognised he was doing it. One day, he wasn't on the scene. The next, they were apparently an item. That was how it had felt. 'I met him in the pub,' she said. 'One Friday after work. I'd gone there for a quick after-work drink with a few members of the Psych team. From what I remember, Graeme was in there with one or two business types— colleagues of his, he reckoned. He started chatting to me at the bar. Made a bit of a bee-line for me in a way—well, that I found flattering, I suppose. I was just beginning to get over what had happened with Ryan. Not ready for a serious relationship or anything like that, but ready to start living again. Graeme's very good at getting you to talk without giving away too much himself. In the end, he persuaded me to give him my phone number.' She shrugged. 'I thought he was probably married. Wasn't really intending to take it any further. But he can be very persuasive.'

'That was always his reputation.'

She was trying to envisage the scene in the pub. There'd been nothing obviously suspicious about it. Just a smooth-talking older man chatting up a woman at the bar. But if Graeme really did know Greg, the whole thing couldn't have been coincidental.

'The question is,' Hulse said, as if voicing her thoughts, 'did Ellis know who you were when he approached you? Had he been tipped off?'

'By Greg, you mean? But why would he?'

'I don't know. But he wouldn't do it without a reason. And that reason would have been more than just a bit of matchmaking. Even assuming that Ellis was that way inclined.'

'What do you mean?'

'I just meant—well, let's just say that, in the days when I knew Ellis, I wouldn't have assumed his primary interest was in the adult female.' He held up his hands before she could respond. 'Not based on any real evidence. Just my impression. And the word on the grapevine.'

She could feel her mental landscape tilting again. 'This file note. Did it mention the nature of my accusations?'

'Not really. You mean—'

'I thought—I still think—that he had an unnatural interest in my son, let's put it that way. Like you, I didn't have any hard evidence. I never really caught him doing anything—inappropriate. Nothing he couldn't talk his way out of, anyway. But there was something about the way he behaved, the way he talked. It began to give me the creeps, to be honest. At first, I persuaded myself I was imagining it. He behaved like the perfect gentleman to me. I could easily have convinced myself I'd found the ideal partner.' She laughed, with just an edge of bitterness. 'That's certainly what my mother thought. But I became more and more uneasy.' She was suddenly conscious that it was fully dark now, and that it was growing cold. 'I know I'd lost it by the end. I was getting hysterical. I can see that now. And Graeme was probably only a part of that. I was feeling stressed at work, and I probably hadn't come to terms Ryan's death as well as I thought I had. But Graeme was one of the triggers. Even after I'd ended it with him, my suspicions kept growing and I felt as if I was losing my mind. Then he turned up one day when I was at work and talked my mother into handing over Jack, pretending he was meeting me.'

'Jesus. What happened?'

'I got home and completely lost it. I called the police. They caught up with Graeme easily enough. I think he'd just intended to use it as a way of trying to lever himself back into our lives, and hadn't expected me to respond so dramatically, so he actually phoned me an hour or so later to let me know where they were. He got a shock when a couple of uniformed officers turned up instead.'

'Serve the bastard right,' Hulse said with feeling. 'Assume he talked his way out of it.'

'He claimed it was all just a misunderstanding. That he'd told my mother where he was taking Jack but she must have not heard, or some such bollocks. That he'd thought it was all agreed with me. Breakdown in communications. All that. Had the police eating out of his hand in the end. Meanwhile, I was a complete wreck. But that just helped convince the police that I was hysterical and that Graeme must be the wronged party.'

'That sounds like the Graeme Ellis I knew,' Hulse said. 'Looking back, though, do you think your suspicions of Ellis were wrong? About him and your son, I mean.'

She surprised herself by responding with no hesitation: 'No, I was right. I'd lost perspective on how to deal with it by the end. But I was right about Graeme.'

'I wouldn't take any convincing,' Hulse said. 'That was always my impression. But he was a manipulative bastard. He and Perry were birds of a feather.'

She gazed back at him, still trying to take all this in. She could see there was something more troubling him. 'Go on. What else?'

'I'm as baffled by all this as you are,' he said. 'I was just struck by another thought. It was when you mentioned your late husband—'

'Ryan?'

'Look, say if you don't want to talk about this. But I saw on your file you were a widow. That your husband had died in service. Some sort of accident.'

'Yeah. Stupid bloody accident. He wasn't even on duty. He'd been out to the pub after work.' She gestured round with her hand. 'Funnily enough, yet another leaving do. Some officer in his team who was transferring. Felt obliged to go—you know, show willing.'

'No wonder this sort of thing isn't your idea of a good time.'

'He hadn't stayed late. Hadn't had a drink.' She took a breath, trying to control her emotions. It was a long while since she'd had reason to tell this story. 'He rode a motorbike in those days. It wasn't long after we'd married. I was working over in South Yorkshire, so he was commuting back over there until I could get a transfer sorted.' She laughed bitterly. 'My new posting was confirmed about two weeks after I no longer needed it. The story was that Ryan lost control up in the Derbyshire hills. Skidded off the road. Nobody could ever quite explain how it might have happened, but sometimes things just do.'

'God, I'm sorry.'

'I got worried when he didn't get back. Got even more worried when I phoned one of his colleagues and found out what time he'd left the pub. Called the police who didn't take it seriously till later that night—kept insisting he must have gone on somewhere else. Even suggested that he might have gone on somewhere he didn't want me to know about. Then in the morning some farmer found the crashed bike and Ryan's body. He'd been dead for hours by the time the police got there.'

'And the police assumed it was an accident?'

'That was the official line. There was no real reason to think any different. There were some oddities. It was a dry clear night, Ryan was an experienced biker, and they reckoned the angle of the skid was a bit strange if he'd just lost control. But, well, like I say, these things can happen.' She hesitated. 'There was one officer who didn't seem quite willing to let it lie. He got their collision analysts to double-check the site. There was some evidence there might have been another vehicle involved, but it wasn't definitive enough for them to pursue it. So the verdict was accidental death.'

'I'm sorry,' he said again.

'I wouldn't say I'd got over it exactly. But I'm coming through. It's not as painful as it was.' She frowned. 'What made you ask about Ryan?'

'It was only when you said the name that I made the

connection. When I read the note in your file, I didn't really think about the detail at all. I'd assumed you'd taken your late husband's name. That he was Ryan Forester.'

'No, I kind of regret it now. But at the time I was full of feminist ideals. Well, I still am, but that's maybe one decision I'd have made differently in retrospect. I kept my own name. He was Ryan McCarthy.'

'Ryan McCarthy. Christ.'

'What?'

'Do you remember what sort of an establishment Ryan was working in?'

'He'd just moved over to Manchester, a few months earlier, which was why we decided that I should look for a transfer. He'd only just got his promotion to Governor grade. Before that he'd been at a place in Lancashire—' She stopped. 'Shit, it was a YOI.'

Hulse nodded. 'I must have already moved on by that stage too. But Ryan was there, Kate. He was there as well.' He paused. 'The thing is, he was the one who made the first complaint against Gregory Perry. He was the one who raised it with me.' There was still the best part of half a pint of beer in his glass. Hulse swallowed it almost in one mouthful. 'I didn't think Perry ever knew who'd first blown the whistle—'

Kate looked up, suddenly fearful for no reason she could explain. It was a Friday night. The car park beyond the garden was packed with cars. There were people coming and going—office workers visiting the pub after work, a few young men getting tanked up for the evening ahead, some already heading home after their regulation couple of halves. Just like the night Ryan died.

She couldn't believe what Hulse was saying. She

couldn't begin to take in the implications. But, in that moment, she was feeling a long way from anywhere that she might call home.

***

Kate arrived back at her mother's later than she intended. She'd sat with Hulse a little longer in that scrubby pub garden, neither of them wanting to return to the glare and noise of the party. For Kate, too many memories had been stirred. For Hulse, she guessed, the over-eager partying would only highlight the bleakness of his prospects. Both recognised that their conversation had opened up a nest of possibilities that, for the moment, neither wanted to examine too closely.

'Look, I'd better go,' she'd said finally, when the silence had stretched longer than she could stand. 'Will you be OK?'

'Tonight or in general?'

'Either. Both.'

'I imagine I'll survive. Tonight and in general.' He sounded unexpectedly determined.

'Are you going to do anything? About what we've discussed?'

'I'm not going to let it lie,' he said. 'Perry's got away with this kind of crap once too often. I've got some ideas. I can't do anything through the official channels, but I might have one or two surprises lined up for him. Maybe sooner than he thinks.'

It sounded like bravado, but it wasn't the moment to challenge him. 'OK', she said, finally. 'But don't do anything stupid. Let's both reflect on it.'

'Yeah, I'll be doing plenty of that. No question.'

She'd half-hoped he might stay outside and watch her

to her car, but hadn't felt able to ask. In the end, she'd been the one who watched him weave his slightly unsteady way back into the pub, and then she'd headed back across the car-park. She was still feeling uneasy as she climbed into the vehicle and started the engine.

Her anxiety did not reduce as made her way back towards the motorway. There was something else. Something nagging at her mind. Something in her conversation with Hulse had stirred a thought or a recollection, but she couldn't pin down what it might be.

At that time in the evening the traffic had been light and she'd arrived at her mother's earlier than she'd feared, although still later than she'd originally planned.

'I had to put Jack to bed,' her mother said, with only a mild edge of rebuke in her tone. 'But I imagine he's still awake, if you want to say goodnight.'

Kate had found Jack very much awake, reading some fantasy book that was apparently all the rage in his year at school. He was growing up already, Kate thought. Becoming his own person, developing his own ideas, moving away from her. She had no problems with that, but she wished she'd been here over the last couple of months to watch it happening. Day by day, she wouldn't have noticed the gradual changes. As it was, each week she seemed to see something new, some side to Jack she hadn't previously registered. But that was coming to an end now, she thought. School was over, the holiday had begun, and Jack was finally coming down to live with her.

'Is it good?' She perched on the edge of his bed and gestured towards the book.

'You're late,' Jack said, bluntly. 'I could have been asleep. Then I wouldn't have seen you.'

'But you're not,' she said, knowing he was right.

'You're reading.'

'It is good,' Jack said. 'The book. I'm going to read the whole series.'

'Not tonight you're not,' she said. 'You're going to sleep soon.'

Jack giggled at the notion of reading the whole series in a single night. 'Can I finish this one, though? I haven't much to go.' He held up the book to demonstrate.

'As long as you turn the light off as soon as you're finished.' She reached across and ruffled his hair. 'Broken up now then?' she said. 'Looking forward to the holiday.'

'Suppose so.' He looked up, a different expression on his face. 'But we're moving. I've got to go to a new school.'

'You'll enjoy it once you settle in. I'll find some other children who go there so you can meet them before you start.' She wasn't even sure if that was possible, but she could ask around among the neighbours. It wasn't the ideal point in the year to change schools, but she hadn't wanted to delay Jack's arrival any longer than necessary. 'You'll soon get used to it.'

Jack looked unconvinced. 'We're not even going on holiday,' he said. 'Just going to your new house.' She'd returned to her mother's every weekend since she'd started her new job, so Jack hadn't yet visited the house.

'Our house,' she corrected. 'And you'll like it. OK, sleepy head, I'd better get down to Granny. Don't forget to turn your light off, and don't stay up too later either.' She kissed him gently on the forehead and then made her way downstairs.

Later, she lay in the darkness herself, listening to the faint ticking of the bedside clock, the soft clicks as the house cooled overnight. Her mind was still running over her earlier conversation with Hulse, trying to identify the detail she hadn't been able to pin down. It had slipped away from her while she'd been talking with her mother, but now the unease crept back into her mind.

Her drifting mind latched on to her dealings with Carl, back in her days working for Greg Perry. Carl who was battling with the emptiness inside his mind, struggling with memories that might one day begin their slow rise to the surface or might remain buried, forever colouring his future.

She sat up in the darkness, suddenly wide awake, her brain racing. She'd recognised the tiny detail that had been tugging at the edge of her mind since her conversation with Hulse. It was nothing obviously significant. So why had it lodged in her thoughts and troubled her so much?

Her laptop was sitting open on the small old-fashioned dressing table under the window. She'd been planning check her e-mails before going to bed, but in the end had felt too tired and woozy from the wine to bother. Now she booted up the machine and opened up her e-mail client, intending to send an e-mail to Hulse to ask him to check the point that had occurred to her. But instead she paused and opened up one of the new messages in her in-box.

Freud was right, she thought. There really was no such thing as coincidence.

She hesitated only for the briefest of moments, then she began to type a response.

CHAPTER TWENTY-TWO

'What do you reckon?' Joe Milton said. The sky was clear but the morning was still chilly, and he was standing hunched against the breeze, his hands wedged firmly in his pockets. They'd come out in a hurry when the call had come from the Control Centre and he'd left his overcoat back in the MIR. Another perfect start to another working weekend.

Murrain had been in the middle of some extended discussion with Wanstead, so Milton had drawn the short straw on this particular one. He'd been more than relieved when Marie Donovan had offered to accompany him. They'd been getting on well over the past week, he thought, but he'd not managed to pluck up the courage to ask her out again, and he still had no idea whether she'd be inclined to say yes. Still, he added optimistically to himself, she'd apparently jumped at the chance to come and view a mutilated body with him. That had to be a positive sign.

'What do you mean? Did he jump or was he pushed?' Donovan was more appropriately dressed for the early morning, wearing a smart-looking beige raincoat. They were standing at the edge of the railway track watching the white-suited SOCOs get on with their work.

'Well, did he jump or did he fall, I suppose. Accident or suicide.'

They'd closed the line to preserve the scene. It was the main Manchester to London line and the trains had been diverted via Crewe, with resulting delays, so there'd be a few fed-up travellers even on a Saturday morning. The protocol was that every violent death was treated as a potential crime until the circumstances were confirmed, which is why Murrain's team were involved. As they could see from the state of the dark-suited body splayed out between the tracks, this was as violent as they came.

'Poor bugger,' Milton observed. 'Don't imagine he knew what hit him.'

'Don't imagine he knew anything,' Donovan agreed. She looked at the scene around them. 'Why was he here?'

'That's the question, isn't it?' Milton examined the damaged fencing behind them. They'd been let into the site by the Network Rail employee designated to meet them. But it was clear there other, less official ways of accessing the tracks.

One of the SOCOs straightened up from examining the prone body and ambled slowly across the tracks towards them.

'Morning, Neil,' Milton said. 'You pulled the weekend shift again, then?'

'You know me. Never one to miss out. It's where you get the interesting ones.' Neil Ferbrache pulled off his protective helmet and nodded to them both. He was a senior SOCO, highly experienced, with an occasional sardonic wit that belied his usually taciturn manner. He was one of the best they had, though, and Milton had learned to trust Ferbrache's judgement.

'Is this an interesting one?' Donovan said.

Ferbrache scratched his nose thoughtfully. 'Not sure, to be honest.' He was, as Milton also well knew, not a man given to offering speculation beyond the available evidence. In many ways, he was Murrain's polar opposite. That was presumably why the two men always seemed to get on so well. 'Slightly odd one.'

'In what way?' Donovan gazed over to where another

SOCO was carefully examining the length of track beyond the body. She could never understand how the SOCOs managed to handle this kind of work, week in and week out. Whether it was an accident or a violent crime, they had to deal with the consequences. Dead and mutilated corpses, decomposing flesh, graphic injuries, and much of it in the most unpleasant working environments you could imagine. And yet for the most part they seemed more sane and balanced than the average copper. Maybe they had to work hard to keep it that way. 'You don't think it was just an accident?'

Ferbrache shrugged. 'Seems most likely. Doc will no doubt confirm but the injuries appear consistent with being struck by a bloody great high-speed train. Only question is why the poor bugger was here at all in the wee small hours of the morning. He's not some drugged-up teenager in a hoodie. Respectable looking chap in a suit. Well, used to look respectable, anyhow. Less so now.'

Milton knew better than to argue with Ferbrache's observations. He gestured towards the broken fence. 'Taking a short cut?'

'Probably.' Ferbrache pointed in the opposite direction across the railway tracks. 'Some evidence of an informal footway over there. There's a residential area beyond that and you can walk into the town from there. Could be where he was heading.'

'Any clues as to his identity?'

'Haven't had chance to move the body yet to check the pockets. Still taking photographs. Will be able to check in a minute, though.' Ferbrache looked as if he was itching to do just that. 'Any word from BTP?'

Milton shook his head. They were liaising with British Transport Police on this one, and they'd had a call in from when the body had first been reported to check whether any driver had reported a collision. 'No. No-one's reported anything. I guess if he was hit at speed the driver might not even have been aware.'

'There'll be a few clues on the body of the train, I'd imagine,' Ferbrache said. 'Scattered between here and Macclesfield. Who found him?'

'Some dog-walker at sparrow-fart,' Milton said. 'Dog went mad. Owner followed it and spotted the body. That was about six-thirty.'

'I reckon he'd been dead a few hours by then. One of the overnight freight trains, I'm assuming. Unlucky bugger, if so. They're not that frequent.'

Milton considered that, and glanced at Donovan. 'Bad luck to pick just that moment to cross the track.' He looked around. The area was thinly wooded, but there was plenty of visibility along the straight track. 'And downright stupidity not to see it coming.'

'These things happen,' Ferbrache said, philosophically. 'Doc'll no doubt confirm, but there's a strong smell of drink about him as well as a strong smell of blood and guts. Maybe too pissed even to spot an oncoming train.'

'Any other possibilities, you reckon?' Donovan asked.

'There's always other possibilities, lass. Suicide. Foul play. That's more your territory than mine. There's nothing much to suggest it wasn't an accident, other than the circumstances.' He paused. 'One thing. See that patch there, just this side of the body? The slight hollow between the tracks.'

Milton peered and nodded. 'Go on.'

'It's a slightly muddy patch. The only bit here that is. Most of the ground's dry, but that spot obviously collects the rain-water. There's a jumble of footprints there. A couple of them seem to match our unintentional commuter over there, but there's at least one that doesn't.'

'And?' Milton knew Ferbrache too well to imagine he was likely to offer any further speculation.

'And nothing much. But they're there. They could—I stress *could*—have been made at roughly the same time as our friend's. But they could be older, or even newer, I suppose. Your dog-walker, maybe?'

'He claims not to have come past the fence. Just saw the body from a distance and went off to call us. But we can check his shoe prints for elimination. You think it might suggest there was more than one person here?'

'It *might*,' Ferbrache agreed. 'Or it might suggest bugger all. Even if there was someone, it might have been some equally pissed mate who took flight when he saw what was happening. Not everyone's a hero in those circumstances.'

'You can't be sure that the footprints are fresh?' Donovan asked.

'They look relatively new but it's hard to be sure. And, judging from the way the ground's trampled, there're obviously a few people prepared to use this as a short-cut.'

'Maybe we'll have more of a clue once we know who he is,' Donovan said.

'No doubt.' Ferbrache gestured towards his colleague by the body, who waved back in acknowledgement. 'Speaking of which, I think we're done with the portraiture. We can move the body and see if we can find out a bit more about him.'

Marie Donovan glanced at Milton who, out of Ferbrache's eye-line, made a face that suggested he wasn't keen to get any closer to the mutilated body than he really had to. She gave him a warm smile in return. That was another thing about her, Milton thought. She didn't seem to care that he was more squeamish about such matters than she was.

'OK, then,' she said, with a final grin in Milton's direction. 'I'm game. Lead on.'

CHAPTER TWENTY-THREE

Kate sat in her mother's neat sitting room to make the call. Her mother and Jack were in the kitchen, baking some cakes. Jack had insisted that Kate should keep out of the kitchen, as the cakes were intended as a surprise.

She shouldn't be doing this, she knew. It was against all the rules. She should refer this upwards, let someone else deal with it. She didn't even know what he wanted, why he'd made contact. She told herself all she had to do was listen, then she could make a decision. And after last night she wanted to know what he might have to say.

The phone rang for so long she'd assumed it would ring out or cut to voicemail. She was considering what message she should leave when, unexpectedly, a voice said: 'Yes?'

'This is Kate Forester. You asked me to phone. Is that Carl?'

There was a moment's hesitation. 'It's Kevin now,' he said. 'But yes.'

'Is that what I'm supposed to call you?'

'I think that's best,' he said. 'I'm not even supposed to acknowledge there ever was a Carl. Live in the present.'

'So why contact me?'

'I wanted to talk to someone,' he said. 'Someone who understands.'

'You must have some sort of official support?'

'I've a probation officer, who I see periodically in conjunction with an officer from the witness protection programme.' He spoke as if reading out a sentence from some official handbook. 'They organised my new life for me. I suppose if I asked for it they'd put me in contact with a suitable professional to talk to.'

'I'm sure they can. They must have people available for this kind of thing. To give you the support you need.'

'It's just that—well, with respect to your colleagues, my experience of dealing with psychologists inside wasn't that great. Present company excepted, of course. From what I've seen, I've no reason to think it'll be better now I'm out.'

'I appreciate that, Kevin. But I can't talk to you in any professional capacity. I don't think it would be ethical. I should probably report this contact.'

There was a longer pause. 'I'm sorry. I shouldn't have put you in this position. It's probably best we both forget it. Forget we ever had this conversation. If you're prepared to do that.'

'Kevin, just tell me why you made contact? Why now?'

'I'm struggling,' he said, finally.

'It was always bound to be hard, Kevin. I can't begin to imagine—'

'It's not the day-to-day stuff,' he said. 'I've got a new life. I've been lucky. That's worked out better than I could have hoped so far. It's not that.'

'So what is it?'

'I'm scared.'

'Scared?'

'I keep having dreams,' he said. 'I'm running through a wood. I'm running forward, threading my way between the trees. I'm heading somewhere. I know it's important, that I've got to get there. But I don't know where I'm going or why it's so critical.' She heard him swallow. 'I feel a hand in mine, as I'm running. A child's hand. As if a child is running along beside me, as if we're both running towards the same destination.'

'Who's the child?' she said, knowing she was already getting herself too deeply involved, recognising the risk of being manipulated.

'I don't know. I try to see who's holding my hand, but for some reason I can't. He's always just out of vision.'

'He?'

Another silence. 'I don't know. I mean, like I say, I can't—'

'But you said "he"?'

'I suppose that's the impression I had. I don't know why.'

'It doesn't matter,' she said. 'Go on.'

'That's really it,' he said. 'Just that scene. Over and over.'

'Why does it scare you?'

'It was the last dream. The last time I had it, I mean. I felt as if I'd reached my destination, finally. There was a clearing. A bright ring of sunlight. And a child's body on the ground. I wanted to help—it, him. But when I reached down he grasped my wrists and pulled me towards him. The next thing I knew my hands were around his throat—the child's throat—and he was pulling them tighter—'

'Is that where the dream ended?'

'No. There was more. I felt a hand on my shoulder. An adult hand, I think. And that's where it stopped. Something woke me.'

'Why did this scare you?'

'I'm afraid it's the truth. That this is my memory finally coming back. That I really did do what everyone says I did.'

'It's not necessarily that simple, Kevin. In fact, it's not usually that simple. Our dreams are rarely straightforward memories.'

'But my circumstances aren't usual, are they?'

'No, but the dream could have all kinds of significance or, more likely, could mean nothing at all.' She wasn't even sure she believed this herself.

'So why do I feel scared?'

'I don't know. You're scared of the future? You're scared of not knowing where you're heading? It wouldn't be difficult to put that interpretation on the dream.' She stopped, wondering whether she should ask the next question. 'Do you have any other reason to think your memory might be returning?' she asked, finally. 'Do you remember any more than you did in those last sessions.'

'I don't know. I've a sense that something is stirring. That was what struck me in the dream. It wasn't so much the obvious stuff. My hands on the child's throat. It was the clearing. The sunlight. The sense I might finally see something. That's what scared me. That I was getting close to the truth.'

'OK,' she said, speaking carefully. 'But that doesn't necessarily mean the truth is bad. It's understandable that you'd be anxious.'

There was silence at the other end of the line, as if Wickham was weighing up what he should say next. 'When I spoke to you, in those last sessions, I felt as if I got closer than I ever had to opening things up. No-one else has been able to help me like that.'

She hesitated. 'If you really think that, then perhaps we should talk. Talk about it properly, I mean.'

'I don't want to put you in a difficult position.'

'I appreciate that. I can deal with that. I don't want to risk compromising you, though. It's your future that matters.'

'I need to talk about this,' he said. 'I need to work out where things stand. Otherwise, I'm not sure I have a future.'

'OK,' she said. 'Let's meet. Where are you living now?'

He told her, and there was another silence. 'Jesus,' she said, 'that's weird. Yes, I know the place.' Knew it only too well, she thought. It was close to where she was living now, and just a mile or two from where Ryan was killed. In the weeks after his death, she'd driven over there a few times, passed through the village up into the hills. She'd stood by the roadside, looking down into the valley, wondering how it could have happened, how he could have lost control that night. Wondering why he'd had to die.

'There's a question I want to ask you, too,' she said. 'I was just going to check the files about it, funnily enough.'

'Ask away.'

'You were moved to a Youth Offenders' Institute at one stage. I remembered that from your file. I wasn't sure which one.'

'Yes, that's right,' he said, 'Weston Grange.'

'That's what I thought,' she said. 'It seems to have been quite the place to be.'

'I don't understand.'

'No, neither do I. It's not important. We can talk about it when we meet.'

They agreed to meet early the following week, lunchtime in a pub in Stockport where no-one was likely to know either of them. Kate knew she'd stepped over a line. Whatever the rules might say, meeting Wickham in this way was unprofessional, unethical. If her career was already in trouble, this might be enough to push it over the edge.

But Wickham's answer had confirmed the thought that had been nagging at her mind the previous evening. When Hulse had mentioned the YOI where Greg, Graeme and Ryan had all worked, it had rung a bell. She knew all the prisons in the north at least by reputation, and she'd visited a number of them in the course of her career. Even though Ryan had been working there when they'd first met, she'd never been there and she'd had no other contact with the establishment as far as she could recall. But she knew she'd come across the name somewhere, quite recently.

It was as she'd finally been dropping off to sleep that the answer had popped into her mind. As sleep stole over her, she'd suddenly visualised the detail that had been troubling her — typewritten, in a file. Part of a list, with background papers attached. Carl's file. She'd been through the file repeatedly during those weeks when she'd been working with him, searching for some clue or trigger that might help her make progress. She must have half-registered the coincidence at the time, but had thought little of it.

The timing would have been about right. As far as she could recall, Carl had been in there up to his 21st birthday. He'd begun his prison career in a secure children's unit, reflecting the original notoriety of his crime. But for some reason he'd transferred into the standard prison system as he reached adulthood. That decision, Kate guessed, would have been influenced by cost. It was much cheaper to keep a prisoner in a YOI than a specialised secure unit. Which would have been in Carl's best interests was an interesting question, but no doubt largely irrelevant to the powers-that-be.

So it was quite possible that Carl had been in the YOI at the same time that Greg, Graeme and Ryan had been there. Perry had never mentioned that he'd encountered Carl before, but it was possible their paths hadn't crossed directly even if they'd been at the same establishment.

In any case, from what she now knew, there were plenty of things that Perry hadn't bothered mentioning to her.

But even if Carl had been there at the same time, so what? She hadn't come across Carl until she'd begun to deal with him in the Open. She hadn't even remembered his name from the original news reports. He'd suffered a brief period of infamy at the time of the original arrest and trial, but, after a year or two, it had been the victim's name that lodged in the public's mind. The name of the perpetrator, however much it was splashed across the tabloids at the time, had become the stuff of pub quizzes. As she worked through the files, the original story had come back to her. Two children. One, a year or two older, had apparently strangled the other in some sort of argument over a games console. Tabloid shock and disbelief that this could happen, now, today, and not in some inner-city slum. But at a Catholic holiday centre on the North Wales coast with both children, victim and killer, from respectable working-class backgrounds. Kate's primary memory, as a teenager herself, only a little older than Carl, had been of an array of pontificating experts on the TV news. Social workers, cultural commentators, academics, police officers and—inevitably—psychologists, giving their largely unevidenced views on how or why this had been allowed to happen.

Kate was never fully able to reconcile her recollections of that news story with the Carl who'd sat in front of her. He'd been presented by the prosecution as an evil and sadistic young man. Yes, he'd been quiet and generally well-behaved at school but they'd teased out some instances that suggested a different side to his character. An attack on a fellow schoolchild, apparently unmotivated; some supposedly inappropriate sexual discussion and contact with another young girl on his school bus; an instance when he'd talked to schoolfriends about torturing animals.

From her own experience as a witness in other cases, Kate knew enough about the adversarial nature of such trials to take much of this with a heap of salt, but there was enough to paint a picture which the jury had been content to accept. The defence team had made some effort to challenge this depiction of Carl's character, as well as highlighting reasons for mitigation – the recent death of his mother, the traumas of her protracted illness. Despite the blank in Carl's own memory, no-one seriously questioned that he was responsible for the killing. He was found sitting next to the body, his hands still holding the other child's shoulders. There were no other serious suspects.

The only question-mark was Carl's apparent amnesia. He could offer no explanation as to why he'd committed the act. He claimed to have no memory of how or why he and the victim had come into the woodland, no recollection of what had prompted the killing. The prosecution's case was that the killing had resulted from an argument over the handheld games console found lying in the grass at the scene. A witness claimed to recall the boys squabbling over the console some days earlier. Carl's father admitted under oath that he'd had to tell Carl he couldn't afford to buy a similar console for his birthday. Several more witnesses testified that Carl had been behaving oddly over the previous few days.

He'd seemed moody, withdrawn, reluctant to interact with others staying in the centre.

The jury had eventually convicted Carl of murder, and he'd been sentenced to detention at Her Majesty's Pleasure with a recommendation that he should serve at least fifteen years. In the event, he'd served that and more. There'd been no attempt to appeal against the conviction or the sentence, and Carl had made no effort to seek an earlier release, although his record inside might have justified it. For the most part, he'd moved through the system as a low-key, well-behaved prisoner. This was the individual Kate had encountered. She'd seen no sign of the disturbed, sociopathic character depicted by the prosecution.

From the next room, she heard the sound of Jack shouting something excitedly to his grandmother. Kate flicked through the numbers on her phone until she found Hulse's mobile. Just a quick conversation, she thought. See how he is today. Ask him whether he had any recollection of Carl's time at the YOI, whether there was any connection with what they'd been discussing the previous night.

She dialled the number but the call went straight to voicemail. That was unusual. Hulse generally left the phone on at all times when he was off-duty in case there was an incident at the prison. Perhaps he was simply on another call.

She ended the call without leaving a message, unsure what she really intended to say. Hope you're not too hungover? Hope you're feeling better about the future? Do you really believe all the things you told me last night? Are you OK?

That was the real question, she thought. She'd never had reason to call his home number before, but Hulse had given it to the management team to help ensure he was always contactable. She hesitated for an instant, and then dialled the number.

A female voice answered, sounding anxious and suspicious. 'Yes?'

'Mrs Hulse?'

The voice sharpened. 'Who is this?'

'It's Kate Forester. I work with Tim—'

'Do you know where he is?'

Kate felt the same chill of fear she'd felt the previous evening. 'I just wanted to speak to him about a work matter. I assumed he'd be at home.'

'He's not here. He didn't come back last night.' There was no obvious emotion in the tone of voice, nothing that Kate could easily interpret.

'I saw him in the pub. After work. Just briefly. He'd had a few. Maybe he stayed over with someone.'

'That's not him. He doesn't do that.' Kate could hear the trace of a north-eastern accent. 'He's always contactable. It's the job, you know. He has to be.'

'Perhaps there's something wrong with his phone.'

'He'd find a way to call. He knows I worry.' She paused. 'And the way things are at the moment—well, he's not been himself.'

'He seemed fine when I spoke to him last night.' The words sounded unconvincing, but Kate could offer no other response. 'Like I say, he'd had a few to drink— difficult not to at a do like that, isn't it? He wouldn't have been in a condition to drive. I imagine he spent the night on someone's sofa.'

'We're not that far away. He normally gets a taxi after a night out. And he'd have phoned—' It was clear she'd spent the night and morning running through all the possibilities over and over in her head. 'I've been calling his mobile all morning. It just goes to voicemail.'

'I'm sure there's some straightforward explanation,' Kate said. 'Maybe there's been some incident at the prison. He might have had to go straight in, been too tied up to let you know what's happening.' She didn't even believe this herself. If there'd been that kind of incident, she'd have been informed. In those circumstances, it was all hands to the pump, even if you were just a psychologist.

'I called the prison. Spoke to the Duty Governor. He hadn't seen Tim. I didn't like to say he hadn't been back last night. I kept thinking he'd phone at any moment.' There was a long silence. 'Do you think I should call the police?'

Kate's every instinct was telling her that this was exactly what the woman should do. She recalled going through exactly this herself, working through all the possible scenarios, trying to find one that would explain why Ryan hadn't contacted her. Knowing finally there could be no explanation other than the worst possible.

She recalled her own hesitations. It was too early, the police wouldn't take her seriously, they'd assume she and Ryan had had some kind of tiff. She'd delayed long enough that in the end she hadn't needed to call. Later that afternoon. she opened the front door to find a policeman and policewoman standing there, and she knew instantly what they'd come to tell her.

'You know Tim,' she said, finally. 'I mean, you know what he's like. If you really think this is out of character, you should call the police. If nothing else, they'll be able to give you some reassurance.'

'They won't think I'm over-reacting?'

'I'm sure they won't. If you really can't see any reason why Tim hasn't been in touch, they'll take that seriously.

They'll help you track him down much quicker than you'd do on your own.'

'I'm sure I'm just being stupid, but you read such stories.'

'I'm sure it won't be anything like that, but you need to know.'

'I didn't catch your name—'

'Kate. Kate Forester. Head Psychologist at the prison. Don't forget when Tim finally turns up to tell him I want to speak to him.' The flip comment felt inappropriate, but she'd wanted to end the conversation on as upbeat a note as possible.

'I will. I'll make sure he calls you straightaway.'

'You do that.'

As the call ended, Kate stood listening to the cheerful sounds of her mother and Jack in the kitchen. The cakes, it seemed, were nearly ready. In her head, she was praying that Hulse's wife would do the right thing, would call the police straightaway, would get them to take this seriously.

But, somehow, she was already convinced it was too late.

She heard nothing more that day. She wondered, once or twice, whether she should call Hulse's wife again to find out if there'd been any further developments. But if Hulse had turned up, whatever the circumstances, neither party would be interested in talking to her. And if he hadn't—well, that didn't bear thinking about, and there'd be nothing she could do but offer worthless platitudes.

She got up late on Sunday morning. The sun had returned, but there was a definite chill in the air. Summer was over. The trees that lined the residential street outside were rapidly shedding their leaves, the crimson-brown drifts accumulating between the parked cars.

Kate showered, dressed and made her way downstairs. Jack and Elizabeth were in the kitchen. 'Mum. We're doing blueberry muffins for breakfast!'

'That's great,' Kate said. 'Though it's probably brunch by now.'

'Turned a bit chilly,' Elizabeth said. 'What time do you want to be off?'

'Up to you. The drive's only a couple of hours. We can get a takeaway tonight, so there's no rush.'

'It won't take me long to sort things out. By the way, your mobile was buzzing away earlier.'

'Was it?' Kate had left her mobile recharging in a corner of the living room. A call and a voicemail, both from the same unfamiliar number. She thumbed to the voicemail menu. 'Kate, it's John. Hodges. Can you give me a call? Use this number. It's my personal mobile.'

It had to be bad news. Why else would be call her on a Sunday morning? She pressed call back and waited. The phone rang once and then was answered.

'Kate?' He presumably had her name and number in his address book.

'John. What is it?'

'I almost didn't call today. Didn't want to disturb people's weekends if I didn't have to. But I remembered you were on leave next week.'

'What is it?'

'Tim. Have you heard the news?'

'I spoke to his wife yesterday. Just briefly. She said he hadn't come home on Friday night. She was tearing her hair out.'

'Yes. Poor Jane. Jesus.'

'Has something happened?'

'They found Tim. Yesterday morning, apparently. By the main London-Manchester railway track. Just a few hundred yards from the pub.'

Kate could picture the expanse of track, a couple of fields away from the car park where she'd sat talking to Hulse on the Friday evening. The West Coast mainline trains ran down there, every twenty minutes in the daytime, a red and silver streak she'd occasionally registered as she drove to or from the prison.

'Jesus. What happened?'

'He was hit by a train, sometime overnight on Friday. They've not said much but it was after the passenger services had stopped running, so they think an overnight freight service.'

'Christ. How could that happen?'

'That's the mystery,' Hodges said. 'It's not the sort of place you'd stumble into by accident. Police aren't saying anything just yet, not even to Jane.' There was a lengthy pause. 'I can only see two explanations. Tim was pretty pissed by the time I left on Friday. I'd been careful so I offered him a lift home, but he said he'd sort a taxi. But I know in the past he's sometimes not bothered with the taxi if it looked like there was going to be a long wait, and he's walked it instead. It's only a couple of miles. And there's a theoretical — but quite illegal — shortcut over the railway line.'

'You think he'd have done that?'

'He was the one who told me about it. But he reckoned he was too cautious to actually use it. Being Tim, he was less concerned about safety than about getting caught. Wouldn't look good: prisoner governor caught in illegal trespass.'

'So why would he have done it on Friday then?'

'Christ knows. Like I say, he was pissed. Maybe

seemed a good idea at the time. I suppose after midnight the risk should be pretty minimal.'

'Poor bastard,' Kate said. 'What would the odds be of being hit at that time of the night?' That was the question, she thought, realising now where Hodges was leading. 'You said two possible explanations.'

'Yes,' Hodges said. 'I mean, either he was there by accident or—' He stopped, reluctant to articulate his next thought. 'Or it wasn't an accident. The other possibility is that he went there deliberately. That he waited until there was a train approaching.' He took a breath, and she could heat the emotion in his voice. 'And then threw himself under the fucking thing.'

CHAPTER TWENTY-FOUR

Milton slumped himself down in front of Murrain's desk. Here they were again, yet another Sunday morning, a quarter of the team turning up unpaid in the hope of making some headway on a case that seemed to be going nowhere. Murrain was looking exhausted, his eyes red from lack of sleep, carrying the air of someone pushing on through will-power alone.

'Anything new?' Milton said.

It seemed to take Murrain a moment to focus on the question. 'Bugger all. Other than this Kevin Wickham stuff.' He'd briefed Milton on the outcomes of the session with Barker and the others.

'You reckon there's any legs in that?'

Murrain hesitated in a way that, to Milton's practised eye, suggested some potential significance. 'My first reaction's to say no. It's just coincidence. Just another possible lead to be eliminated. But—' He paused, again. 'You remember when you called me after you'd been out to that pub in the village?'

Milton stiffened awkwardly. 'Last week, you mean?'

'The Friday night. I was in the car when you called.'

'What about it?'

'When you talked about the people coming in—that Business Forum lot—I felt, just for a moment, something really intense. Stronger than usual. Couldn't make head or tail of what it might mean, but it nearly drove me off the road.'

Milton nodded, clearly following Murrain's train of thought. 'You think Wickham might be part of this

Business Forum? That he might have been one of the people coming into the pub?'

'Who knows? But it might be worth checking with that Brody chap.' Murrain rubbed his eyes and then continued, as if unconscious of any non-sequitur: 'What about your railway body? That going to end up with us?'

'I'm hoping not,' Milton said. They were all conscious how thinly their resources were stretched already. Not just the Ethan Dunn case, but all the other numerous ongoing cases and unfinished business that they had to deal with. 'Ferbrache's view was that it was most like an accident. Or maybe even suicide. There are some reports of trouble at work, apparently. He was a prison governor, of all things. Either way, not likely to end up on our list.'

Murrain rubbed his temples. 'Hope you're right.'

'You've got some feeling about this as well?'

Murrain laughed. 'You shouldn't place too much faith in anything I'm feeling, Joe. You know what it's like.'

'I do. I also know it's usually worth paying attention to.'

'Maybe I'm losing it. Whatever it was. I'm normally sure what I'm feeling, even if I don't know what it means. But in this case it's been all over the place. Nothing there when I might expect it. Then some sort of sensation when it makes no sense. Like with that couple in Hazel Grove.'

'But if the attempted snatching there was linked to the Dunn case, that wouldn't be surprising, would it?'

'Maybe not. But it didn't feel like that. It was something to do with the parents. There was something similar with Dunn's parents.' He paused, thinking. 'The mothers, at any rate.'

'You think they're involved? We've talked to them

countless times now, but there's nothing suspicious.'

'I'm not sure about involved. I've just got the sense that there's something else there. Something they're not saying. Or something one of them's not saying.' He shook his head. 'Maybe nothing. Like I say, I don't know. Anything come from Bert's door to doors with the neighbours in Hazel Grove?''

'Not much so far. She's gone over there again today to try to catch a couple who were out yesterday. But nobody seems to have seen anything.' He stopped and regarded Murrain more closely. 'You OK?'

Murrain pressed his palms against the sides of his head. 'Truth is, I've had a bloody nagging headache ever since the report of that railway body came in. That's not usually a good sign. Feels like a loose connection in the back of my skull.'

'Could be a migraine,' Milton pointed out. 'Or just that you're knackered.'

'The second's certainly a possibility. But—'

Milton nodded. 'Difficult to see any connection with the Dunn case, though.'

'You'd think so. Could well be something else.'

'But you think there's something?'

Murrain shrugged apologetically. 'Didn't want to tread on your toes, Joe. But I put a call into Pete Warwick. Asked him if he could expedite this one. Just to put my mind at rest. We've enough on our plates as it is. Could do without another one.'

Warwick was the pathologist who most commonly supported Murrain's team. 'And what did he say?' Both of them knew that Warwick usually made a point of doing things his way and at his own pace. Which, in fairness, generally meant they were done both rigorously and efficiently, if not always quite at the speed that Murrain would have ideally preferred.

'You know Pete. He huffed and puffed and told me how busy he was. Then I offered him a couple of beers and he said he'd pull it to the top of the list. Truth is, he loves doing the stuff for us far more than his day-to-day work.'

'Well, let's hope he just confirms what Neil Ferbrache thought.'

'Ferby's not often wrong.' Murrain shook his head. 'Jesus, it's coming to something, isn't it?'

'What's that?'

'When we're both sitting here hoping that some poor bastard might have committed suicide.'

CHAPTER TWENTY-FIVE

The news was shocking enough in itself, of course. But what had really shaken her were the echoes of Ryan's death. Echoes that seemed almost too loud, as if someone wanted to be sure she heard. She considered that thought for a moment, then realised how absurd it sounded.

'Mum. Come and try a muffin. They're great.' Jack stopped, his child's intuition recognising that something was wrong.

'Are you all right?' Elizabeth said.

'No.' Kate sat at the kitchen table. 'I just had some news. Bad news.'

Her mother shooed Jack into the sitting room with a plateful of the freshly-baked muffins. 'You go and get started on those. I'll make some coffee for your mother and me and then we'll come and join you.'

Kate waited until she was sure Jack was out of earshot. From the sitting room, she heard the sound of the television being turned on, an explosion of musical noise. 'It's Tim, my boss.'

As she recounted what Hodges had told her, Kate could see that Elizabeth had been struck by the same thought that had occurred to Kate herself. 'Oh, my goodness. How dreadful. I remember—'

'Ryan?' Kate said. 'That's exactly what I thought. The same stupid senseless death.'

'Did he have children?'

Kate nodded. 'Two. Quite young, I think.' She pushed away her half-drunk coffee before her mother could offer any response. 'Let's go and help Jack finish those muffins before he eats them all himself.' she said. 'And then let's get off, shall we? I need to be doing something.'

An hour or so later, they'd packed up and were on the road. They had a slow journey back south, the motorways clogged by weekend roadworks even though the traffic was light. It was late afternoon before they pulled up outside Kate's new home.

'This is lovely,' Elizabeth said as she climbed effortlessly out of the car. 'Beautiful views.'

'That's the Peak Forest canal,' Kate said, trotting out the information she'd accumulated since moving here. 'Part of the Cheshire Ring. And beyond that's the Goyt Valley, with the river down there among the trees. And after that you're into the High Peak.'

'That's nice.' Elizabeth clearly had little interest in her daughter's gazetteer offering. 'And it's an ideal house for you.'

Kate busied herself helping unload her mother's and Jack's cases from the boot of the car. 'Still a bit of a drive to work, but nothing too unpleasant.' Once in the house, Kate ushered Jack into the kitchen and poured him a glass of orange squash. 'What do you think of the place, then?' she asked as he lifted the full beaker to his mouth. It was a question she might have been better asking herself.

'It's nice,' he said. 'Better than granny's. Can we go and look at the canal later? Are there boats?'

'There are narrow boats,' she said. 'Sometimes people actually live on them. I can show you.' She felt as if she were babbling to keep the silence at bay. 'Some of them are painted bright colours.'

Kate left Jack to explore the house with Elizabeth, and stayed by the kitchen window staring on to the small garden at the rear of the house. The garden was backed by a stone wall, a couple of metres high, which looked older that the house itself. She'd been told that it was part of an old farm wall that had formed the boundary of an adjoining estate, but she had no knowledge of the history. Much of the land in the area had belonged to the local landed gentry and had been sold off piecemeal over the years.

The resulting garden was a decent space, though — a sun-trap on summer's evenings, the sun over the hillside warming the stone to create an atmosphere that felt comfortable and secure. Although the summer had been nearly over by the time she moved down here, she enjoyed the evenings she'd spent out there with a glass of wine and a book. Those evenings seemed distant now, and not only because of the approaching chill of autumn.

Jack and Elizabeth had discovered the garden too and were out exploring its charms. There was little out there to interest Jack, just a patch of lawn and a few half-tended flowerbeds. But she could see he was already concocting some fantasy in his head, running up and down the grass, engaged in an adventure only he understood.

As she watched, she was struck by a sudden thought, and the same old fears came flooding back into her head.

She stepped over to the back door. It was firmly bolted and locked, the key of the deadlock secreted safely in her purse. As she knew it had been. She fumbled in her pocket for the purse and found the key, then she unlocked and unbolted the door. Outside, the air was chilly and damp. 'You found the garden, then?' she called to her mother, striving to keep her voice steady. 'Good, isn't it?'

'Lovely,' Elizabeth said, her attention fixed on Jack's

increasingly manic circling of the lawn.

'How'd you manage to get out here?' Kate asked. 'Was the key in the lock?'

Her mother was frowning, her expression baffled. 'I thought you must have been out here already,' she said, after a moment.

'No,' Kate said. 'No, I hadn't been.'

'The patio doors were unlocked. I don't know why I even tried them. It was only because Jack was keen to get out into the garden. But they weren't fastened. I just pushed them open.' She sounded apologetic, as if she'd committed some social *faux pas*.

'God, I'm so stupid,' Kate said. 'I must have forgotten to lock them when I left on Friday morning. It was a bit frantic because I was running late for work.' In fact, she hadn't been in any particular hurry on Friday. She'd been up early and had packed the night before. She was sure she'd checked very carefully that all the doors and windows were locked before she'd left.

Leaving Elizabeth and Jack out in the garden, she walked through to the sitting room and looked around. There was no sign of any disturbance. As far as she could tell, everything was as she'd left it. There were a couple of CDs out next to the stereo system, but those were ones she'd been playing the previous week. There was a small pile of newspapers and magazines and a couple of books on the coffee table in the middle of the room, but as far as she could recall those were all where she'd left them.

She walked upstairs to check the bedrooms Jack and Elizabeth would be using. Both rooms were austere in their furnishings and decor, with little beyond the bare minimum of furniture. Kate had taken no steps to personalise them. She'd entered the two rooms only occasionally, and as far as she could judge both were as she'd last seen them. The bathroom, similarly, looked unchanged.

Finally, she entered her own bedroom. At first glance, it looked as unchanged as the other rooms. The bed was tidy, as she'd left it. There was a book, spread-eagled, on her bedside table—a paperback thriller she'd been reading to help send herself to sleep. The dressing table held its usual scattering of cosmetics, a box of tissues.

There was something else on the table, a square piece of card that caught the last light of the sun through the window. She couldn't remember what that might be.

Kate took a step forward and peered more closely. It was a photograph, the image still obscured by the reflected sunshine.

She had no memory of leaving a photograph on the dressing table. Some nights before, when she'd been feeling low and anxious, she'd dug out an old album of pictures from the early days of her relationship with Ryan. They'd been the last few photographs they'd taken with their old camera in the days before digital cameras had become ubiquitous.

They were mainly holiday snaps, most of them showing only Kate or Ryan, the picture taken by the other. Souvenirs from those happier times—a long weekend in Paris, a rain-sodden week in the Lakes, a languorous week on one of the Greek islands. Some of the photos were already sun-faded. She'd hoped the images of herself and Ryan would help snap her out of her anxieties, but they'd had the opposite effect. The fading colours had felt almost like a metaphor. The past was slipping away even as she tried to make sense of it.

She'd brought a couple of the albums up to the bedroom, almost luxuriating in the self-pity that overwhelmed her as she flicked through the images. She'd had a last skim through them in bed and then slipped the two folders into the bedside drawer.

As she stepped forward, the angle of the sunlight slipped away from the photograph. It was an image that, at first glance, she did not recognise. She picked up the glossy sheet and stared at the picture.

It was a photograph of Ryan, maybe a couple of years older than those she'd been leafing through. He was standing slightly awkwardly, dressed in his uniform, squinting into the camera as if caught off-guard. The photograph itself was inexpertly taken, with the sun apparently partly behind Ryan's body so that his face was partly lost in the shade. There was another figure standing beside Ryan, clearly a prisoner. A young man, slighter than Ryan, with a spade in his hand. His face, too, was only partly visible.

Kate held the photograph before her and peered at the image. It was impossible to be sure, she told herself. The definition was poor. The face was partly obscured by shadow. Even so, she had no doubt.

Carl Hancock. Kevin Wickham. Whoever he might be now, she knew that he was the figure in the photograph.

So how had the picture appeared here?

She had no recollection of seeing it before, though both she and Ryan had kept a few envelopes of random older pictures—most from before they had met—tucked in the backs of the albums she'd been looking through. Perhaps this had simply fallen out of one of those, unnoticed, while she'd been skimming through the pages.

But she didn't really believe that.

Someone, somehow, had been in here. Someone had left this for her as—well, as what? As a message? As a warning?

She looked around her, feeling the same vulnerability she'd felt in the pub car-park. But stronger now, and with more substance. She'd seen this place as a safe haven for herself and Jack, a place where she could start again, rebuild her life. Now, she felt exposed and threatened and she didn't have a clue why.

She should call the police. But what could she say? She had no evidence of any intruder other than an unlocked door and an old photograph. She had no evidence that Hulse's death was anything other than, at worst, self-inflicted. And she couldn't begin to explain the possible significance of this photograph without compromising herself and, more importantly, Wickham.

She stood staring out of the window at the bright autumn sunshine. From the garden below, she could hear the sound of Jack still running tirelessly round the lawn. At last, she took out her mobile and thumbed through her contacts.

The call was answered almost immediately, as if Wickham had been sitting waiting for her call. 'Kate?'

'Kevin, there are some things I need to talk to you about. Sooner rather than later.'

There was a brief silence. 'When I saw it was your number, I thought you were calling to cancel.'

'I've considered that option too,' she said. 'But, no, I think we need to meet. I know it's short-notice, but what about tomorrow. Same place. Whatever times suits you.'

'Fine by me,' he said. 'Lunchtime?'

'About one, then. We can grab a bite.' She tried to make it sound casual but she knew the tension in her voice would be evident.

'Is everything OK?'

'Everything's—well, no, not OK. But we can talk

about that tomorrow.'

'Is this about me?'

'No—or, at least, I'm not sure. It's a long story.' She stopped, conscious how enigmatic she was sounding. 'Look, it's not something you need to worry about. Just something I need clarifying. I'll explain when we meet.'

'If you say so.' He sounded unconvinced. 'Tomorrow, then.'

CHAPTER TWENTY-SIX

Monday morning started badly for Murrain and rapidly became worse.

He was already feeling at his lowest. He'd slept badly, the same insistent headache nagging behind his eyes. He'd tried to describe it to Eloise the previous night — like a loose connection in an electrical circuit, he'd said, sparking and sparking but not producing any power. She'd nodded indulgently over her glass of wine. They both knew that when Murrain was in this state, the only response was to ride it out, wait for the moment either to pass or come to some kind of fruition. There was no way to guess which outcome was more likely.

Eloise had been up before dawn, off to some conference in London where she was due to give a presentation on the force's recent organisational restructuring. How to do the impossible with bugger all money without pissing everyone off, she'd wanted to call it, but had eventually settled for something less provocative. Murrain had dragged himself out of bed to make her coffee and toast, knowing that he was well beyond sleep in any case.

His mood wasn't improved by his journey into the MIR. The Monday morning traffic, worsened by heavy rain, slow moving even at that early hour of the day. He arrived already feeling exhausted and dispirited. The bleak 1970s block of the old police station was no more attractive than the rain-washed grey stone of the surrounding villages. The drop into the valley beyond felt like it might be the end of the world.

Murrain was first in, and he contented himself with sipping on a hot coffee and working his way through the pile of e-mails that had somehow accumulated even since the previous afternoon. Wanstead turned up as always just before eight, and the room slowly filled. It was always interesting to observe the atmosphere in an incident room, Murrain thought. You could almost read the progress of a case from the buzz, or the lack of it, around the place. Today, the place felt almost dead. Milton and Donovan arrived at almost the same time and were chatting with relative animation but, as Wanstead was keen to point out, there might be other reasons for that.

When Bert Wallace arrived, Murrain wandered over to her desk. 'Morning, Bert,' he said, the name as always sticking momentarily in his throat. 'Just wondered if anything came out of your Hazel Grove interviews?'

She looked up nervously, as if expecting him to give her a telling off. 'Not much, to be honest. Spoke to as many of the neighbours as I could track down. Nobody seems to have seen anything. It's not a busy road, but there's enough traffic that no-one registered a van particularly.' She paused. 'There was one thing.'

'Go on.'

'It's probably nothing.' Wallace was still feeling awkward about having drawn Murrain's attention to Kevin Wickham. He'd said nothing more about Wickham since they'd interviewed him, except to tell her that it was in hand. She'd interpreted that as meaning that she'd probably wasted their time, even if Murrain was too polite to say so. 'It was just something that a woman from across the street said. She was a fairly elderly lady. Got the impression she was a bit of a curtain-twitcher, you know?'

'I know.' Murrain smiled. 'They often make the best witnesses.'

'When I mentioned the Morrisons, she looked disapproving. She wouldn't say anything at first, but after we'd chatted for a while she relaxed and became a bit more gossipy.'

Murrain smiled. He knew that Wallace had the skills to get the most out of any interviewee. 'And?'

'She was reluctant to say anything directly. None of her business, all that. But she dropped enough hints. She obviously thinks that Mrs Morrison is having an affair.'

Murrain sat up. He'd caught the same glimpse then, that same half-formed image. The persistent hum in the back of his head had momentarily intensified. 'Really? She'd seen someone at the house?'

'She reckoned so, though there was nothing particularly helpful. I'm sure she's kept watch very dutifully, but all she could say was that there seemed to be a man who turned up at odd times of the day. She'd only seen him from a distance. Fairly big, heavily-built, she reckoned.'

Murrain stretched out his own hefty frame. 'Interesting. The young lad reckoned that the man who tried to grab him looked more my build than Joe's. Don't suppose this mysterious caller was considerate enough to drive a van?'

'Apparently not. Just a car. A shooting-brake, she called it.' Wallace's shrug indicated her bafflement at the phrase.

'What we might call an estate,' Murrain explained. 'And she didn't have the number?'

'No, nothing like that. To be honest, I didn't know how seriously to take it. She was obviously the type who likes bad-mouthing their neighbours, given half a chance. It was all a bit vague, and it wasn't clear that this man had visited much. Could all be perfectly innocent.'

'Could well be,' Murrain agreed. 'But probably worth another chat with Mrs Morrison when we get a moment. Perhaps in the day when her husband's not likely to be around.'

'Shall I do that?'

Murrain nodded. 'Yes, but if I get chance in a bit, I'll try to come with you. I'd like to see her reaction when we raise it.' He smiled, not wanting her to think that he didn't trust her to handle it herself. 'You know what I'm like.'

As it turned out, though, the morning was busier than he'd expected. The first call came just before ten. Murrain had finished working his way through the e-mails and was reviewing the plans and schedules for the investigation when he saw Wanstead gesturing across the room. 'Call for you,' Wanstead mouthed, as he made the transfer to Murrain's phone.

'Kenny? Pete Warwick.'

'Crikey, Pete. Don't expect you to call this early. Thought you'd be on your rounds. Or playing golf or something.'

'I've sacrificed it all for you, Kenny. You know me.'

'I know you only too well, Pete. That's why I don't expect you to do anything just because I've asked you to.'

'Usually I make a point of doing the opposite, obviously. But this time I've decided to make an exception. You asked me to give you a view on this body. The Hulse chap.'

Murrain was genuinely surprised, though he made sure it didn't show in his voice. When he'd asked Warwick to expedite the Hulse case he'd been thinking in terms of days rather than hours. He knew how much pressure Warwick was under. 'Don't tell me you've done it already?'

'Well, not properly. I don't want to start setting any precedents. But I've had a preliminary look.'

'And?'

'I got on to it because — well, to be honest, because I thought I'd be in and out in five minutes. I assumed it was an open and shut case from my point of view. Some poor bugger gets hit by train. Cause of death: being hit by a train. There you go.'

Murrain felt a frisson under his skin. 'I'm sensing a "but" coming.'

'A big one.'

'Namely?'

'That he wasn't killed by the train. Well, not exclusively. I think he was already well on his way — unconscious at least — by the time the train hit him.'

'How come? And how can you be sure?'

'That's the thing. It's a hundred-to-one shot that it was detectable. If the impact of the train had been even marginally different, it would have destroyed any other evidence. You might get Ferby's people to give a view on this, but it looks to me as if, by some fluke, the head avoided the worst impact of the train. Not that it did the poor bugger much good.'

'The head?'

'Yeah. The torso was pretty badly crushed, but head was surprisingly unscathed. Relatively speaking, you understand. Except that on the side of the skull, there was a fairly severe injury that, as far as I can judge, wasn't caused the impact of the train. More likely be some sharp instrument.' There was a silence as Warwick allowed Murrain to digest this. 'I can't be absolutely certain, of course.'

Warwick was famous for surrounding his conclusions with caveats and reservations, just to ensure his own backside was covered if further evidence emerged. Murrain knew that he wouldn't offer a view like this without being absolutely sure of his ground. 'So what are you saying?' Murrain pressed. 'That he was injured before the train hit him?'

'That's the way it looks to me,' Warwick said. 'I'll need to do a full examination, of course, but as I say my initial view is that the injury was caused by a blow to the head from some sharp instrument, with the assailant striking from behind. It would have been a pretty severe blow. Enough to render him unconscious. Maybe enough to kill him, though not immediately. It probably took the train to do that.'

'Jesus,' Murrain said. 'So we're talking murder. Or at least manslaughter.'

'That's your territory, old son. But I'd say so. Hard to see that a blow like that, in that setting, could have happened by accident.' He paused, clearly conscious that his words had been uncharacteristically definitive. 'Like I say, it's impossible to be absolutely certain. But that's where I'd put my money.'

Murrain took a moment to respond. The throbbing in his head had already changed tone. The connection, whatever it might be, was growing stronger. 'I'd like to say I'm grateful, Pete. And I am grateful to you for expediting it. But frankly the last bloody thing I need right now is another murder enquiry.'

'We aim to please.'

The nagging headache was coalescing into something more familiar. A sense of meaning. A sense of connection. Something about the Hulse case suggested it wasn't a one-off, that there was some link, however tenuous, with the Ethan Dunn killing. He couldn't imagine what that link might be but he was already growing increasingly certain it was there.

At the same time, he could provide no substantive evidence to support his hunch. There was no reason to link the two cases. The only option would be to initiate a new investigation, ideally with one of his own team as the SIO. Given the high profile of the Dunn case, DS Winston might need some persuading about the wisdom of their taking on more work. Not that resources were likely to be readily available elsewhere.

Wearily, Murrain gestured to Wanstead to join him so they could set the wheels in motion. The formalities would be dependent on Warwick's confirmation of the apparent cause of death, but there was every reason now to treat Hulse's death as an unlawful killing.

The second phone call came half an hour later, as he and Wanstead were still working their way through the actions needed to kick off the Hulse investigation. Murrain had already set up a meeting with Winston and wanted to make sure he'd got all his arguments prepared in advance.

This time, the call was from the Head of the Force Control room, a police staff member called Tony Willis who Murrain knew slightly, mainly because Eloise had been responsible for Willis's appointment following her restructuring of the FCR a couple of years earlier. A first-rate manager, she'd reckoned, and Murrain knew that those were few and far between in this environment.

'Kenny?' Willis said. 'Sorry to bother you. This isn't the sort of report I'd normally forward straight to you, but in the circumstances—'

'No problem. What is it?'

'We've had a report. A missing child. Just called in this afternoon.'

'You did the right thing, Tony. In the light of the Dunn case, we can't afford to take any chances, even if it's a false alarm.'

'No, well, that's what I thought. But it's not just that. I mean, that's why it was escalated to me. But then the name rang a bell. The child's been reported missing before.'

Murrain sat up straighter and exchanged a look with Wanstead, who was clearly overhearing enough of the dialogue to follow the gist. 'Go on.'

'It's a boy called Myers. Luke Myers.'

CHAPTER TWENTY-SEVEN

Murrain glanced at his two colleagues, and then along the street. 'If he doesn't answer soon, the neighbour's will start asking questions. We don't exactly look like Jehovah's Witnesses.'

'Maybe he's out,' Colin Ashworth suggested.

'Maybe,' Milton said. 'But that's his car parked over there.'

Murrain held up his hand. 'I hear movement.'

After a moment, the door was opened and Kevin Wickham stood facing them. He glanced quizzically between the three men. He had clearly recognised Murrain from their previous meeting, but he'd then focused on Ashworth standing at the rear. He nodded, as if Ashworth's presence had simply confirmed his expectations. 'Mr Ashworth. What can I do for you?'

Ashworth stepped forward. 'Afternoon, Kevin. You don't want us hanging about on the doorstep, do you?'

Wickham held open the door, allowing the party to troop past him. 'Through there,' he said. 'On the left.' It was impossible to read his expression.

The three men traipsed through into the sitting room. It was a neat-looking room, but, apart from a couple of well-stocked bookcases, had the anonymous air of a furnished rental. Murrain and Milton lowered themselves on the two ends of a sofa like ill-matching bookends. Ashworth seated himself at the dining table, and began flicking through a notebook. Without looking up, he said, 'You know what this is about, Kevin?'

'Haven't a clue,' Wickham said. 'You'll have to

enlighten me.'

'Fair enough. You know me, Kevin. And I believe you've met DCI Murrain. This is DI Milton.'

Wickham nodded. 'Go on.'

'You don't need to worry, Kevin,' Ashworth said. 'Or I hope you don't. We just need to ask you a few questions.'

Murrain nodded impatiently. 'Thanks, Mr Ashworth. Shall we take over now?' Without waiting for a response, he turned to Wickham. 'Just so you understand, Mr Wickham, this isn't a formal interview. Not at this stage.'

Wickham nodded, still expressionless. 'But they must be serious questions,' he said, 'especially given that Mr Ashworth's here.'

'We need to handle this with care given your background. Mr Ashworth is here to advise us on those aspects.'

'Ah.' Wickham shifted uncomfortably in his seat. 'So you know?'

'We didn't know before, Mr Wickham,' Murrain said. 'We do now. It rather changes things, don't you think?'

'Not from where I'm sitting. I didn't set out to mislead you. Mr Ashworth will tell you—'

'We understand your position,' Murrain said. 'And we understand why you said nothing. But I'm wondering why you didn't inform Mr Ashworth immediately that we'd been talking to you. That might have been wise. In the circumstances.'

'There aren't any circumstances, as far as I'm aware,' Wickham said. There was an edge to his voice now. 'I've no idea why you're here. I've no real idea why you came here before.'

'We spoke to you in connection with Mrs Susan Myers, Mr Wickham.'

'So you said.'

Murrain looked up at him and said nothing for a moment. 'She has a son. Luke.'

'We talked about this. I hardly know him. Like I told you, I hardly know Sue, really. I've met Luke a couple of times now but that's all.'

'When my officer interviewed you and Mrs Myers originally, she was under the impression you were a couple.'

'We never said that, whatever impression your officer formed. Sue was looking for moral support. She just wanted someone there with her.'

'And you were the only one available?'

'I guess so.'

'I see.' Murrain left the words hanging, eventually forcing Wickham to break the silence.

'Perhaps you'd like to explain why this might be any of your business. Look, I'm sorry, but I've really no idea why you're here.'

Murrain rose slowly to his feet and began to prowl around the room, peering at the rows of books on the bookshelf, the few ornaments arranged artlessly around the room, the scattering of DVDs on the floor beside the television. 'We told you before that we're investigating a murder locally,' he said at last, not bothering to look back at Wickham.

'That little boy. Yes.' Wickham looked across at Ashworth. 'And, of course, now you think I must have something to do with it. I suppose that was inevitable.'

'We're exploring all avenues, Mr Wickham. But that's not the main reason for our visit. The reason we're here is that Luke Myers was reported missing this morning.' He turned and gazed unblinkingly at Wickham, watching his expression. Waiting for some sensation.

Wickham stared back, his face blank. 'Luke—' He stopped. 'I don't understand.'

'Neither do we, Mr Wickham. Luke apparently disappeared from home this morning. His mother was upstairs. It's half-term, so she'd got someone else working in the shop. She left Luke playing in the back garden. Just for a few minutes, apparently, while she went to bring down some washing. When she came down, he'd disappeared. That's all we know at the moment.' He paused, still watching Wickham closely. 'It took her longer than it should have done to report it because of the previous false alarm. She didn't want to look a fool. She went round checking with the neighbours. Phoned his friends. Phoned her ex. Couldn't see why he'd have left the garden without telling her.' He paused. 'She didn't call you?'

Wickham's eyes flicked from Murrain to Ashworth. 'To be honest, I've been screening her calls since you and your colleague came round to interview me. When I saw her number this morning, I just turned the phone off. I thought it was all getting too complicated.' He gestured towards Ashworth. 'In the circumstances.'

'Tell us about your relationship with Mrs Myers.'

'Look, I keep telling you, it was hardly a relationship. We only met a short while ago, part of a get-together in the local pub. Finlan Brody's so-called Business Forum.'

Murrain exchanged a glance with Milton, who nodded. 'But you got to know her?'

'Well, we got on, or I thought we were getting on. And now I imagine it's over. That's it. All there was to it.'

Ashworth looked up for the first time since Murrain had interrupted him. 'Did you know she had a child? When you took up with her, I mean.'

'For what it's worth,' Wickham said, 'as I told Mr

Murrain here, no, I didn't. Not when I "took up" with her, as you put it. I met her in the pub. She was a pleasant woman of roughly my own age. I knew she was divorced but she never mentioned a child. We went out together a couple of times. That's the whole story.'

'She didn't mention she had a child?' Murrain this time, speaking softly. 'That seems a little odd.'

'You'd have to ask her,' Wickham said. 'I'm guessing she was holding it back until we'd got to know each other better. She never actually lied to me. I just didn't ask.'

'But you found out when Luke supposedly went missing the first time?'

'I've told you all this.'

'Indeed.' For the first time, Murrain looked across at Milton, who opened a laptop bag he'd been holding on his knee and pulled out a plastic wallet. 'Some mix-up between Mrs Myers and her ex, wasn't it? Youngster left kicking his heels in the rain.'

'Something like that,'

'There was some suggestion that, while he was waiting in the rain, young Luke got scared by someone watching him. Someone in a van.'

'So you told me,' Wickham said. 'That was what Finlan Brody said. He was one who found Luke. I wasn't there. There's nothing more I can tell you.'

Murrain leaned forward on the sofa. 'Let's go back to Mrs Myers. You form a relationship with a divorcee who has a child of the same sex and age of the child you were convicted of killing—'

'Now wait a minute—'

'I'm simply stating the facts. You seem to have inveigled your way into her life in a very short time.'

'There was no "inveigling". We got to know one

another. That's all.'

'A lonely woman with a son of a certain age.'

'That's not how it was.' Wickham stopped. 'Look, I can understand why you'd want to talk to me. I can see this is the first place you'd look. But if Luke's gone missing, it's nothing to do with me.' He gestured expansively. 'Search the place. Search wherever you want.'

'Thank you, Mr Wickham. We'd like to do that. Just so we can all be reassured.'

'Search wherever you like. You've my full permission. You'll find nothing here.'

'Thank you for your co-operation, Mr Wickham. I'm sure it'll make it easier for all of us. We'll need to search your car and the garden too. I presume that won't be a problem?' Murrain knew they could obtain a warrant if need be, but Wickham's offer would make the process much quicker.

'Whatever you want,' Wickham said.

Murrain turned to Ashworth, as if he'd only just remembered his presence. 'You're happy with that, Colin?'

Ashcroft's expression suggested that he was never likely to be happy again. 'Best we can do, I suppose,' he said. 'We need to protect Kevin's identify as far as we possibly can. It won't be in anyone's interest for this to hit the press without good reason.'

'Quite so,' Murrain said. 'Well, let's hope there is no good reason.' He turned to Wickham, who was still standing awkwardly by the window. 'And let's hope you don't have any nosy neighbours.'

***

Wickham sat hunched in a chair in a corner of the living room as they listened to the tramp of heavy shoes up and down the stairs and across the floors of the rooms above. Colin Ashworth was sitting on the sofa pretending to read a newspaper he'd pulled out of his briefcase. He clearly hadn't known whether to stay or go and Murrain had shown no intention of enlightening him. Milton had already had a couple of officers standing by ready to conduct the search, knowing Murrain was likely to succeed in provoking Wickham to agree to it voluntarily.

Murrain himself was at the opposite end of the sofa, showing no signs of restlessness or boredom even though they'd been sitting there for the best part of ninety minutes. He'd been content to leave the supervision of the search to Milton, wanting to spend time in Wickham's company. The familiar nagging headache had been there since they'd entered the house, but had never intensified in the way he might have expected.

'Their instructions are to leave things as tidy as possible,' Murrain had commented. 'But it'll be a thorough search.'

'The more thorough the better, as far as I'm concerned. I just want to prove to you that I've nothing to do with this.' He paused. 'Apart from anything else, I want you to stop wasting time with me and devote your energies to trying to find Luke.'

They'd sat in silence for a long period after that, hearing the irregular stamping of footsteps through the house. Eventually Milton stuck his head around the door. 'Kenny,' he said to Murrain. 'Can I have a word?'

Murrain looked across at Ashworth, tacitly instructing him to keep an eye on Wickham. He left the room and returned a few moments later, holding a small plastic bag delicately between his fingers.

'Mr Wickham,' he said, with a new formality in his tone. 'I wonder whether you can offer us any explanation for this?' He held out the plastic bag in front of Wickham's face.

Wickham peered at the contents. A folded piece of cardboard, deep blue. 'What is it?'

'Part of the cover of a school exercise book,' Murrain said. 'Not in good condition. But enough to read the name of the front. Luke Myers. Any explanation, Mr Wickham?'

'Where the hell did that come from? I've never seen it before.'

'It's a mystery, isn't it, given that Luke's never been in this house. That's what you told us?'

'It's true,' Wickham said. 'Where did you find that? Maybe Sue dropped it.'

'Anything's possible.' Murrain took the evidence bag back, and then, with the air of a magician performing his climactic trick, he produced a second identical bag from behind his back. This bag contained a folded white sheet of paper, dog-eared at the corners. 'I won't ask you to play guessing games with this one, Mr Wickham. It's one of those letters that schools send out to their pupils. The kind that sit in their blazers or school-bags for months because they've forgotten to pass them on to their parents. This one was about a PTA meeting a couple of months ago.'

Wickham shook his head. 'I don't know what you're talking about.'

'The letter is addressed to Luke Myers. But I imagine you'd already guessed that. The real question is, once again, how it came to be in your possession.'

'I've never seen it before—'

'Both these items look to me as if they might have, say, fallen accidentally out of a school-bag, or perhaps a pocket.' He glanced at Ashworth, who was watching the exchange with an increasingly horrified expression.

'I think,' Murrain continued, 'that we need to continue this discussion in a more formal setting. We can do this the easy way or the hard way at this stage, Mr Wickham. I can invite you to be interviewed voluntarily under caution, or I can arrest you on suspicion of the abduction of Luke Myers.'

'I keep telling you that I've done nothing. I'll co-operate with you every step of the way if it helps prove that.'

'That's good, Mr Wickham. I'm sure it'll make all our lives much easier.'

CHAPTER TWENTY-EIGHT

Kate was preparing to leave the house for her meeting with Wickham when she heard the insistent buzzing of the mobile phone in her handbag. She fumbled for the handset but the call had already run to voicemail. As she'd half-expected, it was Wickham. 'Kate, really sorry but I'll have to postpone our get-together. Something rather major's come up. Will be in touch.' There was something odd about the tone of voice, she thought. As if he'd been trying to convey some meaning he couldn't express openly.

Second thoughts? Well, it seemed likely. Maybe he'd just thought through the implications of their meeting and felt it wasn't worth the risk. But she wanted to see him now. She pressed 'call back', but the phone went straight to voicemail. She cut the call without leaving a message, unsure what to say.

As she held the phone to her ear, she'd been half-watching the television screen as the lead news stories were summarised. Elizabeth had left one of the news channels running with the volume down, parading its images of the usual endless struggles in the Middle East, tensions between the US and Russia, some Government Minister pontificating about who knew what.

Suddenly she found herself staring at a landscape she recognised. The low sweep of the Pennines, a fast-flowing river under a stone bridge, the slow progress of a narrow boat over a canal. One of the nearby villages. The village where Wickham was living, she realised. The banner at the bottom of the screen read starkly: 'Breaking News: Missing Child.'

She fumbled for the remote control from the coffee table and thumbed up the volume, initially too loud so that Elizabeth and Jack, who were engaged in some board-game in the corner of the room, looked up startled. '...Now missing for over twenty-four hours. Police say that they are pursuing a number of leads but have no far released no further details. Local people have been organising their own searches of surrounding countryside, but a police spokesman today requested that any such activity should be conducted only under police direction.'

Kate felt a sinking in the pit of her stomach. The village where Kevin Wickham was living. 'Something rather major's come up.' It might mean anything but whatever it meant was unlikely to be good.

She cut the sound on the TV again, but remained staring at the screen. The reporter was interviewing locals who no doubt had little of substance to offer but were keen for their moment of fame.

Then she froze. For the briefest of seconds, as the TV reporter was interviewing two earnest-looking women who'd been involved in a search of nearby woodland, she'd caught sight of another face in the background. Just the merest glimpse of a figure passing the camera, then turning away hurriedly as if perhaps concerned about being caught on television. She told herself there was no way she could be certain, not in that short instant.

But she was.

Graeme.

He was there, somehow, for some reason, in that village. A village close to where she was living.

A village in which a child was missing.

***

Murrain and Milton had played nice and nasty cop in various permutations for most of the afternoon but made little progress. Wickham hadn't yet been arrested, but was being interviewed under caution as a potential suspect. He had, for the moment, declined legal representation. The police had agreed that Ashworth could sit in on the interview, assuming Wickham had no objection.

'You can't offer any explanation as to how those items came to be in your house?'

'I've told you. I've never seen them before. If they were in my house, I've no idea how.'

'Luke Myers has never entered your house.'

'I've only met Luke briefly, and that was at his mother's house. Nowhere else.'

'You can offer no explanation as to how that piece of his exercise book and that letter came to be in your house?'

'No.'

And so on, in endless circles. Murrain knew there'd come a point, probably fairly soon, when this became counter-productive. They'd have to make a decision about whether to arrest Wickham or to let him go. They probably had enough grounds to make an arrest, and in normal circumstances that would have been Murrain's preferred option. But Wickham's circumstances were anything but normal, and the consequences of placing him under arrest would be substantial. They needed something more than the flimsy circumstantial evidence currently in their possession.

They went backwards and forwards over his relationship with Sue Myers. They asked him about the night that Luke had first been reported missing. He repeated that he'd known nothing until Sue had called him. He'd stayed with her until Luke was found, and then, at her request, he'd joined her at the meeting with PC Wallace the next day. And, no, he hadn't encountered Luke in the street that night. Whoever Luke had seen, if he'd been talking to anyone, it wasn't him. He offered nothing.

Eventually, Murrain and Milton rose, and beckoned Ashworth to follow them out of the room. 'That's fine for the moment, Mr Wickham. We'll be back shortly.'

Outside, Murrain said: 'We're getting nowhere.'

'What's your feeling?' Milton said, glancing at Ashworth.

'I don't know. My instinct is that he's not our killer. But there's definitely something there.' Murrain was silent for a moment, trying to make sense of what felt almost like a host of distant voices howling almost out of earshot. Nothing. Nothing coherent, at any rate.

'What's the next step?' Ashworth intervened. 'Are you planning to arrest him?'

'That's the question, isn't it, Mr Ashworth? If he were anyone else, my inclination would be to do that. Turn the heat up a bit and see if we can get anything out of him. But if we do—'

'The proverbial will hit the fan.' Ashworth nodded grimly. 'I know.'

'And if we don't, and it turns out he is our man, we'll all be covered in the proverbial,' Murrain said. 'Welcome to our world, Mr Ashworth.' He turned to Milton. 'I may live to regret this. But I think we should let him go for the moment and keep an eye on him. If he has taken Luke, then we've got to hope that the boy's not been harmed so far. If Wickham's our man, he might lead us to him. If Luke is being held somewhere, keeping Wickham here won't help him. But get someone from our team to stick with him. Not just a uniform. Someone who knows what they're doing.'

That something was still buzzing away in the back of Murrain's head, like a fly incessantly hitting its head on a pane of glass. Some connection that wasn't quite being made. A dead and a missing child. Kevin Wickham. Another man lying crushed on a rail track. An attempted child snatching in Hazel Grove. A circuit that wasn't quite being completed.

Rubbing his temples, he picked up the phone and dialled Bert Wallace, who was working back in the MIR. She answered on the first ring.

'Bert,' he said. 'This thing with the Morrison woman in Hazel Grove. What the neighbour said. I'm not going to get free for a while, but I want you to go out there now. Talk to Mrs Morrison. Don't let her off the hook. Find out if there's anything in this gossip or not.'

'You really think it's relevant?'

'I think it might be. I don't know how or why, but I want it checked out.' He could sense the puzzlement at the other end of the line, and he allowed himself a faint smile. 'You know how it is, Bert. It's just a feeling.'

***

Kate had been clutching the phone in her hand and answered it on the first ring.

'It's Kevin. Kevin Wickham.'

'Are you OK? I've just seen the news—'

'It's a long story,' he said. 'I need to talk to you. Could you come over here? To my place, I mean.'

'Are you sure that's all right? I thought you preferred

to meet somewhere more anonymous.'

'Like I say, it's a long story. I'd rather not leave the house. And I think our meeting up is the last thing the authorities will care about just at the moment.'

'What do you mean?'

'The police were here,' he said. 'In connection with Luke's disappearance. I knew his mother. They took me in for questioning.'

'But surely they can't think—'

'What would you expect them to think? Of course, they're going to want to talk to me. They know the background now.' She could hear the bitterness in his voice. 'That's one reason I need to talk to you.'

'I'll come straight over,' she said. 'I need to talk to you too. I don't understand it, but I've a feeling we might want to talk about the same things.'

She arrived twenty minutes later. As he let her into the house, she glanced down the street. It was already late afternoon, and the sun was setting behind the woodland opposite. Further down the road, a figure was standing in the shadows. Probably a plain-clothes cop keeping an eye on Wickham and his movements. She could imagine they'd be checking her registration number even as she entered the house. It was madness being here, but it was too late for her to think about that now. And maybe it no longer mattered.

'You're OK?' she said. 'You're looking well.'

'As well as can be expected,' he said. 'I'll apologise in advance for the mess. The police aren't very domesticated.'

'So what's happened?' She'd been tempted to launch straight into her own story, but she recognised that Wickham needed to talk.

He ran through the whole story—meeting Sue, the

first incident with Luke, and then today's visit from the police.

'You've no idea how those items of Luke's might have got into your house?'

'None at all. Depends where the police found them, of course. They were playing that close to their chest. But if Sue had dropped them I don't see why I wouldn't have found them earlier.' He hesitated, as if unsure how to frame his next words. 'Do you think it's possible that I could have put them there without knowing? That I could be doing things I don't remember—'

She stared back at him, understanding the significance of what he was asking. 'I can't say that anything's impossible,' she said, finally. 'Do you believe that might have happened?'

'I don't know. I feel as if I don't know anything any more.'

'The thing is,' she said, 'something similar's happened to me. I've found something in my house that shouldn't be there.' She briefly recounted finding the photograph in her bedroom. 'Perhaps we're both going mad.' She regretted the flippancy of the words as soon as she'd spoken.

'That would be your considered professional opinion, would it?' He smiled, but there'd been no humour in his tone.

'I'm like you,' she said. 'I feel as if I don't know anything any more.' She paused, wanting to move the conversation on. 'You wanted to tell me about your dream. You felt you were getting nearer the truth.'

'That's exactly what I felt—feel. It seems so weird that it's happening at the same time as all this.'

'Jungian synchronicity?' she said, and this time she offered the smile.

'Who knows? But the dreams have been there for weeks, months. Probably longer than I realise. I told you about the clearing, the first sight of sunlight? And then, just last night—'

'Go on.'

'It went further. I knew, for the first time, that it wasn't me that had my hands on the child's throat. There was someone else. An adult. In the dream, I mean.'

'What do you think that means?'

'It could mean anything. I suppose it could mean that the adult me is finally taking responsibility for what I did as a child.'

'But you don't believe that?'

'No. I can't justify what I'm feeling. I can't give you any proof or evidence. But I think I'm finally remembering what really happened.'

'You might just be deluding yourself.'

'Of course I might. But then I'd be deluded, so I wouldn't know, would I?' He laughed. 'And people say psychology's a waste of time.'

'But you seem confident.'

'I still can't recall what happened that morning. But my feeling is that the dream is true. That I didn't kill Ben Wallasey. But that somehow, by accident or design, I ended up in the frame.'

'Whatever the truth, it sounds as if psychologically you're moving in the right direction.'

'And that sounds as if you're saying, very politely, that you don't believe me.'

'I believe what you're saying,' Kate said. 'But I don't know how much it means. You still don't remember anything more of what actually happened?'

'Not yet. But I feel as if it's slowly returning. Like

someone gradually turning up a dimmer switch.'

Kate sat back and swallowed the last of her coffee. The sun had almost set behind the row of houses, casting deeper shadows across the valley. The twilight was thickening. 'I haven't a clue how any of this knits together,' she said, finally. 'But I've got a few stories of my own to tell you. And, somehow, you seem to be at the heart of them.'

'Me?' Wickham blinked in surprise. 'Tell me.'

Slowly, with no real sense of where the narrative was going, Kate began to recount all the events that had happened since her last sessions with Wickham. The relationship with Graeme, and her growing distrust of him and his motives. Her own apparent breakdown after she'd thought Graeme had taken her son. The change in jobs and the move down here. Greg Perry. Tim Hulse. That last fateful conversation with Hulse, and what had happened afterwards. Her growing paranoia. Finally, as she realised how absurd the whole thing sounded, she told him about her apparent glimpse of Graeme on the television — somewhere here, now, in this village.

'You think I've not recovered from the breakdown,' she said. 'That I'm still out of my head. It sounds like that to me, now I've said it all out loud.'

'No.' He paused as if considering the question seriously. 'Look, you're more of an expert than I am, but you strike me as a very stable person. Even that supposed breakdown doesn't sound like much more than acute stress. You were already doing a very stressful job. You had the pressures of dealing with my case. You were afraid of this guy, Graeme. Afraid for your son. And no-one seemed ready to believe you. Enough to drive anyone over the edge.'

'You're being very kind,' she said. 'But you still think

I'm off my trolley.'

'I'm trying to look at it all objectively. No-one knows better than I do about the vagaries of memory. I don't know how or whether any of that stuff really does link together, or whether you're being paranoid.' He smiled. 'Just like you don't know whether I'm right about my memory coming back. But a lot of what you've told me is substantive enough.'

'What do you remember about the Youth Offenders' place? Somehow, we keep coming back to that.'

Wickham involuntarily rubbed his hands across his face as if the memories were physically painful. 'Jesus, that place. It was my worst time inside. The only really bad time I had, to be honest.'

'In what way?'

'In every way. The staff. The other prisoners. Things kicking off every ten minutes because some spotty little tosser has too much testosterone gushing through him. You name it. I'd been in a special unit up to that point, I guess because of the notoriety of the case. I hadn't realised how much I'd been sheltered.'

'Why did they take you out of the special unit? I'd have thought in a case like yours it wouldn't be unusual to spend most of your sentence there. At least up to twenty-one.'

'Who knows? Someone thought it was the right decision. I suppose, looking back, that's an interesting question in itself. They supposedly gave me anonymity — at least, they'd given me a false name to use, though no other real preparation — but someone must have known or guessed. I argued against the decision for a while, but I was too young and nobody on the outside, not even my dad, was very keen on fighting my corner.' She could see he was tracking back through his memories. 'But the place was awful. You'll have looked back at my file. There was a period, just one, when I stopped being a model prisoner. It was while I was there, and it was because I had no choice.'

'Why?'

'Because some bastard, or maybe more than one bastard, had it in for me. Really had it in for me. It wasn't something I'd been used to. But I was attacked three, four times in the first few weeks. I wasn't even sure who was behind it. But it wasn't just the stupid scrotes who were putting the boot in. It felt organised. Suddenly, for whatever reason, there'd be no staff around. It was like someone was trying to take me out.'

'How did you get through it?'

Wickham shrugged, mock modestly. 'I learned to look after myself. I don't just mean that I fought back, though I did that too. Bullying in prison's like bullying anywhere else. They pick on the weak and the vulnerable. If you show you're neither of those things, they eventually move on. I was smart enough to make the right friends, too. Prison is about cliques and alliances. I learned fast. You get the right people on your side, and the rest don't take you on.'

'What about the staff? What were they like?'

'I remember your husband,' he said, finally. 'Mr McCarthy.' He smiled. 'I'd never made the connection, obviously. But he was one of the good guys. I'm not just saying that. There weren't many of them in there, so you tended to remember them. He tried his best to look after me. Not just me. Everyone. Not in a soft way, but, you know, professionally. Tried to do his job like it ought to be done. He actually used to talk to me. Proper conversations. There weren't many did that. The others—well, they were a mixed bunch, of course, but most of them tend to blur into one mass of unpleasant brutality, to be honest. A lot of them had become institutionalised themselves. Some of them just enjoyed exploiting the youngsters' vulnerability.'

'You mean—?'

'I mean in every way. Bullying, mostly. But in some cases sexually as well. There were various scandals that never saw the light of day.'

'Do you have any recollection of Greg Perry or Graeme Ellis? From your days in the YOI, I mean.'

'When I saw Perry at the Open, I knew I'd come across him before but couldn't remember where. He was relatively senior so I'd only encountered him once or twice. I don't have any real memory of Ellis. But, as I say, a lot of the officers just tended to blur into one. You just knew there were a lot of unpleasant bastards around. There were a few of them only too happy to turn a blind eye when someone was having a go at me.' He frowned. 'But I do remember Ellis's name. That's because, later on, there was some gossip about him. That he'd got the boot for some reason. Sexual assault was the word on the landings, but then it would be. That was usually the claim whenever any officer moved on.'

'That was what Tim reckoned, too.'

'It would tie in with your fears about him,' Wickham said. 'Maybe that time there was fire as well as smoke.'

'It's not getting us very far, this, is it?' she said, after a pause. 'I'd somehow expected some kind of alchemy, I suppose. That we'd share what we each know, and somehow all the pieces would fit together and it would all make sense. But we're in the same place as before.'

'What about this last thing?' Wickham said. 'You reckoned you spotted this guy Ellis on TV?'

She paused before responding, asking herself if she

really could be sure it had been Graeme she'd seen in that instant on the television screen. But she had no doubt that it was him. 'I'm sure of it,' she said, finally. 'It was him.'

'What would he be doing round here?'

'Christ knows. That was always one of the problems with Graeme. You never really knew what he was up to. One of those ducking and diving types. Always cagey about his work. Cagey even about where he lived. He had some flat up north when I knew him. He took me back there a few times, but it gave me no sense of who he was. It felt like an anonymous rental. He was something in import-export, he said, so he was always travelling. Supposedly.' It had all sounded reasonable at the time, even after she'd started to become suspicious of Graeme. Now she wondered how she could ever had believed any of it.

'Do you have any pictures of him? It's a long shot, but if he's living round here now, I might recognise him.'

'Funnily enough, I do,' she said. She wasn't a great one for taking photographs, and Graeme had seemed almost psychotically camera-shy. But she had a couple of pictures of Jack that had Graeme caught in the background. She hadn't deleted them, even she'd tried to remove all other traces of Graeme from her life, because she'd wanted to keep the images of Jack. She pulled the phone from her handbag and flicked through to the images.

'That's him.' She slid the phone across the table to Wickham.

Wickham peered at the screen. He said nothing for a long moment, then he looked up at Kate. 'That's not Graeme Ellis,' he said. 'Or not only Graeme Ellis. I know exactly who that is.'

CHAPTER TWENTY-NINE

Mrs Morrison had shooed Charlie upstairs to play on his computer, and now sat on the sofa, her body contorted as if in pain, opposite Bert Wallace.

'I don't know why you want to talk to us,' she said. 'Charlie's told you everything he could.'

Wallace tapped gently on her notebook with her pencil. 'It's not Charlie I want to talk you, Mrs Morrison. It's you.'

'Me? There's nothing I can tell you.'

Wallace had known that her presence was unwelcome from the moment Mrs Morrison had opened the front door. There had been no offer of coffee this time, and Wallace had had the impression that Mrs Morrison simply wanted her out of the house as quickly as possible.

Wallace glanced at the clock on the mantelpiece. 'What time does you husband usually get back from work, Mrs Morrison.'

'I don't—' She stopped, unsure of her ground. 'About five thirty. But I don't—'

'Then we've got a bit of time. I'll try to be gone before your husband gets home.'

'I don't understand.' But the obvious relief in Mrs Morrison's eyes told Wallace everything she needed to know. She felt confident in pushing this harder now.

'I think you do understand, Mrs Morrison. I think there's been something you've not told us.'

'I don't—'

'Let's not play games. We're conducting a murder enquiry. We're currently searching for a second missing child. If you're withholding information that's pertinent to our investigations—' Wallace left the consequence unstated, but she could see that the point had struck home.

'But it's not relevant—' Mrs Morrison stopped, conscious that she'd already said too much.

'What is it you've not been telling us, Mrs Morrison?'

There was no immediate response, but Wallace was content to let the silence build. She tapped gently and rhythmically on her notebook. Finally, Mrs Morrison said: 'My husband doesn't need to know, does he?'

'Until I know what the information is, I can't offer you any guarantees, Mrs Morrison. But we won't make anything public unless we need to.'

'It's nothing,' Mrs Morrison said. 'It's really nothing. But, well, it's embarrassing—'

'Go on.' Wallace could see now that Mrs Morrison wanted to talk, wanted to get something off her chest. She would need little more than encouragement.

'I should have known better. I don't know what I was thinking—'

'Start from the beginning, Mrs Morrison. That may be easiest.'

'I had—' She stopped. 'Well, it was hardly even an affair. Not even a fling. It was just stupid. This man was pestering me for ages. Very persuasive type. Wouldn't take no for an answer. And, well, he was flattering and he played to my ego.' There were tears in her eyes now and for a moment Wallace thought she would begin crying. 'Talked to me in a way that my husband had forgotten.' She shrugged and smiled. 'You know?'

'I can imagine,' Wallace said.

'I fended him off for ages, but then eventually—'

'This is recent?'

'The last couple of months. He's been coming here in the daytime when my husband's at work. Not often. Just three or fours times. But often enough.' She dropped her head into her hands, as if thinking about what she'd just said. Then she looked back up at Wallace. 'How did you know?'

It was Wallace's turn to shrug. 'We didn't. My colleagues just sensed that there was something you weren't telling them.' There was no point in stirring up any bad blood with the nosy neighbour. The interesting question, she thought, was why Mrs Morrison had been so anxious about her secret when Murrain and Milton had spoken to her. 'The day this incident happened with your son—'

Mrs Morrison nodded. 'He'd been here earlier. We'd been, well, you know. He'd stayed a bit longer than we intended.' She offered a weak smile. 'Lost track of the time. He'd not been gone long when Charlie arrived home.'

'So when my colleagues spoke to you—?'

'I just thought it was all bound to come out. I couldn't bear it. I've been so stupid.'

'And when Charlie said he thought the man looked like someone he'd seen leaving the house—?'

Mrs Morrison was staring at her with dead eyes. 'Yes, it's possible. The first time he came to see me at home he was leaving just before Charlie arrived home. He was just visiting that day. Just came to see how I was, he reckoned. Nothing had happened, you understand?' She spoke as if it were vital that Wallace accepted this point.

'I'm not sure I do see exactly, Mrs Morrison. Who is this man?'

Mrs Morrison took a breath. 'This doesn't need to come out, does it? I mean, my husband doesn't—'

'I can't make any promises. It depends on how pertinent this is to our investigations. But we'll do our best to handle this discreetly.'

Mrs Morrison nodded. 'It started with my mother, you see. She died last year. She'd been in a care home for the last couple of years. Alzheimer's. After dad died, it just got to the point where we couldn't take care of her properly any more—'

'And this man?' Wallace prompted.

'I met him at the care home. He was very solicitous—'

I bet he was, Wallace thought. 'This was after your mother died?'

'Well, I met him before that, you understand. He's the manager or owner, I'm not sure which. He was very thoughtful and supportive when mum was ill.' She allowed herself a thin smile. 'More than my husband was. That was partly the point. Then after she died— well, he was helpful in sorting out all the arrangements. I thought he just wanted to help, you know?'

Wallace didn't know, but she could easily imagine. Just as she could imagine the kind of man who might prey on a woman when she was at her most vulnerable. 'I understand. And one thing led to another?'

'I suppose. He turned up here, a few weeks later. Just wanted to see how I was bearing up, he said. And he wanted to know how Charlie was coping—'

'Charlie?'

'Yes, you know. Losing his gran and all that. Truth was, I think, Charlie was really a bit young to take it in. But, you know, I just felt that there was someone who was genuinely interested in us. In me.'

Yes, Wallace thought, that's generally how these things are worked. She leaned forward. 'I'm afraid we will have to talk to this man, Mrs Morrison. Especially after what Charlie told my colleagues.'

'Yes. Yes, I understand.'

'We'll need his contact details.'

Mrs Morrison nodded. 'Yes, of course. His name's Brody,' she said. 'Finlan Brody.'

***

'Finlan Brody,' Wickham said. 'Finlan fucking Brody.' He flicked backwards and forwards between the two images. The same face from two slightly different angles.

'Who's Finlan Brody?'

'Local noise. Runs the retirement home, up the hill. Jesus.' It was clear that some other thought had just struck him.

'Go on.'

'He was the one introduced me to Sue Myers in the first place. He runs some local business group. Meet in the pub on Friday nights. I was encouraged to go along. Ended up sitting next to Sue—'

'Sounds not a million miles from how I met Graeme. Funny that.' She took the phone from him, staring at the screen herself. 'You're sure it's him?'

'Pretty certain,' Wickham said. 'It's one of those images that make you do a double-take because it looks like it should be a different person. The clothes, the whole style looks different. But the face is the same. It took me a moment, because I was thinking: 'Where the hell do I know that face?' I couldn't connect it with Brody at first.'

In the picture Graeme was dressed, as he usually was, in relatively formal attire. A dark grey business suit, incongruous in the context. The only concession to informality was the unusual absence of a tie. Otherwise, that was how Graeme always dressed.

She could sense that some other thought was troubling Wickham. 'What is it?'

'Brody,' he said. 'I've just realised. He's been in here. A couple of days back. Popped in for a chat. Supposedly some work he was pushing in my direction. Ran into the police on his way out, funnily enough.'

'You think he could have planted those things of Luke's?'

'I don't see how else they could have got in here. Brody was the one who claimed to have found Luke when he went missing that first time. He could have got stuff out of Luke's schoolbag then, maybe. It was Brody who claimed Luke had been scared by someone in a van. No-one else saw it. As far as I know, no-one ever asked Luke to confirm it. The WPC who came wanted to talk to Luke, but Sue wasn't keen. Luke was very vague about the whole thing and nobody thought it was worth pursuing.'

'If Brody really is Graeme, he could probably have persuaded Luke it had happened anyway,' Kate said. 'Graeme could persuade you night was day. Christ, we need to do something.'

Wickham fumbled in his pocket for the business card Murrain had given him. 'First thing we do is tell the police.'

'You think they'll believe it?'

'I don't know. I think this guy Murrain might, or at least be prepared to listen to us. They've nothing much to lose by following it up.'

'As long as they do it quickly.'

'If they don't do something, we do. But we tell them first, OK?'

***

'Finlan Brody?' Murrain said, disbelievingly.

'The very same. The guy we met at Wickham's.'

The headache felt almost as if needles were being drive into his temples. He could almost hear the crackle of electricity. 'And she admitted this?'

'Eventually,' Bert Wallace said. 'Denied everything to start with. So I reminded her we were conducting a murder enquiry and said we'd take a dim view of anyone withholding what might be relevant information.'

'And that did the trick?' Murrain could envisage exactly how Wallace would have handled the conversation. He didn't imagine Mrs Morrison would have felt she was left with much choice.

'Eventually. Didn't want her husband to know. I said I couldn't make any promises.'

'Quite right. We'll have a job keeping it quiet if Brody's involvement really is significant,' Murrain observed. 'How did she meet him?'

'Her mother was in the residential home. Suffered from Alzheimer's. She reckons Brody was very—I think "solicitous" was her word.'

'I bet he was. Did she ever take her son over there?'

'Sometimes. School holidays and the like. She reckons Brody was keen to know how Charlie was coping with his gran's death, that kind of thing. Very caring. But, when I probed her a bit about what Brody had asked, it sounded to me like he might have weaselled out a lot of stuff about Charlie. What his daily routine was. How he got home from school, that sort of thing.'

Murrain sat back, drumming his fingers on the table. For a moment, as Wallace had been speaking, he'd almost seen something, some image behind his eyes. A flicker in an electrical storm. 'Well,' he said, 'this is certainly an interesting coincidence.'

Wallace was smiling. 'And I've another one for you.'

'Go on.'

'It occurred to me to do a bit of checking up. I phoned up the residential home and had a discreet conversation with one of their admin people. It turns out that Mrs Morrison isn't the only one who had a relative in Brody's place. Ethan Dunn's grandfather's was in there, too, until he died a couple of months back. His mother was another regular visitor.'

Murrain always struggled to find the language to describe his feelings. Now, the tenor of his headache had changed. His mind felt like the air on a humid summer's evening, the pressure slowly building as the weather prepares to break. This wasn't the end, he thought. More was coming.

He was about to speak when his mobile buzzed on the desk. He glanced at the screen then thumbed the call button. 'Yes?'

'It's Kevin Wickham. I've something to tell you.'

More to come. Even sooner than he'd expected. 'Is this a confession?'

'Not from me,' Wickham said. 'I'm phoning about Finlan Brody. You know, the guy at the care home.'

There was a long pause. 'Well, talk of the devil,' Murrain said, finally. He raised an eyebrow to Wallace who was listening intently to the conversation. 'Now the coincidences really are starting to pile up. As it happens, I've just been talking about Mr Brody for quite another reason. What can you tell me?'

'That he's not Finlan Brody, for a start. Or not only Finlan Brody. He's also known as Graeme Ellis. And he has a history.'

Murrain listened as Wickham recounted what Forester had told him. 'And you're sure, are you? That Brody and Ellis are one and the same?'

'As sure as I can be,' Wickham said. 'They're not particularly clear photographs of him, but I'd swear it's the same guy.'

'OK. I think we need to go and talk to Mr Brody. But if you're yanking my chain, Wickham, you'll be back behind bars whatever happens. You understand that?'

'Clearly. All I want to do is help you find Luke before it's too late.'

'Then we're of one mind.'

Murrain ended the call and sat for a moment, staring at nothing. As he'd been talking to Wickham, he'd sensed the image again. Two figures. An adult and a child. Just two shapes in an intermittent darkness. He blinked, as if returning to consciousness.

'You've done brilliantly, Bert,' he said, finally, his tone suggesting he'd only just remembered her presence. 'Go and see if you can dig anything more up on Brody. And do a check on this Graeme Ellis, too. Anything, any kind of record. Maybe check with the Prison Service as well.' He paused, his brain making another half-connection. Another flicker of light in the darkness. 'That guy Hulse. The railway line death. He worked for the Prison Service, too, didn't he?'

'Think so,' Wallace said. 'Though I've not been involved. Is that likely to be relevant?'

'God knows,' Murrain said. 'At least I hope he does. Because I sure as hell don't. OK, Bert. You go and dig whatever dirt you can on our friend Brody a.k.a. Ellis. And Joe and I will go and pay him a visit.'

***

By the time Murrain and Milton left the MIR, it was almost dark and the weather was beginning to turn. The wind was growing stronger and there was a first scattering of rain. They took Milton's car and headed down through the village towards the edge of the moors. The residential home was harder to find in the murky evening, set back among the trees in an unlit stretch of road. Finally, Murrain spotted the illuminated sign and signalled for Milton to turn into the car park. Beyond the squat building, there was open moorland, a bleak empty space with only a few distant lights visible.

The receptionist looked up in surprise as they entered, Murrain waving his warrant card. 'We need to see Mr Brody,' he said. 'Urgently.'

She blinked. 'I'm afraid you've just missed him. Half an hour or so.'

'Do you know where he's gone?'

'I don't—' She stopped, her expression confused, on the edge of tears. 'He's been in a state all afternoon. Said something had gone wrong, but tore me off a strip when I asked if there was anything I could do. He's not usually like that—'

Murrain turned to Milton. 'Maybe he got wind of Bert's call here.'

'Or maybe the Morrison woman contacted him and told him we'd become interested.'

'And you've no clue as to where he might have been heading?' Murrain said to the receptionist. 'Could he be heading home?'

She shook her head. 'He lives here. Has a self-contained flat at the back. He just went off in the van. Didn't say a word.'

'Van?'

'There's a van belongs to the home. We use it to get stuff from the cash-and-carry mainly. He's been in and out to it all afternoon.'

Murrain exchanged a glance with Milton. 'Get an alert out on this van. I'll check Brody's office and meet you outside. I don't think we can afford to waste time.'

When Murrain emerged from the building some time later, Milton was waiting by the entrance, speaking urgently into his mobile phone. He finished the call and gestured across the car-park. 'We've got company.'

Murrain squinted into the darkness. 'Who the hell's that?' A car had been parked next to their own, and two silhouetted figures were tramping towards them across the gravel.

'Mr Murrain—'

'What the hell are you doing here, Wickham?'

Kevin Wickham blinked at the floodlights illuminating the exterior of the building. 'I'm sorry. We just thought that, if Brody starts denying things, it might speed things if he were to meet Kate here. She'll confirm who he is. She knew him as Ellis.'

'It's academic anyway for the moment,' Murrain said. 'Brody's not here. Seems we've just missed him.' He looked back at Milton. 'Nothing much in the office. Though it looks as if he might have left hurriedly. His flat was locked up but they had a spare set of keys. Nothing untoward in there as far as I could see. You've got the alert out?'

Milton nodded. 'Receptionist had a note of the van reg, luckily.'

'Where is he?' Kate asked. She was looking past the two police officers, through the brightly-lit reception.

'Supposedly drove off hurriedly about an hour ago.'

'You believe us, then?' Kate said.

Murrain looked at her in apparent surprise. 'I think I've believed Mr Wickham here from the start. Just an instinct. But as it happens we'd just become interested in Mr Brody for another reason.'

'You think he's got Luke with him?' Wickham asked.

'It's possible. There's nowhere here than he could be concealed without the staff being aware. There's not a lot more we can do till we get a sighting of the vehicle.'

Wickham looked past him at the open moorland. 'They'll take some finding if they're out there somewhere.' None of them wanted to raise the question of whether Luke was likely still to be unharmed. They could do no more than hope for the best.

'Receptionist reckons he went down towards the village,' Murrain said. 'But that doesn't get us very far. He could be heading towards Manchester or the other way up into the Pennies. Or, quite frankly, anywhere.'

Kate was staring into the darkness, as if seeing something that was invisible to the rest of them. 'I've an idea,' she said, speaking more to herself than the others.

Murrain was watching her. 'Go on.'

'I was thinking about how those items of Luke's got into Kevin's house. It seemed inexplicable, until we realised that Brody had been in there. Brody could have taken them from Luke when he took him in that first time, and then left them when he visited Kevin—'

'And?'

'Similar things have happened to me. I found things in my house that shouldn't have been there. I had a sense that Graeme had been in there. I thought I was just being paranoid. But it's just struck me. Only one person could have let him know where I was living now. Only one person had a spare copy of my keys.' She stopped, as if thinking through the implications. 'My mother.'

Murrain was watching her carefully, as if he could read her thoughts in her expression. 'You really think that your mother might have given Brody access to your house?' The words were sceptical, but the tone less so. Murrain could feel the rising pulse that suggested there was something in what Forester was saying.

'I don't know. It's just a feeling. I thought I'd finally persuaded my mother I wanted nothing more to do with Graeme, especially after my breakdown. But he was capable of anything. What if somehow he still managed to talk her round? What if he'd somehow persuaded her that he was going to win me back, if only she'd help him? I know what he was like. He could make you believe whatever he wanted. It's partly about control with him. Game playing. He'd want to set it up so that he could walk into my house whenever he wanted. Do enough to disconcert me. Make me doubt my own judgement. Maybe even get access to Jack whenever he liked—' She was looking at Murrain with something close to panic in her eyes. 'He could be down there now. With my son. Who's the same age as Luke.' She spun round and fixed her eyes on Wickham. 'Who's the same age as the child that Kevin was supposed to have killed all those years ago.'

'But there's no reason to think—' Milton began.

'I don't pretend I'm entirely following this,' Murrain interrupted, 'but I'm feeling that we should check it out.' As she'd been speaking, he'd had that same flash of an image. The sudden glare of a mental flashbulb. Three figures, one large, two small.

'*Please*,' Kate begged. 'I'm probably making a complete fool of myself. But if I'm not—'

'OK,' Murrain said. He turned to Milton, who looked as if he was about to intervene. 'Instinct, Joe, instinct. That and the fact that we don't have a clue what else to do next anyway. We've nothing to lose.'

***

They left Kate's car parked outside Brody's house and headed down in the police vehicle, Milton driving. The road through the village was narrow, with the rows of parked cars allowing only a single line of traffic through the centre. Milton, who'd long ago accepted the need to go with the flow of his boss's eccentricities, didn't stint on turning on the siren and lights whenever the conditions demanded. Fifteen minutes later they were approaching the turn off past the canal that led to Kate's house.

He pulled into Kate's driveway, and the four of them scrambled out. The house was ablaze with light, every window uncurtained, every room lit, but there was no other sign of life. The wind was booming along the canal, the rain coming down harder.

Murrain peered around him, then pointed. 'There.' There was a dark-coloured van parked further along the street. 'Is that Brody's?'

Milton moved to check the registration and then nodded.

'Instinct,' Murrain said to Kate. 'Whatever it means, it looks like you were right.'

'I wanted to be wrong,' she said. '*Shit.*'

Murrain gestured for Kate and Wickham to stand back while he and Milton approached the front door. Kate knew he was being sensible—none of them knew what they might find in there, and Milton had already called for back up—but she wanted to push past and rush in there herself. The door was ajar, light streaming from the hallway out on to the wet path.

Murrain stepped slowly inside, Milton a step behind. The house was silent, except for the rattle of rain against the window, the occasional roar of the wind gusting down the chimneys. The interior felt chilly and a breeze touched his cheek as he stepped into the hallway. He paused momentarily to touch the hall radiator and check that the central heating was on. The cold was coming from elsewhere.

With Milton still close behind, he stepped into the hallway and listened. Nothing. He gestured to Milton to check the living and dining rooms while he continued into the kitchen. The downstairs rooms were deserted. The back door, like the front, was ajar—the source of the chill breeze blowing through the house. Murrain opened it and peered briefly out, but could see nothing. 'Let's check upstairs first, then we'll try outside.'

It took them only a few more minutes to confirm the upper floor of the house was an empty as the downstairs. Jack's room looked undisturbed, with no sign that he or anyone else had been in there since the morning.

Murrain gestured for Kate and Wickham to join them in the hallway. 'Wait here,' he said. He and Milton made their way back through the kitchen, Milton pulling a heavy flashlight from the inner pocket of his overcoat.

Murrain turned off the kitchen light and allowed a few moments for their eyes to adjust to the darkness. Then Milton shone the torch beam around the small rear garden. At first, both officers thought that the garden was as deserted as the house. It was only a small plot, given mostly to lawn, with a couple of flower beds and a few small bushes.

'There,' Murrain said, suddenly. 'What's that?' He took Milton's wrist and guided the beam slowly back. The largest of the garden's bushes stood alongside the far corner of the house to the left of where Murrain and Milton were standing. When the beam had first touched it, Murrain had thought the odd shape below the bush was simply an effect of shadows. But it hadn't looked right. Now, as Milton moved the beam up and down, he saw that the patch of darkness was something else, something large, below and behind the bush.

The two officers stepped out into the damp air. The garden was sheltered from the worst of the wind, but the rain was coming down heavily now. Milton pulled back the foliage and both men peered forward as he shone the torch into the cavity behind.

CHAPTER THIRTY

It was an elderly woman, her body twisted, her white blouse soaked with blood. With another flick of the torch-beam, Milton illuminated the large kitchen knife protruding from her stomach. Murrain leaned down and checked the pulse, but it was clear they were already much too late. 'Christ,' he said. 'Who could do that?'

'Somebody not in their right mind,' Murrain said. 'The more important question is: where the hell are they?'

They made their way back into the house and, while Milton phoned for back-up and an ambulance, Murrain ushered Kate and Wickham back into the hallway. 'I'm afraid it's your mother,' he said, briefly. 'We're too late to help her. I'm very sorry.'

Kate raised a hand to her mouth as if she were holding back a scream. 'Oh, Jesus—' She made a move to push past Murrain, but he held her firmly by the shoulder. 'Please don't touch anything. All of this is a crime scene now. There's no sign of your son out there.'

'But where is he?' Kate was looking desperate now. 'What the hell's happened to Brody?'

'That's what we need to find out,' Murrain said. 'I want you both to stay right here. Don't move till back-up gets here.' He stepped out of the front door and peered into the darkness. Other than the rhythmic swaying of the trees, there was no sign of movement. As he turned to re-enter the house, Kate, her face drained white, pushed unexpectedly past him and hurried to the front gate. 'Jack! Where are you? Jack!' Her voice was loud but almost immediately whipped away by the wind.

Murrain called after her, but before he could move she was already out of the garden and heading along the canal. He knew he should catch up with her, stop her and insist she return to the house. But he also knew, in his heart, that she was right. He could feel it, that familiar insistent buzzing, telling him they needed to act. Whatever was happening here, every second was vital. There was no point in waiting for a back-up team to arrive if all they found were more bodies.

Instinct. It was Murrain's joke, the line he often used to deflect attention from his working methods. But, at a moment like this, he had nothing else. He waited a moment longer, then, leaving Milton with Wickham, he followed Kate out into the darkness.

***

Kate paused as she reached the canal-side. She didn't know what had happened back at the house. But she knew it was Brody she was looking for. He had Jack. He had Luke. Kate didn't know why or where, but she knew it was true.

Where would he have gone, if he wasn't in the house. He'd know the area, know that the road to the left led down into the village centre, and he would have wanted to avoid that. Kate's best guess was that he would have headed along the canal, but which way?

The canal path to the right led to a brightly-lit pub, a favourite of the narrow-boat users, visible once you walked a few yards up the tow-path. The path to the left led into darkness and, fairly soon, open country. Another quarter of a mile or so the canal descended through a flight of locks. Then you reached the river valley, which the canal crossed through a dramatic aqueduct, a testimony to the remarkable ambition of the Victorian era.

That way, it had to be that way.

She stumbled along the muddy tow-path, her eyes gradually adjusting to the darkness. Even away from the residential parts of the village, the blackness was far from complete, low clouds reflecting the pale orange glow of the distant Manchester lights. She made her way cautiously down past the endless locks, trying not to lose her footing on the uneven ground. She should have stopped to find herself a torch, but had been afraid that Murrain would try to stop her. She still couldn't understand why he hadn't.

After a few hundred yards the ground levelled and she was able to make her way more easily along the path. The canal was a black trench to her right, the water invisible in the darkness. To her right, there were stone walls, then undergrowth, a patch of woodland, patchy darkness.

Suddenly she was at the edge of the valley, the land falling away on both sides, the narrow stone ramparts of the aqueduct stretched out ahead. She was struck by the emptiness and distance, the wind buffeting her face and body. Across the valley she could see the scatterings of light from farm buildings and houses, and beyond that the denser glow of a neighbouring village.

She'd been for walks down here once or twice at weekends, and even in the calm of a sunlit afternoon the place had terrified her. She had no head for heights, and something about the sheer drop on each side of the aqueduct combined with the blackness of the canal itself had felt oddly unnerving. She'd tried to walk along the tow-path but it had felt like walking a tight-rope and she hadn't made it more than a quarter of the way along before turning back. The thought of crossing the aqueduct in the rain-soaked night seemed unbearable.

There was something out along the aqueduct, though. In the windy darkness, at first it was nothing more than a lighter blur, a cluster of pale shapes by the canal.

She took a few tentative steps out on to the stone pathway, feeling the tight clutch of fear in her stomach. The wind was even stronger now, blasting past her ears, whipping the breath from her mouth. She walked another ten or fifteen yards, her hand grasping tightly to the stone wall which felt much too low for its purpose. She felt as if, at any moment, the gale might pick her up bodily and toss her over the parapet into the emptiness below.

Then the blurred shape ahead began to make sense, and the breath was wrenched from her body for quite another reason.

There were three of them. Three pale bodies in the darkness.

Three figures.

Three figures perched like birds on a telegraph wire, sitting on the stone wall of the aqueduct, as casually as if they were sightseers admiring the view.

One larger figure in the centre, two smaller ones on each side. A parody of a loving family group.

Brody. Luke. And Jack.

Sitting on the edge of the aqueduct, nothing between them and the sheer drop down to the valley floor below.

Any fear Kate felt for her own safety had dissolved as soon as she realised what she was seeing. Now, she felt nothing but sheer terror for Jack and for Luke.

She glanced back, hoping that, somehow, help might be at hand but she could see nothing. Somewhere in the distance she thought she detected the flicker of a blue light, but if back-up had finally arrived it was much too far away to help her now. She turned back and focused intently on the three figures, motionless on the edge of the wall.

As she did so, the blasting wind unexpectedly dropped and the night fell eerily silent, as if the elements themselves were holding their breath. In the sudden quiet, Kate became uncomfortably aware of her own movements, the sounds as her feet crunched on the gravel, her hand rasped against the wall.

Finally, Kate was close enough to hear Brody's voice. He was speaking softly, the voice of a kindly uncle telling a bedtime story to children slowly drifting into sleep, though she could make out none of the words. Just a steady rhythmic monotone.

Afterwards, Kate couldn't be sure what happened. Her memory had blurred the detail, the moments too terrifying to recall. Brody had continued speaking in the same gentle unvarying voice, but she had seen or sensed some movement, some tremor in his body that she knew meant the moment had come. That he was about to drop into that pitiless void.

She had thrown herself forward instinctively, making a grab for Jack's coat. For an awful moment, she couldn't get a grip of the thick fabric and thought Brody was going to drag the small body with her. Then, suddenly, mercifully, she was holding Jack tight, dragging him back from the wall, pulling him down with her into the safe shelter of the stonework. She had no idea how Brody had managed to keep the boy so calm while she had sat with him on the wall. Now, he was sobbing, choking back a scream.

It was only then she remembered Luke.

There was nothing she could have done, she told herself, her head buried in the warmth of Jack's back. She'd had time to grab only one of the boys, and of course, without even considering the matter, she'd reached for her own son. No-one could blame her for that.

But she had killed Luke. She had sent him to his death.

Her arms still wrapped around Jack's sobbing body, she lifted her head. Murrain was prone on the path beside her, his own arms wound in the same way around Luke's crying figure.

'Instinct,' Murrain said, breathlessly. 'It's all I have.'

CHAPTER THIRTY-ONE

'If you think you need some kind of counselling,' Murrain said, slowly, stirring his coffee, 'I'm sure we can organise it. I can't imagine what sort of impact all this must have had.'

Kate Forester was sitting on the sofa, her body clenched as if she were wary of being physically struck. 'I don't think I'm even at that stage. I just feel numb.'

'I'm not surprised,' Murrain said. 'We're still struggling to work it out.' He sat in silence for a few moments. He felt that Kate wanted to talk and he was content to let her. It seemed to be helping her, and it was helping him to make sense of what was emerging. And, if he was honest, he had his own traumas to work through. Small beer compared with what Kate had faced, but troubling enough.

'Brody killed that boy,' she said, finally. 'He killed that boy in the holiday centre, and they let Kevin take the blame—' She trailed off, for a moment.

'I'm not sure we'll ever prove it definitively, but it looks that way,' Murrain said. 'We've confirmed that they were both working there at the time—Graeme Ellis and your colleague Gregory Perry. Two of a kind. A nasty kind, by all accounts. It was just a student job for them but probably a good place to find their young victims. It doesn't even seem to have been a sexual thing. Not primarily, anyway.' He shrugged. 'You probably understand this kind of stuff better than I do. It seems to have been about humiliation. Control, like you said. It looks as if there were some complaints about their behaviour at the time, but nothing was done. There's no way now of knowing exactly what happened with Ben Wallasey. Some game that went too far, presumably. No-one made the connection later but Perry was actually called as a witness at the trial. He was one of those who'd turned up, along with a couple of other convenient witnesses, and supposedly found Wickham with the dead boy.'

She shuddered. 'Greg knew Ellis all the time. Knew everything about Graeme and Kevin.' She stopped. 'But how come they both ended up in the Service. That can't have been premeditated, surely?' Her tone suggested she'd been worrying at these issues, but hadn't resolved them.

Murrain wondered quite how far her thinking had so far taken her. 'I think it was probably just coincidence at first,' he said. 'Perry was the bright one. He'd applied to the Prison Service as a fast-track governor after university. I don't know what his motives were or whether it was accident or design he ended up working in the YOI, but I'm guessing it suited his purposes. They were advertising for officers. Ellis had dropped out of university, but he applied for the officer role and got the job, maybe with Perry's help. Surprised they passed all the security checks, but I guess things weren't as rigorous in those days. And neither had any kind of record. Like I say, my impression is that Perry was the smarter of the two—he seems to have been adept at digging himself out of trouble at least—but Ellis was maybe nastier and more manipulative. And, I suspect, less in control of his own urges.'

'But why pursue Kevin after all those years?'

'I imagine they came across Kevin by accident initially. Perry would have recognised him, whatever name he was using. I imagine Perry saw him as a vulnerability, a loose end they'd not tied up. They were safe as long as Kevin didn't recall what had happened that day. Kevin was attacked in the YOI and reckons it was set up. I think Perry and Ellis instigated that, but maybe it didn't go the way they'd planned. After that, Kevin became smarter and probably the authorities realised he needed to be better protected. That was probably their last chance to deal with it that way.'

There was another silence. 'What about Ryan?' she said.

'Something else we'll never prove, I'm afraid. From what I understand from Kevin, he talked to Ryan more openly than he had to any other officer.'

She smiled faintly. 'That was Ryan. But Kevin wouldn't have been able to tell him anything.'

'I imagine not,' Murrain said. 'But Perry and Ellis might have been concerned at anyone getting close to Kevin.'

'You really think they might have silenced Ryan for that?'

'Probably not in itself, no. But I suspect he was gathering evidence on other activities that Ellis and Perry were up to. From what I understand, Ellis was dismissed subsequently for "inappropriate behaviour". Looks like Perry was smarter and came away with his record unblemished.'

'That was what Tim Hulse implied,' she said. 'And he shafted Tim later for similar reasons. You think they did the same to Tim?'

'What I do know is that Hulse had already gathered and submitted a detailed portfolio of evidence about Gregory Perry. It was already too late for Perry though he wouldn't have known that at time of Hulse's death.

From what I'm told, there was enough in the material that Hulse had collected not just to dismiss Perry but maybe even to put him inside himself. Not an attractive prospect for a former prison governor, I imagine.' He paused and looked at her. 'And I imagine it wasn't coincidence that you ended up dealing with Kevin's case in the months before his release. My impression is that Perry was skilled at manipulating events to his own ends.'

She nodded, her eyes dull. 'When I was looking for promotion, he approached me about working with him at the Open. Reckoned he'd heard good things about me on the grapevine.'

'That way, I guess he could keep an eye on you and Kevin in the months before his release. Assess the level of risk to him and Ellis.'

'What about Greg? Surely, he'll give you a route to proving some of this?'

Murrain leaned forward, conscious that what he was about to say would be news to her. 'Perry's gone missing. Disappeared the same day that Ellis killed himself. That morning, he'd been informed by HR that he was being suspended from duty pending the investigation of a number of allegations. His phone records suggest he'd phoned Ellis to tell him the game was up. Our investigations were getting close to Ellis as well, but that phone call may be what pushed Ellis over the edge.' Murrain realised only after he'd spoken that the metaphor was all too appropriate. 'But my guess is Ellis was already getting out of control. We're fairly sure he was responsible for Ethan Dunn's death—we've found traces of Dunn's DNA in Ellis's van. Again, we don't know the whole story. But we think we may be able to link him to at least one other child murder in the region. And maybe others.'

'They were trying to frame Kevin?'

Murrain shrugged. 'I'm not sure it was that premeditated. I think it was mostly an urge that Ellis just couldn't control. He liked controlling people, manipulating them—not just children but women too. It was all one big awful game to him.'

She nodded, her eyes blank. 'That was what he did to me. Or tried to do.'

'We don't know what exactly happened with Ethan Dunn, any more than we know what happened with Ben Wallasey. But it looks as if, after Ethan Dunn's killing, Perry saw it as an opportunity to put Kevin in the frame. If Kevin was identified as Dunn's murderer—or probably even if he just became our prime suspect—that would take Ellis out of the frame and mean that no-one was likely to revisit Kevin's original conviction.' He paused, giving her a moment to take in what he was saying.' As for Gregory Perry, we've had a report that his car's been found abandoned. On the North Wales coast. Near the site of a former holiday centre.' He shrugged. 'We're still looking, but I have a feeling that we won't find him. Not alive anyway.'

'I thought he was a friend,' Kate said. Her voice drifted away. She was still staring blankly over Murrain's shoulder at nothing in particular. 'What about Kevin? What happens to him?'

'The case has been reopened. There's enough to raise doubts about the original conviction. Between these four walls, it looks as if corners were cut in the original investigation. I think as a minimum, there'll be a retrial. He may even just be given a pardon. There are various worm-filled cans here than I suspect the powers-that-be may prefer to remain unopened.'

Somewhere in the next room, Murrain could hear the sound of the television. Jack, seemingly none the worse for his ordeal, was watching some noisy children's programme. Murrain wondered whether Kate was in a fit state to take proper care of the boy, but he couldn't bring himself to take any steps that might result in their being separated.

He took another mouthful of his coffee, allowing the silence to build, expecting that Kate would want to continue talking. But she sat staring into space, watching nothing and no-one.

So much for her wanting to talk, he thought. So much for instinct.

'Look, I'd better go,' he said, at last. 'You sure you'll be OK?'

'Yes, I'm fine,' she said, in a tone that suggested the opposite. 'Don't worry.'

'Think about that counselling,' he said. 'And I'll call in again. Keep you updated.'

'Thanks,' she said. 'That's kind of you.'

***

By the time Murrain arrived back at the MIR, Wanstead was already beginning to arrange its closure. There was plenty of work still to complete on the case but it was mainly administration which they could carry out just as effectively back at the ranch. There was something poignant about seeing all the equipment, which had so recently been critical to their work, being prepared for packing.

'Marty Winston called,' Wanstead said. 'Offers his congratulations.'

'For what?' Murrain said. 'We've got more dead

bodies than the last act of Hamlet, and we still don't know for certain who did what.'

'We're pretty sure who killed Ethan Dunn,' Wanstead pointed out. 'And we know the killer is well and truly dead. That's all Winston cares about. And you're a hero. That's always good PR.'

Murrain snorted. 'Some hero.'

'There'd be another child dead without you,' Wanstead said.

'I'm still not sure that Ellis intended to take the two boys with him. He didn't make any effort to hold on to them when he dropped. It was almost like he was just saying goodbye.'

'Still, two terrified kids out there in the dark. If you and Forester hadn't gone down there—'

'Just lucky,' Murrain said. 'Right place at the right time.'

'But that's your knack, isn't it, Kenny? When the rest of us are lost in the mire, you know what's what.'

'I wish that were true, Paul. You know as well as I do I've been wrong too many times. Sometimes when it mattered the most.' He sat down at his desk, knowing there was no merit in pursuing that chain of thought. 'How's Luke's mother taken it?'

'Difficult to know,' Wanstead said. He gestured towards Marie Donovan, who was sitting chatting to Joe Milton at the far end of the room. 'Love's young dream over there went out to see her. Reckoned she'd come through it OK. Though wasn't sure she'd really taken in what nearly happened to Luke. More shocked by the revelations about Kevin Wickham than anything, apparently.'

'Which revelation? That he might have been a killer, or that he most probably isn't?'

'Either. Both. Must be a shock that you've let someone into your life without knowing who they really are, whatever the outcome.'

'From what I understand of Graeme Ellis's track record, there'll be a few women facing that kind of shock at the moment. And probably with more cause than Sue Myers. But, yes, that's always the risk when you let somebody new into your life, isn't it?' He paused. 'Speaking of which, what's with all the love's young dream stuff?'

'Those two,' Wanstead waved his hand towards Donovan and Milton. 'I may not have your special gifts, but I can sense when two people are getting closer than professional demands might require. If you get my drift.'

'I get your drift. Their business, though. For the moment, anyway.' Murrain made a mental note to have that promised discussion with Joe Milton just as soon as the dust settled. It was their business, as long as it didn't start interfering with their work. As for Milton's existing relationship, assuming there still was one — well, that was even more his business. But he might need some emotional support, however things worked out.

He reached out and booted up his computer, knowing that the best option now was to lose himself in the endless administration that would be needed to close down the case. He realised that Wanstead was watching him curiously. 'And, you know what, Dave?' Murrain said finally. 'Good luck to them. Just at the moment, I could do with any ray of sunshine I can find.'

***

After she closed the front door behind Murrain, Kate had returned to the living room and stood staring out of the window, watching as he climbed into his car and drove off. Her mind was still fixed on that one moment, when she'd grabbed Jack's coat and dragged him back from the wall. She hadn't moved past that, or begun to make sense of how she'd reached that point. She hadn't even begun to think properly about her mother, who had died trying to protect Jack from the man she'd unknowingly allowed back into their lives.

Murrain had been generous with his time. Well beyond the call of duty, she suspected, and she'd been grateful to him, even while she was failing to absorb much of what he'd been saying.

Kate stood at the window and shivered, reliving in her head, over and over again, the moment when, against all the odds, she had held on to Jack.

The previous day, Kevin Wickham had visited and, as a gift, had left her a CD. He'd been hesitant as to whether it was tactful or appropriate, but said it was the song his own mother had sung to him as a child. She'd sung it as a lullaby, and he'd heard it, always, as a prayer or incantation to keep him safe. He heard it that way still, despite everything that had happened.

Kate turned on the CD player. She was familiar with the song from the polished Simon and Garfunkel version, but this was something different, more primitive. She listened to the rough, English voice singing those strange, incantatory verses. And then it finished:

'*...When he has done and finished his work.*
Parsley, sage, rosemary, and thyme:
Oh, tell him to come and he'll have his shirt,
And she shall be a true lover of mine.'

She sat in silence afterwards, the muffled noises of the television carrying through from the next room. Then, finally, she picked up her phone and began to dial Wickham's number.

THE END

About Alex Walters

Alex has worked in the oil industry, broadcasting and banking and now runs a consultancy working mainly in the criminal justice sector including police, prisons and probation.

As Michael Walters, he has published three crime novels set in modern-day Mongolia. As Alex Walters he has written two books set in and around Manchester and featuring the undercover officer, Marie Donovan, *Trust No-One* and *Nowhere to Hide*, and *Candles and Roses*, a serial killer story set on Scotland's Black Isle (the first in a series featuring DI Alec McKay and DS Ginny Horton).

Late Checkout was the first in a series featuring, alongside Marie Donovan, the rather distinctive DCI Kenny Murrain. *Dark Corners* is the second book in the series.

Alex lives in Manchester with his wife, occasional sons and too many cats.

Twitter: @mikewalters60
Facebook: www.facebook.com/alexwaltersauthor/
Blog: https://mikewalters.wordpress.com/

Printed in Great Britain
by Amazon